PUFFIN BOOKS
The Silver Branch

'Rome is falling, my children . . . If I can make this one province strong enough to stand alone when Rome goes down, then something may be saved from the darkness.'

But in spite of warnings from Justin and Flavius, the two young soldier cousins, the dream of Carausius, the remarkable Roman Emperor of Britain, was cut short when he was assassinated. When they too were threatened the young men fled, trying to reach Gaul and safety – but then they met Paulinus, and saw that they could serve Rome, and Carausius's memory, better by staying hidden in Britain and organizing resistance.

Then Paulinus too was betrayed and killed, and the cousins had to continue alone. Would help ever come from Rome? And if it did, what part could their motley army play, made up as it was of their throng 'of legionaries gone wilful-missing, farmers and hunters with wrongs to right, a sneak thief, a ship-master, a gladiator and Emperor's Fool'.

It was Cullen, the Fool, with his strange musical instrument of silver apples, who brought a most unexpected message that vindicated Justin and Flavius – and it was Cullen, too, who found the battered remains of an old Eagle which was a standard and a hope to the Lost Legion as they faced the final struggle.

The Silver Branch continues the story begun in *The Eagle of the Ninth*, which is also available in Puffin.

Rosemary Sutcliff

THE SILVER BRANCH

Illustrated by Charles Keeping

Puffin Books
in association with Oxford University Press

Puffin Books, Penguin Books Ltd, Harmondsworth,
Middlesex, England
Penguin Books, 625 Madison Avenue,
New York, New York 10022, U.S.A.
Penguin Books Australia Ltd, Ringwood,
Victoria, Australia
Penguin Books Canada Ltd, 2801 John Street,
Markham, Ontario, Canada L3R 1B4
Penguin Books (N.Z.) Ltd, 182–190 Wairau Road,
Auckland 10, New Zealand

First published by Oxford University Press 1957
Published in Puffin Books 1980

Made and printed in Great Britain by
Richard Clay (The Chaucer Press), Ltd,
Bungay, Suffolk
Set in Linotype Pilgrim

Historical Note

More than a hundred years went by after the time of this story, before Rome fell; before the last of the Legions were withdrawn from Britain and Rutupiae Light went out and the Dark Ages had begun. But already the great days were over. Rome was harassed by the barbarians all along her frontiers, while at home generals fought to become Emperors and rival Emperors struggled among themselves for power.

Marcus Aurelius Carausius was a real person; so were Allectus the Traitor and the Legate Asklepiodotus; and so of course was the Caesar Constantius, whose son Constantine was the first Christian Emperor of Rome. For the rest :– The body of a Saxon warrior buried with his weapons was found in one of the ditches of Richborough Castle, which was Rutupiae in the days of the Eagles. The Basilica at Calleva was burned down towards the end of the Roman occupation and later roughly rebuilt, and the eagle which I have already written about in another story was discovered during excavations in the ruins of one of the courtrooms behind the Main Hall. At Calleva also – Silchester as it is now – there was found a stone with a man's name carved on it in the script of the ancient Irish; and the name was Evicatos, or Ebicatos, which means 'Spear Man'.

Contents

1 The Saxon Shore   9

2 A Whisper down the Wind   24

3 The House on the Cliffs   34

4 The Sea Wolf   44

5 Nightshade!   57

6 Evicatos of the Spear   64

7 'To the Fates,
   that they may be Kind'   75

8 The Feast of Samhain   89

9 The Sign of the Dolphin   103

10 The *Berenice* Sails for Gaul 117
11 The Shadow 132
12 A Sprig of Broom 144
13 The Silver Branch 160
14 An Ancient Ensign 175
15 Return to the Legions 187
16 'Carausius! Carausius!' 199
17 Eagle in the Flames 208
18 Triumphal Garlands 225
  Place Names in Roman Britain 237

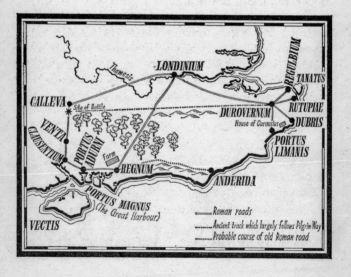

Roman roads
Ancient track which largely follows Pilgrim Way
Probable course of old Roman road

1

The Saxon Shore

ON a blustery autumn day a galley was nosing up the wide loop of a British river that widened into the harbour of Rutupiae.

The tide was low, and the mud-banks at either hand that would be covered at high tide were alive with curlew and sandpiper. And out of the waste of sandbank and sour salting, higher and nearer as the time went by, rose Rutupiae: the long, whale-backed hump of the island and the grey ramparts of the fortress, with the sheds of the dockyard massed below it.

The young man standing on the fore-deck of the galley watched the fortress drawing nearer with a sense of expectancy; his thoughts reaching alternately forward to the future that waited for him there, and back to a certain interview that he had had with Licinius, his Cohort Commander, three months ago, at the other end of the Empire. That had been the night his posting came through.

'You do not know Britain, do you?' Licinius had said.

Justin – Tiberius Lucius Justinianus, to give him his full name as it was inscribed on the record tablets of the Army Medical Corps at Rome – had shaken his head, saying with the small stutter that he could never quite master, 'N-no, sir. My grandfather was born and bred there, but he settled in Nicaea when he left the Eagles.'

'And so you will be eager to see the Province for yourself.'

'Yes, sir, only – I scarcely expected to be sent there with the Eagles.'

He could remember the scene so vividly. He could see Licinius watching him across the crocus flame of the lamp on his table, and the pattern that the wooden scroll-ends made on their shelves, and the fine-blown sand-wreaths in the corners of the mud-walled office; he could hear distant laughter in the camp, and, far away, the jackals crying; and Licinius's dry voice :

'Only you did not know we were so friendly with Britain, or rather, with the man who has made himself Emperor of Britain?'

'Well, sir, it does seem strange. It is only this spring that Maximian sent the Caesar C-Constantius to drive him out of his Gaulish territory.'

'I agree. But there are possible explanations to these postings from other parts of the Empire to the British Legions. It may be that Rome seeks, as it were, to keep open the lines of communication. It may be that she does not choose that Marcus Aurelius Carausius should have at his command Legions that are completely cut away from the rest of the Empire. That way comes a fighting force that follows none but its own leader and owns no ties whatsoever with Imperial Rome.' Licinius had leaned forward and shut down the lid of the bronze inkstand with a small deliberate click. 'Quite honestly, I wish your posting had been to any other Province of the Empire.'

Justin had stared at him in bewilderment. 'Why so, sir?'

'Because I knew your father, and therefore take a certain interest in your welfare ... How much do you in fact understand about the situation in Britain? About the Emperor Carausius, who is the same thing in all that matters?'

'Very little, I am afraid, sir.'

'Well then, listen, and maybe you will understand a little more. In the first place, you can rid your mind of any idea that Carausius is framed of the same stuff as most of the six-month sword-made Emperors we have had in the years before Diocletian and Maximian split the Purple between them. He is the son of a German father and a Hibernian mother, and that is a mixture to set the sparks flying; born and bred in one of the trading-stations that the Manopeans of the German sea set up long since in Hibernia, and only came back to his father's people when he reached manhood. He was a Scaldis river-pilot when I knew him first. Afterwards he broke into the Legions – the gods know how. He served in Gaul and Illyria, and under the Emperor Carus in the Persian War, rising all the time. He was one of Maximian's right-hand men in suppressing the revolts in eastern Gaul, and made such a name for himself that Maximian, remembering his naval training, gave him command of the fleet based on Gesoriacum, and the task of clearing the Northern Seas of the Saxons swarming in them.'

Licinius had broken off there, seeming lost in his own thoughts, and in a little, Justin had prompted respectfully, 'Was not there a t-tale that he let the Sea Wolves through on their raids and then fell on them when they were heavy with spoil on their h-homeward way?'

'Aye – and sent none of the spoil to Rome. It was that, I imagine, that roused Maximian's ire. We shall never know the rights of that tale; but at all events Maximian ordered his execution, and Carausius got wind of it in time and made for Britain, followed by the whole Fleet. He was ever such a one as men follow gladly. By the time the official order for his execution was at Gesoriacum, Carausius had dealt with the Governor of Britain, and proclaimed himself Emperor with three British Legions and a large force from Gaul and Lower Germany to back his claim, and the sea swept by his galleys between him and the executioner. Aye, better galleys and better seamen than ever Maximian could lay his hand to. And in the end Maximian had no choice but to make peace and own him for a brother Emperor.'

'But we have not k-kept the peace,' Justin had said bluntly after a moment.

'No. And to my mind Constantius's victories in North Gaul this spring are more shame to us than defeat could have been. No blame to the young Caesar; he is a man under authority like the rest of us, though he will sit in Maximian's place one day ... Well, the peace abides – after a fashion. But it is a situation that may burst into a blaze at any hour, and if it does, the gods help anyone caught in the flames.' The Commander had pushed back his chair and risen, turning to the window. 'And yet, in an odd way, I think I envy you, Justin.'

Justin had said, 'You liked him, then, sir?'

And he remembered now how Licinius had stood looking out into the moonlit night. 'I – have never been sure,' he had said, 'but I would have followed him into the mouth of Erebos itself,' and turned back to the lamp.

That had been almost all, save that at the last Licinius had stayed him in the doorway, saying, 'If you should at any time have speech with the great man himself, salute him from me, and ask him if he remembers the boar we killed below the pine-woods at the third bend of the Scaldis.'

But it was scarcely likely, Justin thought, that a Junior Surgeon would have the chance to give any message to the Emperor Carausius.

He came back to the present with a jerk, to find that they had entered a world of stone-and-timber jetties, ringed round with sail-lofts and armourers' shops and long-boat sheds, threading their way among the galleys

that lay at anchor in the sheltered water. The mingled
reek of pitch and salt-soaked timber and hot metal was in
his nostrils; and above the beat of the galley's oars and
the liquid rush of water parting under the bows, he could
hear the mingled myriad beehive hum of planes and saws
and hammers on anvils that was the voice of a dockyard
all the world over. And above him towered the ramparts
of Rutupiae; a grey prow of ramparts raw with newness,
from the midst of which sprang the beacon-crested tower
of the Light.

A while later, having landed and reported to the Commandant and to the Senior Surgeon, having left his kit in
the lime-washed cell in the officers' block that had been
assigned to him, and set out in search of the bath-house
and lost his way in the crowded unfriendly immensity
of the huge fortress, Justin was standing close before that
tower.

The thing was no match for the Pharos at Alexandria,
but seen at close quarters it was vast enough to stop one's
breath, all the same. In the centre of the open space rose
a plinth of solid masonry four or five times the height of
a man, and long as an eighty-oar galley, from the midst
of which a tower of the same grey stonework soared
heavenward, bearing on its high crest the iron beacon
brazier that seemed to Justin, staring giddily up at it,
almost to touch the drifting November skies. The gulls
rose and fell about it on white wings, and he heard their
thin, remote crying above the busy sounds of the fortress;
then, with his head beginning to swim, brought his gaze
down as far as the top of the plinth. Curved ramps for
the fuel-carts led up to it at either end, and from them
roofed colonnades ran in to the base of the tower itself;
and now that he had got over the stupendous size of the
thing enough to take in the details, he saw that the
columns and cornices were of marble, enriched with

statues and splendid carvings, but that they were broken
and falling into decay, which was strange, here in the
midst of a fortress so new that in places they were still at
work on the walls. But there was broken marble everywhere, some of it roughly stacked as though for use at a
future time, some clinging yet to the stark grey walls that
it had once covered. A small piece that must have fallen
from its fellows when being carried away lay almost at
his feet and, stooping to pick it up, he saw that it was
part of a sculptured laurel-wreath.

He was still holding the fragment of marble and gazing
up at the great tower from which it had fallen, when a
voice behind him said, 'Pretty, isn't it?' and he swung
round to find standing at his elbow a very dusty young
man in Centurion's uniform, with his helmet under one
arm; a stocky, red-haired young man with a thin, merry
face and fly-away eyebrows, who seemed friendly.

'It is half ruined,' Justin said, puzzled. 'What is it? I
mean, I can see it is a pharos, b-but it looks as though it
was meant to be something else as well.'

A shadow of bitterness crept into the young Centurion's
voice. 'It *was* a triumphal monument as well – a triumphal monument to the might of Imperial Rome and her
conquest of Britain. Now it is just a pharos, and we break
up the fallen marble for rubble in the walls that we build
to keep the Saxons out ... There's a moral somewhere in
that, if you like morals.'

Justin glanced down at the fragment of marble laurel-
wreath in his hand, then tossed it aside. It fell with a
little sharp clatter, raising a puff of dust.

'Would you be looking for anyone or anything?' in-
quired his new acquaintance.

'I was looking for the bath-house,' Justin told him; and
then, by way of giving an account of himself, 'I am the
new Junior Surgeon.'

'Are you so? Well, truth to tell, I thought you might

be.' The other glanced at the uniform without armour, which Justin wore. 'You have reported to the Commandant?'

'And to the Senior Surgeon,' Justin said, with his rather hesitating smile. 'He called me a fledgling butcher and turned me off until an hour before sick parade tomorrow.'

The young Centurion's eyes had become dancing slits. 'Vinicius must be in rather a mellow mood; he called your predecessor a ham-fisted assassin and threw a pitch-pot at his head, so I've heard. I wasn't here myself then . . . Well, if it's a bath you want, you had best come with me. I'm just going to shed this harness, and then I'm for the bathhouse myself. We'll just have time for a plunge and splash about before dinner if we're quick.'

Retracing his steps with his new acquaintance, between the busy workshops and crowded barrack rows, it seemed to Justin that the great fortress had all at once put on a more friendly face; and he looked about him with a quickened interest. 'This place seems very big and busy to me,' he said. 'I spent my year as a surgeon's Cub at Beersheba, and that is a single Cohort fort. It could g-get lost in this one.'

'They're all monsters, these new Saxon shore fortresses,' said his companion. 'They have to be; they are fort and shipyard and naval base in one. You'll grow used to it after a while.'

'Are there many of them, then? Great new forts like this?'

'A good few, from the Metaris round to the Great Harbour; some of them altogether new, and some built over old ones, like Rutupiae. They are all part of Carausius's defences against the Sea Wolves.'

'Carausius,' Justin said, with a touch of awe in his tone. 'I suppose you will have seen Carausius often?'

'Zeus! Yes! This is his headquarters, though of course he's all over the Province too, in between whiles. Not one

to let the turf smoulder under his feet, our little Emperor.
You'll see him yourself this evening, in all likelihood; he
most often feeds in Mess with the rest of us.'

'You mean – he's here now?'

'Surely. And so are we. Come up and sit on the bed. I
shall be but a few moments.'

And so, a short while later, Justin was sitting on the
edge of the cot in a limewashed cell exactly like his own,
while his new-found acquaintance laid aside sword and
helmet and set to work on the straps of his breastplate,
whistling softly and very cheerfully through his teeth as
he did so. Justin sat and watched him. He was a friendly
soul himself, but he was always gratefully surprised at any
sign of friendliness from other people, and with his gratitude, his liking went out, hesitant but warm, to the red-
headed Centurion.

The other slipped the last buckle free, and broke off his
whistling. 'So you're from Beersheba, are you? A long
march, you have had. Ah, thanks.' (This as Justin reached
out and took the heavy breastplate from him.) And his
next words were muffled in the folds of his leather
harness-tunic as he dragged it over his head. 'And where
before that? What part of the Empire do you spring
from?'

'Nicaea, in southern Gaul.'

'So this is your first sight of Britain?'

'Yes.' Justin laid the breastplate down on the cot beside
him. 'But my people are from Britain, and I have always
had a mind to c-come back and see it for myself.'

The young Centurion emerged from the leather folds,
and stood up in his uniform tunic of fine crimson wool,
looking, with his red hair on end, suddenly much more of
a boy and less of a grown man. 'What part of Britain?'

'The South. Somewhere in the Down Country towards
C-calleva, I believe.'

'Famous! All the best people are from the Down Country; the best people and the best sheep. I am myself.' He eyed Justin with frank interest. 'What is your name?'

'Justin – Tiberius Lucius Justinianus.'

There was a moment's silence, and then his companion said very softly, 'Justinianus – *is* it so?' And with a swift gesture pulled something off his left hand and held it out to Justin. 'Have you ever seen anything like that before?'

Justin took the thing and bent his head over it. It was a heavy and very battered signet ring. The flawed emerald which formed the bezel was darkly cool, holding the surface reflection of the window as he turned it to catch the light, and the engraved device stood out clearly. 'This Dolphin?' he said, with a dawning excitement. 'Yes, I have, on – on the ivory lid of an old cosmetic box that belonged to my grandmother. It was the badge of her family.'

'That proves it!' said the young Centurion, taking back his ring. 'Well, of all the –' He began to do strange calculations on his fingers, then abandoned the attempt. 'Nay, it is beyond me. There have been more marryings than one between your house and mine, and it would take my Great Aunt Honoria to unsnarl such a tangled skein – but we are undoubtedly cousins of some kind!'

Justin said nothing. He had risen from the cot, and stood watching the other's face as though suddenly unsure of his welcome. It was one thing to take casual pity on a stranger and bring him back to one's quarters on the way to the bath-house, but it might be quite another to find oneself saddled with him for a kinsman.

That unsureness, though he did not know it, was one of the things that years of being a disappointment to his father had done to him. He had always been miserably aware of being a disappointment to his father. His mother, whom he could scarcely remember, had been beautiful; but Justin, always unfortunate, had continued to be both very like her and very ugly, with a head too large for his thin shoulders, and ears that stuck out defiantly on either side of it. He had spent a good deal of his childhood being ill, and as a result, when the time came for him to go into the Legions, as the men of his family had always done, he had failed to come up to the needful standard of fitness for the Centuriate. He had not minded for himself, because he had always wanted to be a surgeon; but he had minded deeply for his father's sake, knowing himself more than ever a disappointment; and became even more unsure of himself in consequence.

And then it dawned on him with delight that the red-headed young man was every whit as glad of the astonishing discovery as he was himself.

'So, we are kinsmen,' he said. 'And that is good. And I am Tiberius Lucius Justinianus – but still I do not know by what name to call you.'

'Flavius,' said the red-headed Centurion. 'Marcelus Flavius Aquila.' He reached out and caught Justin by the shoulders, half laughing, half incredulous still. 'Oh, but this is most wonderful, that you and I should meet like this on your first day on British soil! It must be that the Fates mean us to be friends, and who are we to fly against the Fates?'

And suddenly they were both talking together, in breathless, laughing half-sentences, holding each the other at arm's length the better to look at each other, caught up in delight at the thing that had happened, until Flavius broke off to catch up the fresh tunic which the orderly had left for him on the foot of the cot. 'This is a thing that we must celebrate royally by and by; but if we aren't quick we shall neither of us get a bath before dinner – and I don't know about you, but I've been on wall building duty all day and I'm gritty from head to heel.'

*

The Mess Hall was already crowded when Justin and
Flavius entered it, and men stood talking idly in groups,
but as yet nobody had taken their seats at the long tables.
Justin had been rather dreading his entry alone into a hall
full of strangers. But with Flavius's arm across his
shoulders he was swept at once into a group of young
officers. 'Here's our new Junior Surgeon – what Vinicius
has left of him, and he's a kinsman of mine!' And immediately appealed to to take sides in an argument about
oysters, the plunge was over almost before he knew it.

But soon after, the hum of talk in the long room fell
abruptly silent, as steps and a quick voice sounded outside in the Colonnade, and as every man straightened himself on his feet, Justin looked with eager expectancy towards the door.

At first sight the man who entered with his Staff
Officers behind him was a disappointment. A short, thick-
set man of immensely powerful build, with a round head
set on a neck of extraordinary thickness, and crisp brown
hair and beard as curly as a ram's fleece. A man who
looked as though he would have been more at home in
leather frock and seaman's bonnet than the fine linen he
wore, and who advanced into the hall with the unmistakable rolling step of a man used to a heaving deck under
his feet.

'But I have seen the like of this man a score of times –
a hundred times before,' Justin thought. 'You can see him
on the deck of any galley in the Empire.'

The Emperor had halted at the upper end of the room,
his gaze moving over the faces of the men gathered there;
and his eyes under their thick bar of brows met Justin's.
'Ah, a new face among us,' said the Emperor, and crooked
a finger. 'Come here, boy.'

He heard the Camp Commandant speak his name and
position quickly to Carausius. Then he was saluting before

the man who had risen from a Scaldis river-pilot to be
Emperor of Britain; and suddenly he knew that he had
been wrong. He had never seen the like of this man before.

Carausius set a hand on his shoulder and turned him
– for it was dusk by now – to get the lamp-light on his
face. After a long unhurried scrutiny, he said, 'So you are
our new Junior Surgeon.'

'Yes, Caesar.'

'Where did you serve your Cubhood?'

'With the third Cohort of the Fretencis, at Beersheba in
Judea,' Justin said. 'Fulvius Licinius, who commands the
garrison, bade me salute you from him, and ask you if you
remember the boar that you and he killed below the pine-
woods at the third bend of the Scaldis.'

Carausius was silent a moment. Then he said, 'I remember that boar, yes – and Licinius. And so he's in
Judea, is he? He was senior to me in those days; and now
he commands the garrison at Beersheba, while I wear this'
– touching the mantle of Imperial Purple that he wore
clasped by a huge ruby at the shoulder. 'There's naught
so odd as life. Maybe you haven't noticed that yet, but
you will, you will, if you live long enough ... So my
brother Emperors send me a Junior Surgeon from the
Fretencis. There have been several postings from overseas
to the Legions here in Britain, lately. Almost like old
times. – Yet they showed themselves none so friendly this
spring, as I remember.' Voice and manner were musing,
nothing more, the hand on Justin's shoulder barely tightened its grip, there was no change in the blunt, straight-
featured face so near his own, save that perhaps for a
moment the eyes seemed to grow a little paler, as the sea
whitening before a rain-squall; and yet suddenly Justin
was cold afraid. 'Can you read me the riddle, I wonder?'

Somehow he held his ground under the light, deadly
hand on his shoulder, and gave back the Emperor's look
without wavering.

A voice – a pleasantly cool voice with a laugh in it – protested lazily, 'Excellency, you are too hard on the boy. It is his first night among us, and you will put him off his dinner.'

Carausius paid not the faintest attention. For a few moments he continued that terrible raking stare; then a slow, straight-lipped smile spread over his face. 'You are so right, my dear Allectus,' he said; and then to Justin, 'No, you have not been sent to play the spy, or if you have, you do not know it.' His hand slipped from the young surgeon's shoulder, and he glanced about him. 'Shall we begin dinner, my friends?'

The man who had been called Allectus caught Justin's eye as he turned away, and smiled. Justin returned the smile, grateful as always for kindness, and slipped back through the crowd to Flavius, who greeted him half under his breath with a swift 'Eugé! That was well done!' which warmed him still further.

And a little later he was sitting between Flavius and another Centurion at the foot of the table. His right-hand neighbour was too busy eating to have any conversation, and he was free to give his whole attention to the highly irreverent account of the great ones at the upper end of the table, with which Flavius was favouring him under cover of the general hum of talk.

'You see that one with the sword-cut down his cheek?' said Flavius, dealing with a pickled herring. 'That's Arcadius, the captain of the *Caleope*, our biggest three-bank galley. He came by that mark in the Arena. A bright lad, Arcadius, in his young days. Oh, and the melancholy fellow beside him is Dexion, a Centurion of Marines. Never,' said Flavius, wagging his head, '*never* shake the dice with him unless you want to lose the tunic off your back. I don't say he doesn't play square, but he throws Venus more often than any mere mortal has a right to.'

'Thanks for the warning,' Justin said. 'I'll remember.'

But his eyes strayed with an odd fascination, as they had done more than once before, to the man whom the Emperor had called Allectus, who now sat among Carausius's staff officers near the head of the table. He was a tall man with a cap of shining fair hair greying a little at the temples; a man with a rather heavy face that would have been good to look at but that it was too pale; everything about him just a little too pale – hair, skin, and eyes. But even as Justin watched, the man smiled at something his neighbour had said, and the smile, swift and completely charming, gave to his face all that it lacked before.

'Who is the tall very fair man?' he murmured to Flavius. 'The Emperor called him Allectus, I think.'

'Carausius's Finance Minister and general right-hand man. He has a vast following among the troops, as well as the merchants and moneyers, so that I suppose after Carausius he's the most powerful man in Britain. But he's a good enough fellow, in spite of looking as though he'd been reared in a dark closet.'

And then, a few moments later, something happened; something so slight and so ordinary that afterwards Justin wondered if he had simply let his imagination run away with him – and yet he could never quite forget it, nor the sudden sense of evil that came with it. Roused perhaps by the warmth rising from the lamps, a big, soft-winged night-moth had come fluttering down from the rafters to dart and hover and swerve about the table. Everyone's attention was turned towards the Emperor, who was at that moment preparing to pour the second Libation to the gods. Everyone, that is, save Justin and Allectus. For some unknown reason, Justin had glanced again at Allectus; and Allectus was watching the moth.

The moth was circling wildly nearer and nearer to one of the lamps which stood directly before the Finance Min-

ister, its blurred shadow flashing about the table as it
swooped and spun in dizzy spirals about the bright and
beckoning flame, closer and closer, until the wild, ecstatic
dance ended in a burst of shadows, and the moth spun
away on singed wings, to fall with a pitiful, maimed fluttering close beside Allectus's wine-cup. And Allectus, smiling faintly, crushed out its life under one deliberate finger.

That was all. Anybody would crush a singed moth – it
was the obvious, the only thing to do. But Justin had seen
the pale man's face as he watched the dancing moth,
waiting for it to dance too near, seen it in the unguarded
instant as he stretched out that precise forefinger to kill.

2

A Whisper
down the Wind

As the days went by, Justin grew used to the great
fortress that was the heart and headquarters of
Carausius's defence against the Saxons. Under the tall
grey pharos that had once been triumphant with bronze
and gleaming marble, the galleys and the merchantmen
came and went; and all day behind the noises of the fortress, behind the parade-ground voices and the trumpets
and the tramp of marching feet, sounded the ring and
rasp of adze and hammer from the dockyard below the
rampart walls. And behind the hum of the busy dockyard sounded always the sea.

Three times that autumn, before winter closed the seaways, there were brushes between the British fleets and
the black-sailed ships of the Saxons; and Justin had much
practice for his skill when the wounded were brought in,
and won grudging praise from the irascible Senior Surgeon,
which made him happy.

That was a good autumn for him in other ways too, and
for Flavius, with whom he spent a good deal of his off-
duty times. The quick liking of their first meeting had
grown into a close and enduring friendship. They were
drawn together by a common loneliness; for Flavius,
brought up by a widowed Great-Aunt after the death from
pestilence of both his parents, had loneliness behind him
also. That autumn and the winter that followed they
hunted boar together in the Great Forest, and took their

birding bows out after wild-fowl in the marshes, and poked about the fishing village that considered itself a town, with its added huddle of shops and temples and beer-sellers' bothies beneath the fortress walls.

One place that they haunted a good deal was a shop close under the North bastion, kept by one Serapion, a little withered man, half British, half Egyptian, with jewel-bright eyes and pointed fingers like a lizard. A veritable dog-hole of a shop, viewed from outside, but inside, filled with delights; with little bundles of dried herbs and pots and jars of unnamed substances, with fragrant oils in little crystal flasks, and dried and shrivelled things that one did not care to guess at too closely. It was a shop much frequented by the garrison; here one might buy scented oils and unguents for oneself, or a stick of perfume for a girl.

Flavius went there for the sake of Serapion's rubbing-oil, which was good when one was stiff and tired from the hunting trail, and for some unguent which he vainly hoped would make his hair lie down; Justin went because Serapion's concoctions interested him, and the man's talk of healing and harming herbs and the influence of the stars interested him still more.

On an evening just after Saturnalia, Justin and Flavius turned in through the low doorway of Serapion's shop, to find the little Egyptian serving another customer; and by the light of the small hanging lamp, recognized Allectus. Justin had seen him many times, by now, in the Emperor's train; this tall man with the ashy-fair head and the heavy face that lightened so pleasantly at his ready smile, who was, after Carausius, the most powerful man in Britain. He had never told Flavius about the moth – after all, what was there to tell, when one came to put it into words? 'I saw him kill that moth, and he enjoyed doing it.' That was all. And as time went by he had almost, though never quite, forgotten the whole thing.

Allectus looked round at their entrance, with that swift, pleasant smile of his. 'Ah, I trust you are not pressed for time. I fear I am lamentably slow to make my choice, this evening.' Then he turned back to the matter in hand, which seemed to be the choice of a phial of perfume. 'Something out of the common – something that will be at once a gift and a compliment, for the lady's birthday.'

Serapion bowed, smiled, touching with one pointed finger the fine alabaster flask that he had set on the table before his noble customer. 'This is the perfume that I blended especially to your order last time, Excellency. Was the lady not pleased?'

'Yes, but this is a different lady,' said Allectus, with that cool note of laughter in his voice; then, tossing the words casually over his shoulder to the two young men in the gloom behind him, 'Never give the same perfume to two different women at the same time – they may meet. That is a thing for you to remember, my young cockerels.'

'Ah, now I understand, Excellency.' The little Egyptian bowed again. 'If your Honour could give me until to-morrow to blend something worthy of the lady whom Allectus honours with his gift –'

'Do I not tell you her birthday is tomorrow, and I must send it off tonight? Show me something that you have here ready blended.'

Serapion was still a moment, considering, then turned, and moved, silent as a cat, into the farthest shadows, to return holding something between his cupped hands. 'I have this,' he said – 'this, the perfume of perfumes. Blended by myself, ah yes, as I alone can blend the precious essences into one exquisite whole.' He set the thing down on the table, and it stood there, a small crystal flask, glowing under the lamp like a green-gold jewel.

'It is a charming flask,' said Allectus, taking it up and turning it in strong white fingers.

'A charming flask, ah, but the fragrance within – the

flowering essence of a thousand summers caught in amber! Wait now, I will break the seal and you shall judge.'

He took back the tiny flask, and with a sharp thumb-nail peeled away the film of wax about the neck, and withdrew the stopper; then dipped in a thin glass rod, and touched Allectus on the back of the hand he held out for the purpose. Instantly, as the drop of precious liquid ran on to the man's warm skin, a wonderful scent arose, strong but delicate, engulfing the other odours of the place.

Allectus held his hand to his nostrils. 'How much?'

'A hundred sesterces, Excellency.'

'That is a great price for a very small flask of perfume.'

'But such perfume, Excellency! The cost of such ingredients is very great, and I assure you a hundred sesterces allows me but a very small reward for my time and skill.'

'So. I still think it a great price, but I'll take it. Seal it up for me again.'

'Allectus is most good and gracious.' Serapion bowed, and continued his plaint as he warmed the stick of wax he had taken up, and again sealed the neck of the flask. 'Aye, aye, costly they are indeed, such ingredients as these – sheer liquid gold. And on so many of them one must pay a king's ransom in duty, to bring them into the province. Ah me, they come hard upon a poor man, these new taxes of the Emperor's.'

Allectus laughed softly. 'Maybe you should lay the taxes at my door, friend. Who else should take the blame if not the Emperor's Finance Minister?'

'Why of course, your Excellency. See, here is the perfume.' Serapion handed it over, glancing up under his thin lids as though to judge how far he might venture. 'But is an Emperor always guided by his Finance Minister? They say in the market-place that sometimes a Finance Minister might be – not altogether at one with his Emperor in all things; that the taxes might be less harsh if –'

'It is generally foolish to listen to market-place talk,' said

Allectus. 'And generally foolish to repeat it.' He slipped the flask into the breast of his fine woollen tunic, shaking his head with smiling impatience at the Egyptian's protestation that he meant no harm. 'Nay, man, we all let our tongues run away with us at times. Here, take your hundred sesterces.' And with a courteous good night, which included the two young men, he gathered the folds of his cloak about him and was gone into the wintry darkness.

Serapion the Egyptian stood looking after him, with an expression of sly understanding in his little bright eyes. Then he turned back to the two young men, with a face empty of everything except willingness to oblige.

'And now, young sirs – I regret that you have been kept waiting. Is it some more of the muscle oil – or maybe a gift for the ladies at home? I hear that you go on leave together in a few days' time.'

Justin was startled, for it was only that morning that Flavius had managed an exchange with another Centurion, so that they could take their leave at the same time.

Flavius laughed. 'Does ever anyone sneeze in Rutupiae that you don't know about it within the hour? No, just the muscle oil.'

They made the purchase, thinking no more of the little scene that was just past, and returned to barracks. And a few days later, when their leave fell due, set out together on the long two days' ride westward, to spend it at the old farm in the Down Country that was Flavius's home.

'It is no good pushing on to Calleva,' said Flavius, 'because Aunt Honoria will be at Aqua Sulis taking the waters, at this time of year. So we'll head along the chalk to the farm, and descend on Servius. He'll be glad to see us – and so will the farm.'

And then, as Justin looked at him sideways, he grinned, but said seriously enough, 'The farm is always pleased to

see the people it is fond of, and who are fond of it. You
can feel it being pleased – like an old wise hound.'

And when, towards dusk on the second day, with the
frost crisping in the ruts of the wagon-way, they came
through a little wood of oak and birch and wild cherry,
and saw the house with its farm buildings at the head
of the long downland valley, Justin knew what he meant.
He felt the welcome reaching out to them, and knew that
it was for him also, as though, stranger as he was, the place
knew him for one of its own, and was glad of his coming.

Presently there were other welcomes: from Servius the
old steward who had been an Optio under Flavius's father;
from Cutha his wife, and Kyndylan his son when he came
up from the cattle; from the other farm-hands, free men
and women, all of them. 'Aunt Honoria has a few old
slaves,' Flavius said. 'But we have always farmed with free
labour. It makes it difficult at times, but we manage.
Couldn't change.'

They spent five days at the farm, and it was during those
five days that Justin first really discovered Britain. The
bare winter woods dappled like a partridge's breast, the
slow, broad voices of the farm hands, the lapwings on the
winter ploughland; the low, long house itself, built on to
by succeeding generations but holding still at its heart
the smoke-blackened atrium, used as a store-room now,
that had been the original houseplace, built by another
Marcus Flavius Aquila making a home for himself and
his British wife and the children that came after – these
were all Britain to Justin.

He had that other Marcus Flavius Aquila much in mind
during those days while, with Flavius, he poked happily
about the byres and barns, or helped old Buic the shepherd
in the lambing-pens. It was as though, because he also was
of Marcus's blood, the old house, the whole downland
valley was a link between them.

He was thinking about that Marcus the last evening of all, as he and Flavius leaned side by side on the wall that kept the Downs from sliding into the vine terraces on the warm southern slope. From where they were, they could see the whole farm lying clear down to the shores of the forest that closed the valley at last, all quenched and quieted in the first faint thickening of the winter twilight.

'It is queer, you know, Justin,' Flavius said suddenly, 'I've never been here for more than a few weeks at a time, since – since I was very small; but ever since I can remember it has been home to me.' He propped himself more comfortably against the old dry-stone wall. 'The place looks well enough, all things considered.'

'What particular things?' Justin asked.

'Me being away with the Eagles, for one thing,' Flavius said. 'I ought really to have stayed at home and helped Servius run the farm. But you know how it is with us; the old Service is in all our blood; look at you, you're a surgeon, but you couldn't break away from the Eagles, even so. Luckily Servius is a better farmer than I could ever be – but it isn't an easy world for farmers and the small estates nowadays. Things must have been so much simpler when my namesake first cleared this valley and made his home here.'

They were silent a few moments, and then Flavius added, 'You know, I've so often wondered what lay behind the starting of our farm.'

'How do you mean?'

Flavius hesitated a moment. 'Well, see now,' he said at last. 'He – Marcus – was only a very junior Centurion, if family accounts be true, when he was lamed in some tribal rising or other, and invalided out; and yet the Senate gave him the full land grant and gratuity for a time-expired Centurion. That isn't like the Senate.'

'Maybe he had a powerful friend on the Senate benches,' Justin suggested. 'Such things do happen.'

Flavius shook his head. 'I doubt it. We aren't a family that collects powerful friends.'

'A reward, a special p-payment of some kind, then?'

'That seems more likely. The question is, what was it for?'

Justin found that the other had turned his head to look at him, clearly hesitating on the edge of saying something. 'You have an idea about that?'

'I'm – not sure.' Flavius most unexpectedly flushed up to the roots of his fiery hair. 'But I've always wondered whether it could have been anything to do with the Ninth Legion.'

'The Ninth Legion?' Justin said, a little blankly. 'The one that was ordered up into Valentia in the troubles, and was never seen again?'

'Oh, I know it sounds far-fetched. I wouldn't speak of it to anyone but you. But his father disappeared with the Ninth Legion, remember; and there's always been a vague story in the family of some sort of an adventure in the North in his wild young days before he married and settled down. It's just that, and a sort of – feeling I have – you know.'

Justin nodded. He knew. But he said only, 'I wonder ... You know most of this is quite new to me. You must have the family history at your finger-tips.'

Flavius laughed, the odd seriousness of the moment dropping from him as swiftly as seriousness generally did. 'It is not me. It is Aunt Honoria. Nobody sneezed in the family for two hundred years that our Aunt Honoria doesn't remember all about it.' He leaned forward to call to Servius, who had appeared on the lowest of the three vine terraces. '*Sa ha!* Servius, we're up here.'

The old man looked up and saw them, and altered course toward them, marching up between the trained vines with a long legionary swing that seemed to carry with it the unheard jingle of accoutrements. 'I see you.'

He halted just below them. 'Cutha has the supper almost ready.'

Flavius nodded. 'We are coming,' but he made for the moment no move, lingering as though unwilling to abandon his vantage point and come indoors on this last evening of his leave. 'We were saying that the farm looks good,' he said after a moment.

'Aye, none so bad, all things considered.' Servius unconsciously echoed Flavius's words of a short while before. 'But it is in my mind that we are falling behind the times. I'd like fine to see one of those new-fashioned water-mills down below the pool; we've enough head of water to turn the wheel.'

'I'd like it too,' Flavius said. 'But it cannot be done.'

'And well I know it. With the corn tax gone up to where it is, it is as much as we can do to hold our own, let alone rise to any new thing that we can do without.'

Flavius said soberly, 'Don't grudge the corn tax. If we are to have a fleet and coastwise forts to keep the Saxons out, we must pay for them. Do you remember before Carausius took command, summer nights when we saw the coastwise farms burning, and wondered how much farther inland the Sea Wolves would come?'

'Aye,' Servius growled. 'I remember well enough; no need that you remind me. Nay then, I'm not complaining at the corn tax, for I see the need of it – though mind you they do say that that right-hand man of the Emperor's who sees to such things is none so much of the Emperor's mind in the matter of taxes, and would find ways to ease them if he might.'

'Who says?' Flavius said quickly.

'Folks. One of the tax-gatherers himself was talking about it at Venta a week or so back.' Servius pushed himself off from the wall. 'See, Cutha has lit the lamp. I'm away down to my supper, if you aren't.'

And he went swinging off into the softly gathering dusk, toward the light that had sprung up marigold-coloured in the houseplace window.

The two cousins watched him for a moment in silence, then turned, as by common consent, to look at each other. There it was again, that vague half suggestion that Allectus and not Carausius was the man to follow, the man who had the people's good at heart.

Justin, with a little cleft deepening between his brows, was the first to speak. 'That's the second time,' he said.

'Yes,' Flavius said. 'I was just thinking that. But he shut Serapion up firmly enough.'

Justin was thinking back over that little unimportant scene in the shop under the walls of Rutupiae, realizing something that he had not noticed at the time. 'He did not deny it, though.'

'Maybe it was true.'

'I don't see that that makes any d-difference,' said Justin, who had his own rigid code of loyalty.

Flavius looked at him a moment. 'No, you're right, of course it does not,' he said slowly, at last. And then in sudden exasperation, 'Oh Hell and the Furies! We are getting as fanciful as a pair of silly maidens up here in the dusk! First it was the Ninth Legion, and now ... Come on, I want my supper.'

He shook himself off from the wall and went striding down the steep path through the vine terraces towards the light in the window below.

Justin followed, forbearing to point out that it was not he who had had the idea about the Ninth Legion.

3

The House
on the Cliffs

DURING their time at the farm, the weather had been
gentle, green winter weather shot through with the
promise of spring, but no sooner were they on the road
than winter swooped back with the snow on its wings.
That meant hard travelling, but there were still two
hours of daylight left when, on the second day, Justin
and Flavius changed horses at Limanis and set out on the
last stage. The road skirted the forest of Anderida, and
they rode with their ears full of the deep-sea roaring of the
wind in the branches, heads down against the stinging
sleet. And when, a couple of miles farther on, the road
dipped to a paved ford beside which squatted a little forest
smithy, the red glow of the forge fire seemed a kind of
shout of warmth and colour amid the grey moanings of
the storm-lashed woods.

Through the sleet scurry they could make out a small
group of dismounted cavalry before the smithy; and
Flavius said, 'Someone's horse has cast a shoe, by the look
of things.' And then with a low whistle, 'Name of
Thunder! It's the Emperor himself!'

The Emperor it was, sitting very composedly on a fallen
tree-trunk beside the way, with the sleet in his beard and
the eagle-feathers of his helmet crest, and sleet whitening
the shoulders of his purple cloak; and a small cavalry
escort standing by, holding their horses, while Nestor, his
big roan stallion, slobbered at the shoulder of the smith,

who held one great round hoof between his leather-aproned knees.

The Emperor looked up as the two young men drew rein, and raised thick brows under his helmet rim. 'Ah, Centurion Aquila and our Junior Surgeon. What brings you riding these wintry roads?'

Flavius had already swung down from his horse, slipping his arm through the rein. 'Hail Caesar. We are on our way back from leave. Can we be of any service, sir?'

'Thank you, no. Nestor has cast a shoe, as you see, but Goban here has the matter well in hand.'

A stinging blast of sleet whipped their faces, making every man shiver in his cloak, and causing the horses to swerve sideways, turning their heads from the gust. And the Decurion in command of the escort said beseechingly, 'Excellency, will you not take one of my men's horses and ride on? The man can bring Nestor after us.'

Carausius settled more comfortably on his tree trunk, drawing the shoulder folds of his cloak about his ears. 'A little sleet will not shrink me,' he said, and eyed the Decurion with distaste. 'Possibly, however, it is not so much my health that concerns you as that of your men – or possibly even yourself.' And ignoring the poor man's stuttering denial of the charge, turned his gaze back under a cocked eyebrow to the two cousins. 'Are you two due in Rutupiae tonight?'

'No, Caesar,' Flavius said. 'We allowed an extra day, but we have not needed it.'

'Ah, an extra day for a winter journey, that is always a wise precaution. And this is certainly the most wintry of winter journeys.' He seemed to consider for a moment, then nodded as though in full agreement with himself. 'Surely it would be a cruel thing to drag ten men on a needless ten mile ride in such weather as this ... Decurion, you may remount and take your men back to Limanis. I shall remain quietly here until Nestor is re-shod, and then ride on with these two of my Rutupiae officers. They will be all the escort that I shall need.'

Justin, who had dismounted also by this time, and stood holding his horse on the fringe of the group, cast a somewhat startled glance at Flavius, who was staring straight before him as though he were on parade. The Decurion stiffened. 'You – you are dismissing your escort, Caesar?'

'I am dismissing my escort,' agreed Carausius.

The Decurion hesitated an instant, swallowing. 'But Excellency –'

'I bid you farewell, Decurion,' said Carausius. His tone was gentle, but the Decurion whipped to the salute, and turned away in desperate haste, with the order to his men to mount.

It was not until the little escort had swung on to their horses and were clattering away with the wind and sleet behind them down the Limanis road, that the Emperor turned back to the two young men, who stood by, holding their mounts. 'I fear that I forgot to ask you whether you would accompany me,' he said.

Flavius's lip twitched. 'Does one refuse to ride with an Emperor?'

'If one is wise, one does not.' Carausius's blunt seaman's face answered the laughter for an instant, harshly. 'Also, observe; the wind is rising, Rutupiae is all of fifteen miles away, and my house, for which I was bound when Nestor cast his shoe, rather less than five, and once there I can offer you an open fire, and better wine than any they keep in Rutupiae.'

And so some two hours later, fresh from a hot bath, Justin and Flavius were following a slave across the courtyard of a great house on the cliff edge high above the sea, to the chamber in the North Wing where the Emperor waited for them.

The great square chamber was bright with lamps in tall bronze stands, and a fire of logs burned British fashion on a raised hearth, so that all the room was full of the fragrance of burning wood. Carausius, who had been standing by the fire, turned as they entered, saying, 'Ah, you have washed the sleet out of your ears. Come you now, and eat.'

And eat they did, at a small table drawn close before the hearth; a good meal, though an austere one for an Emperor, of hard-boiled duck eggs and sweet downland mutton broiled in milk, and wine that was better, as Carausius had promised, than anything they had at Rutupiae; thin yellow wine that tasted of sunshine and the south, in flasks of wonderful coloured glass, iridescent as the feathers of a pigeon's neck, and wound about with gold and inset jewels.

They were served by soft-footed table slaves of the usual kind, but behind Carausius's chair, to serve him personally, stood a creature whom they had glimpsed once or twice before, distantly, at his lord's heel, but never seen at close quarters.

He was a very small man, lightly built as a mountain cat, his legs sheathed in close-fitting dark hose, his body in a woollen tunic of many coloured chequer that clung to him like a second skin. Straight black hair hung in heavy locks about his cheeks and neck, and his enormous eyes were made to seem still larger and more brilliant in his narrow, beardless face by the fine blue lines of tattooing that rimmed them round. About his waist was a broad strap of crimson leather set with bright bronze studs like a hound's collar, and into this was thrust a musical instrument of some kind, a curved rod of bronze from which hung nine silver apples that gave out a thin and very sweet chiming as he moved. But the strangest thing about him only appeared when he turned away to take a dish from another slave, and Justin saw that hanging from his belt behind, he wore a hound's tail.

The odd creature served his master with a kind of proud and prancing willingness, a slightly fantastic flourish that was very different from the well-trained impersonal bearing of the other slaves. And when the third course of dried fruits and little hot cakes had been set on the table, and Carausius dismissed the serving slaves, the creature did not go with them, but laid himself down, hound-wise, before the fire. 'When the Lord of the House is away, Cullen sleeps in the warm cook-place. When the Lord of the House comes home, Cullen sleeps beside his lord's fire,' he said composedly, stretching himself out on one elbow.

The Emperor glanced down at him. 'Good Hound, Cullen,' he said, and taking a cluster of raisins from the red samian dish, tossed it down to him.

Cullen caught it with a swift and oddly beautiful gesture of one hand, his strange face splitting into a grin which reached from ear to ear. 'So! I am my Lord's hound, and my Lord feeds me from his own table.'

The Emperor, turning again in his chair, one hand out to the wine-flask, caught Justin's fascinated and puzzled gaze on the little man, and said with that straight, wide-lipped smile of his, 'The High King of Erin has his Druth, his Household Fool, and should the third-part Emperor of Rome lack what the High King of Erin has?'

Cullen nodded, eating raisins and spitting the pips into the fire. 'Wherefore my Lord Curoi bought me from the slavers up yonder on the coast of the Western Sea, that he might not lack what the High King of Erin has in his Halls at Tara – and also, it is in my mind, because I was from Laighin, even as my Lord. And I have been my Lord's hound these seven summers and winters past.' Then, spinning over and coming to his knee in a single kingfisher flash of movement, he took from his belt the instrument that Justin had noticed before.

Sitting cross-legged now beside the fire, while above him the talk drifted on to other matters, he tipped the thing with a curious flick of the wrist, and a kind of ripple of bell-notes ran from the smallest apple at the tip to the greatest just above the thick enamelled handle and up again, in a minor key. Then, very quietly, and clearly for his own pleasure, he began to play – if playing it could be called, for there was no tune, only single notes, falling now soft, now clear, as he flicked each silver apple with knuckle or nail; single notes that seemed to fall from a great height like shining drops distilled out of the emptiness, each perfect in itself.

It was a strange evening; an evening that Justin never forgot. Outside, the beat of the wind and the far-down boom of the sea, and within, the scent of burning logs, the steady radiance of the lamps, and the stains of quivering coloured light cast upon the table by the wine in its iridescent flasks. He held his hand in one such pool, to see it splashed with crimson and emerald and living peacock-blue; and wondered suddenly whether these wonderful flasks, whether Carausius's great gold cup and the hangings of thick Eastern embroideries that shut off the end of the room, and the coral-studded bridle-bit on the wall behind him, had all known the hold of a black-winged Saxon longship. Outside, the wild wings and the voices of the storm; and within, the little flames flickering among the logs, and facing each other around the table, Flavius and himself and the little thick-set seaman who was Emperor of Britain; while the strange slave Cullen sprawled hound-wise beside the fire, idly touching the apples of his Silver Branch.

It had been for little more than a despot's whim, Justin knew, that Carausius had dismissed his escort and ordered the two of them to ride with him instead; but far down within him he knew also that after this evening, though they never met again like this, there would be something between them that was not usually between an Emperor and two of his most junior officers.

Yes, a most strange evening.

Carausius had most of the talk, as was fitting, while the two young men sat with their cups of watered wine before them, and listened. And indeed it was talk worth listening to, for Carausius was not merely an Emperor, he had been a Scaldis river pilot, and the commander of a Roman Fleet, a Centurion under Carus in the Persian War, and a boy growing up in Laighin, three days south from Tara of the Kings. He had known strange places, and done strange things, and he could talk of them so that they came to life for his hearers.

And then, as though suddenly tired of his own talk, he rose and turned to the curtained end of the room. 'Ah, but I have talked enough of yesterday. I will show you a thing that is for today. Come here, both of you.'

Chairs rasped on the tesserai, and Justin and Flavius were close at his shoulder as he flung back the hangings glimmering with peacock and pomegranate colours, and passed through. Justin, the last to follow, was aware of a grey, storm-lashed window and a sense of the wild night leaping in on them with a shout, and stood an instant holding the rich folds back, uncertain whether they might need the light of the room behind them for whatever it was that they were going to see. But Carausius said, 'Let the curtains fall. Can't see with the lamplight dancing in the panes.' And he let the dark hangings swing across behind him.

As he did so, and the lamplight was cut off, the world outside sprang out of the darkness into a hurrying, moon-shot clarity. They were standing in the bay of a great window such as Justin had never seen before, that swole out with the curve of a drawn bow; a window that was a veritable watch-tower, a falcon's eyrie, clinging as it seemed to the very edge of the cliff.

A ragged sky of grey and silver went racing by, the moon swinging in and out of the storm-scuds, so that one moment the whole sweep of the coast was flooded with swift silver radiance, and the next, all would be blotted out by a curtain of driving sleet. Far below them the white-capped waves charged by, rank on rank, like wild white cavalry. And far away to the eastward, as Justin looked along the coast, a red petal of fire hung on the dark head-land.

'This is my look-out,' Carausius said. 'A good place to watch my shipping come and go, with Dubris light and Limanis and Rutupiae lights to guide them safely in their coming and their going.' He seemed to sense the direction of Justin's gaze. 'That is the pharos at Dubris on the head-land. Limanis light one can see from the hill behind the house. Now look out to sea – yonder on the edge of the world south-eastward.'

Justin looked, and as a sleet-squall passed away from the sea, leaving the distance clear, saw, very far off, another spark of light on the skyline.

'That is Gesoriacum,' said Carausius.

They were silent a moment, remembering that last winter Gesoriacum had been within the territory of the man beside them. And in that silence, above the mingled voices of wind and sea, the ripple of Cullen's Silver Branch sounded in the room behind them, faint and sweet and somehow mocking.

Flavius said quickly, as though in answer to that silver mocking of bells, 'Maybe we are better off without Gesori-acum. An outlying post is always something of a liability.'

Carausius gave a harsh bark of laughter. 'It is a bold

man who seeks to console his Emperor for past defeat!'

'I did not mean it as consolation,' Flavius said levelly. 'I spoke what I believe to be true.'

'So? And you believe rightly.' Justin could hear that straight, wide-lipped smile of Carausius's in his voice. 'Yet it is truth that wears one face for him who seeks to make a single province strong, and quite another for him who would strengthen and enlarge his own hold on the Purple.'

He fell silent, his face turned towards that spark of light, dimming already as another sleet-squall came trailing across the sea. And when he spoke again, it was broodingly, more than half to himself. 'Nay, but whichever it be, either or – both, the true secret is in sea-power, which is a thing that Rome has never understood ... In greater fleets, manned by better seamen. Legions we must have, but above all, sea-power, here with the sea all about us.'

'Some sea-power we have already, as Maximian found to his cost,' Flavius said, leaning a shoulder against the window frame and looking down. 'Aye, and the black-sailed fleets of the Sea Wolves also.'

'Yet the Wolves gather,' Carausius said. 'Young Constantius would be hard put to it to take his troops from the German Frontier *this* spring to drive me from Gesoriacum ... Always, everywhere, the Wolves gather on the frontiers, waiting. It needs only that a man should lower his eye for a moment, and they will be in to strip the bones. Rome is failing, my children.'

Justin looked at him quickly, but Flavius never moved; it was as though he had known what Carausius would say.

'Oh, she is not finished yet. I shall not see her fall – my Purple will last my life-time – and nor, I think, will you. Nevertheless, Rome is hollow rotten at the heart, and one day she will come crashing down. A hundred years ago, it must have seemed that all this was for ever; a hundred

years hence – only the gods know ... If I can make this
one province strong – strong enough to stand alone when
Rome goes down, then something may be saved from the
darkness. If not, then Dubris light and Limanis light and
Rutupiae light will go out. The lights will go out everywhere.' He stepped back, dragging aside the hanging folds
of the curtains, and stood framed in their darkness against
the firelight and the lamplight behind him, his head yet
turned to the scudding grey and silver of the stormy night.
'If I can steer clear of a knife in my back until the work
is done, I will make Britain strong enough to stand alone,'
he said. 'It is as simple as that.'

As they turned back to the lamplit room, Flavius said
swiftly and urgently, 'Caesar knows that for all the worth
that there is in us, we are Caesar's men for life or death,
Justin and I.'

Carausius stood for an instant, the curtain still in his
hand, and looked at them. 'Caesar knows,' he said at last.
'Aye, Caesar knows that, my children,' and let the dark
folds fall between the lamplight and the scudding moon.

4

The Sea Wolf

SEVERAL times as that winter drew on to spring, Justin and Flavius went out together after wild fowl in the marshes: the strange border country between land and sea, that had for Justin the magic of all half-way things.

Their usual hunting ground was Tanatus, the great marsh island across the shipping lane from Rutupiae, but about mid March there were reports of a Saxon ship hovering in the seaways that had somehow eluded the patrol galleys, and Tanatus was put out of bounds to the fortress because of the ease with which stray, wild-fowling Legionaries might be cut off there by the Sea Wolves. And so, in the dark of a certain March morning, Justin and Flavius made their way out to the forsaken fisher village at the southernmost tip of the mainland marshes.

And now they were crouching among the reeds in the lea of the old dyke that had once served to keep back the sea from the village, their bows ready strung, and the small birding bolts stuck barb-down in the turf before them.

The dawn was coming. It was in the smell of the little knife-edged wind that shivered and sang through the hairy grasses and about the crumbling turf walls of the abandoned village; in the calling of curlew and sandpiper; in the faint, sheeny paleness creeping up the eastern sky and the fading of the red iris-bud of flame that was Rutupiae light. Slowly the light gathered and grew; any moment now they would hear the wing-beats of the wild duck rising into the wind; the steady throb of wings that was the beginning of the dawn flight.

But before it came, another sound caught their straining ears; a sound so faint and so swiftly stilled that it might have been almost anything, or nothing at all. Yet there was about it a suggestion of being human and a suggestion of stealth that made it alien among the other sounds of the marsh.

Flavius stiffened, staring away to his left through the thin curtain of reeds that they had left between themselves and the outer world.

'What is it?' Justin whispered. And the other made a quick gesture for silence; then, timing the movement of his hand with a gust of wind, swayed back a few of the tall reeds. And Justin saw.

A man was standing not more than a spear-throw from them, his head turned to watch another who had that moment emerged from the willow-break farther inland. The water-cool light, growing every moment stronger, showed them the round buckler between his shoulders, and the wiry yellow gold of his hair and beard; and his sword-side being towards them, they could see the saex, the short Saxon thrusting-sword, in its wolfskin sheath at his belt. And as the second man drew nearer, Flavius gave a long, soundless whistle. 'Name of Thunder!' he whispered. 'It is Allectus!'

Justin, crouching frozen beside him, was without any surprise. It was as though he had known.

Allectus had come up with the other man now. The Saxon said something in a low, angry growl, and he replied more loudly, 'Aye, I know it is dangerous after cock-light. If I could have come sooner I would have done so – for my own skin's sake. After all, it is I who run the chief risk. You have but to lie hid until the *Sea Witch* puts in for you ... Now this is what I have to say to your lords who sent you.' But even as he spoke, the two men had turned away together, and their voices sank to a formless murmuring.

Justin strained every sense to catch what they were saying, but could make nothing of the low mutter. Indeed he had a feeling that they had abandoned Latin and were speaking in a tongue that he did not know. He scanned the ground ahead of him, searching desperately for some means of getting closer without being seen, but once out of the reeds there was no cover for a curlew, let alone a man.

And then suddenly it seemed that the two men had reached the end of whatever it was that they had to say to each other. The Saxon nodded, as though in answer to some order; and Allectus turned away in the direction from which he had come. The Saxon stood a few moments looking after him, then, with a shrug, turned himself about and bending low so as not to break the skyline, set off along the old thorn windbreak, heading westward for the wildest and most solitary part of the marsh.

Among the reeds Justin and Flavius took one look into each other's faces. There was no time to think, no time to weigh one thing against another and decide what was best to do. They must make an instant decision, and abide by it wherever it led them.

'Wait till he rounds the end of the windbreak,' Flavius muttered, his eyes narrowed as he stared out through the parted reeds. 'If we go after him now, and he cries out, it will warn friend Allectus.'

Justin nodded. From where he was he could no longer see the retreating Saxon, and so he watched Flavius crouching with a knee drawn under him like a runner poised for the start of a race, watched him grow tense on the edge of movement ...

'Now,' Flavius breathed.

They were out from the reeds like an arrow from a bow, running low for the end of the windbreak. By the time they reached it the man had disappeared from sight, but a few moments later, as they checked uncertain, he came into view again at the curve of a dry dyke, and glancing once behind him, struck out into the open over the tawny levels.

'He's probably got a hideout somewhere among the dunes,' Flavius said. 'Come on!'

And again they were out after him. There was no possibility now of keeping under cover – when he looked back he was bound to see them, and it would be a matter of speed against speed, and nothing else. At least they must be well out of earshot of Allectus by this time.

They had almost halved the distance between them when, on the edge of a clump of wind-twisted thorn trees the Saxon checked and glanced back, as they had known he must before long. Justin saw him freeze for one instant into intense stillness, like an animal that scents the hunter; then his hand flew to his sword-hilt, and next instant he had sprung away, running like a hare with the two young Romans on his trail.

As though realizing the danger of such country, lacking all shelter, and veined by the wandering arms of the sea that might cut him off at any moment, the Saxon changed course almost at once, and began to swing away from the coast, heading inland for the forest fringe; and knowing that once he gained the trees they would almost certainly lose him, Justin and Flavius lengthened their stride, straining every nerve to come up with him before he reached shelter. Flavius was drawing slowly away from his kinsman, slowly nearer to the desperate quarry, while Justin, who was not much of a runner, came pounding doggedly along in the rear. The smoke-grey shoreline of the bare woods was very near now, and Justin was far behind, snatching at his breath in great gasps. He felt horribly sick, and he was deaf with the drubbing of his own heart; but the only thing in his mind was that away ahead of him, Flavius with only a little dagger was alone on the heels of a desperate man running with a naked sword in his hand.

On and on, the two figures in front were running almost as one now. They were into the furze and blackthorn scrub, when suddenly – he could not see quite what happened, he was too blind with his own running – the foremost figure seemed to stumble, and instantly the other was upon him. Justin saw them go down together, and put on one last heart-tearing burst of speed. Flavius and the Saxon were locked together in a struggling mass as he reached them; and through the buzzing haze before his eyes he caught the gleam of the naked blade upon the tawny grass, and Flavius's hand gripping white-knuckled about the Saxon's sword-wrist. He dropped upon it, twisted the sword out of the man's grasp and sent it spinning sideways. Flavius, with a hand now to spare, drew it back and hit the Saxon cleanly under the ear, and the fight went out of him in one gasp.

'So – that is better,' Flavius panted. 'Now help me bind his hands. The spare bow-strings will serve.'

They got his arms behind him and lashed his wrists together with the thin, strong bow-string which Justin, still sobbing for breath, dragged out from his belt; and rolled him over on his back. Flavius had struck only hard enough to quieten the man for the moment, and he was coming to himself already. His eyes opened, and he lay staring up at them stupidly, then his lips parted in a snarl, his teeth showing little and pointed in the gold of his beard, and he began to fight like a wild beast at his bonds.

Flavius had a knee on his chest, and slipping the dagger from his belt, held it to his throat. 'No use to struggle, my friend,' he said. 'Never wise to struggle with a hand-span of cold iron against your windpipe.'

Justin, still feeling very sick, but with the breath beginning to come back into him, crossed to the Saxon's sword where it had fallen among the roots of a gorse-bush. He picked it up and turned again to the other two. The Saxon had ceased to struggle, and lay glaring at his captor.

'Why do you set on me?' he demanded at last, speaking in Latin, but with a thick and guttural accent that made it almost unintelligible. 'I do no harm – I am from the Rhenus Fleet.'

'And you with the gear and weapons of a Saxon pirate on you,' Flavius said softly. 'Go tell that tale to the sea-mews.'

The man was silent a moment, then he said with sullen pride, '*Sa*; I will tell it to the seamews. What do you want with me?'

'What passed between you and the man you met back yonder by the ruined fisher-huts?'

'That is a thing between the man and me.'

Justin said quickly, 'It doesn't m-matter much for now. Whatever his orders or his message are, he won't be passing them on, and someone else can get the truth out of him later. Our job is to get him up to the fortress.'

Flavius nodded, his eyes never leaving the Saxon's face. 'Yes, you are in the right of it. The main thing is to get him back; otherwise it is but our word against Allectus's.' He lifted his knee from the man's chest. 'Up, you.'

Rather more than an hour later, they stood before the Commandant in his office, their captive between them, his eyes darting and sliding from side to side in search of a way of escape.

Mutius Urbanus, Commandant of Rutupiae, was a thin, stooping man with a long, grey face a little like a tired old horse's; but his eyes were shrewdly alert as he leaned back in his chair surveying the three before him. 'So, one of the Sea Wolves,' he was saying. 'How did you come by him?'

'We were out on the marshes by the old fisher-huts, sir,' Flavius said, 'lying up among the reeds for the duck, and we saw a meeting between this man and – a man of our own. After they parted we gave chase to this one, and – here he is.'

The Commandant nodded. 'And this man of our own. Who was he?'

There was a silence, and then Flavius said deliberately, 'We did not know him, sir.'

'How then did you know him for a man of our own?'

Flavius never blinked an eyelid. 'He was in uniform, sir.'

'Centurion Aquila,' said the Commandant, 'I am not sure that I believe you.'

'I am sorry, sir.' Flavius looked him straight in the eye, and pressed on to the next thing. 'Sir, I believe the Emperor is expected this evening? Will you apply for us – Justin and myself – to have speech with him as soon as may be after his arrival, and meanwhile have this man bestowed in the Guard-house to await his coming?'

Urbanus raised his brows. 'I scarcely think that this is such a matter as need go to Caesar.'

Flavius came a step nearer and set a hand on the littered table, desperate urgency in both face and voice. 'But it is, sir. I swear to you that it is. If it doesn't go to Caesar, and that quickly, and without anyone else meddling with it first, the gods alone know what the consequences may be!'

'So?' The Commandant's gaze turned on Justin. 'And you also are of that opinion?'

'I also,' said Justin.

'And you do not know who the other man was. More

than ever I am not sure that I believe you, Centurion Aquila.' The Commandant tapped his nose gently with the butt end of his stylus, a trick of his when thoughtful. Then he said abruptly, 'So let it be; you shall have your speech with the Emperor. But your reason for this mystery, whatever it may be, had better be a good one, for if it is not, and you make me look a fool, the gods may have mercy on you, but I'll have none.' He raised his voice to the Optio of the Guard standing at the door. 'Optio, take this man down to the cells. You two had best go and see him safely under lock and key. After that I suggest that you change into uniform. I will send for you when you may speak with the Emperor.'

'Thank you, sir. At once, sir.' Flavius drew himself up and saluted, followed by Justin; and behind the two Legionaries of the Guard who had appeared to take their places on either side of the captive, marched out from the Commandant's office across the Praetorium Courtyard into the parade-ground of the fort. They were just crossing the Via Principia when they met a party of horsemen clattering up it from the main gate and the Londinium road; and drawing aside to give them the crown of the way, Justin saw that the tall man in civilian dress riding in their midst was Allectus.

He glanced down at them as he passed, and his glance lighted on the face of the Saxon captive – and seemed to hang there an instant before it moved on; and to Justin it seemed that his face stiffened for that instant into a mere smiling mask. But he gave no sign, and rode by without a second glance; and the little party moved forward again, hobnailed sandals ringing on the cobbles, down between the workshops where the armourers were busy, and so to the Guard-house by the gate.

'It is a most hideous piece of ill fortune that Allectus saw him,' Flavius said, as they recrossed the parade-ground

towards their quarters. 'I suppose he has come on ahead
of Carausius – leastwise it's meant to look like that.'

'He can't know for sure that we saw him with the
Saxon,' Justin said. 'We might have come on the man
afterward. And anyway, there can be little enough that he
can do about it without b-betraying himself still more
completely.'

'I don't know. I can't think of anything; but then – I'm
not Allectus.' And Justin saw that his kinsman was very
white in the thin March sunlight.

In the pressure of work that waited for him in the
hospital that day, Justin had little more leisure to think
about Allectus, even when he heard in the distance the
clatter of hooves and the sound of trumpets that heralded
the Emperor's arrival. He was measuring a draught for
one of his patients when at last the Commandant's summons reached him, and he finished the task with great
care and exactness before he went clattering down the
stone stairway after the messenger, hastily making sure
that nothing was amiss with his uniform tunic and the
clasp of his belt was dead centre.

Outside he met Flavius hurrying to answer the same
summons and they went on together.

The two young tribunes on duty in the Ante-room of
the Emperor's quarters looked at them with interest.
Clearly the story of their having brought in a Saxon captive that morning had gone the rounds. And one of them
rose and disappeared into the inner chamber, returning
in a few moments to stand aside, leaving the door open.
'Go in now, the Emperor will see you.'

Carausius had done no more than lay aside crested helmet and heavy mud-sparked cloak before turning himself
to his writing-table, on which various papers awaited his
attention. He was standing beside it now, an open scroll in
his hands; he looked up as they entered. 'Ah, you two

again. The Commandant tells me that you would speak
to me on a matter of urgency. Surely it must be a matter
of very great urgency that even at this late hour it cannot wait for the morning.'

'Caesar, it is a matter of very great urgency,' Flavius
said, saluting, as the door closed behind them. His gaze
went past the Emperor to the tall figure lounging in the
farther shadows. 'Caesar, we would have speech with you
alone.'

'If the matter be indeed as urgent as you appear to think
it, speak and have done,' Carausius said. 'You can scarcely
expect that I shall dismiss the chief among my ministers
like a dog to his kennel at your behest.'

Justin, standing at Flavius's shoulder, felt him stiffen,
felt the resolve take shape and harden in him. 'Be it as you
say, Caesar; I will speak and have done. This morning we
two were lying up in the reeds by the old fisher-huts, waiting for the duck. There we saw – though we could make
out little of what passed – a meeting between one of the
Sea Wolves and a certain man of our own camp.'

Carausius let the scroll he was holding roll back on itself with a snapping sound. 'That much I have already
gathered from the Commandant Urbanus,' he said. 'What
was the little that you made out to pass between
them?'

'Nothing to much purpose. The Saxon seemed to protest at the other man's lateness, and the other said, "I
know it is dangerous after daylight. I would have come
earlier if I could, for my own skin's sake. I run the chief
risk; you have but to lie hid until the *Sea Witch* puts in
for you." That is as near as I can remember it. And then
he said, "Now this is what I have to say to your Lords who
sent you," and after that they turned away together and
we could hear no more.'

'And this – certain man of our own camp. You told the

Commandant that you did not know who he was. Was that the truth?'

The split moment of silence seemed to tingle. Then Flavius said, 'No, Caesar, it was not.'

'Who was he, then?'

'The chief among your ministers, Allectus,' Flavius said.

His words seemed to fall into the stillness like a pebble in a pool, and Justin had a vivid awareness of them spreading out and out like ripples across the waiting silence, until they burst and shattered as Allectus sprang up from the couch on which he had been lounging, with an exclamation between rage and sheer amazement.

'Roma Dea! If this be a jest –'

'It is no jest,' Flavius flung back at him. 'I give you my word of that.'

And then Caesar's voice came like a naked blade between them. 'Let me be clear about this thing. With what, exactly, do you charge my chief minister Allectus?'

'With holding secret converse with the Sea Wolves, who are our enemies,' Flavius said.

'So, that is clear at all events.' Carausius turned a bleak stare upon Justin. 'You make the same charge?'

With his mouth uncomfortably dry, Justin said, 'I saw what Flavius my kinsman saw. I make the same charge.'

'And what defence has Allectus my chief minister to set against that?'

Allectus seemed to have got over his first astonishment and to be now merely angry. 'The thing is so – so outrageous that I scarce know what to say. Am I to seriously defend myself from such a preposterous charge?'

Carausius gave a mirthless bark of laughter. 'I scarcely think so.'

Flavius took an impulsive step forward. 'Caesar, the matter does not rest on our word alone. The Saxon is held captive in the Guard-house at this moment; let him be brought face to face with Allectus, and assuredly the truth may be laid bare!'

'So – it seems that you have plotted this thing with remarkable care!' Allectus exclaimed; but Carausius's voice drowned the sentence.

'Centurion Aquila, will you open the door behind you and summon me a tribune?'

Flavius did as he was bid, and a moment later the tribune stood saluting on the threshold. 'Excellency?'

'I wish the prisoner in –' Carausius turned to Flavius, who replied to the unspoken question, 'Number five cell.'

'Ah, the prisoner in number five cell brought here immediately, Tribune Vipsanius.'

Tribune Vipsanius saluted again, and withdrew. They heard his clipped footsteps through the Ante-room, and voice as he issued an order outside.

In the Emperor's quarters an utter silence settled; a silence that was complete and oppressive, as though they were inside a giant gong. Justin, standing with Flavius near the door, was staring straight before him, seemingly at nothing. Yet he was aware of all kinds of details that he remembered afterwards. The perfect shadow of Carausius's great helmet – every eagle-feather of the crest sharply distinct – thrown on the lamplit wall; a little muscle twitching in the angle of Flavius's set jaw; the colour of the evening sky beyond the window, peacock blue, filmed with a kind of murky gold-dust haze by the great pharos beacon. And then a sound grew in the stillness, a small insistent rapping and drumming; and turning his eyes in the direction from which it came, he saw that Allectus, still standing by the couch from which he had risen, had begun to beat a tattoo with long, strong fingers on the wooden couch-head beside him. His face, pale as always in the lamplight, showed nothing but the set mouth and frowning brows of anger with difficulty held in check. Justin

wondered what was going on behind the pale, angry mask;
was it the fear and fury of the trapped – or only a cool
brain making or changing plans? The tattoo seemed to
grow louder and louder in the stillness, and then it was
joined by another sound: the urgent beat of footsteps,
half marching, half running. The footsteps of two men,
Justin thought, not more.

A few moments later Tribune Vipsanius again stood in
the doorway, and with him the Centurion of the prison
guard breathing heavily through his nose.

'Excellency,' said Tribune Vipsanius, 'the prisoner in
number five cell is dead.'

5

Nightshade!

JUSTIN had a physical sensation as if he had been jolted in the stomach, and yet in an odd way he knew that he was not surprised. Allectus had ceased his drumming. Carausius set down the scroll on the table, very softly and exactly, and demanded, 'How comes that about?'

The Tribune shook his head. 'I do not know, Caesar; he's just – dead.'

'Centurion?'

The Centurion stared straight before him. 'The prisoner was well enough, though dumb sullen, when his evening food went in to him an hour or so since; and now he's dead, same as the Tribune said. That's all I know, Caesar.'

Carausius stood away from the table. 'It seems that I must come and see for myself.' Then to Justin and Flavius, 'You will accompany me.'

As the little group turned to the doorway, Allectus stepped forward. 'Caesar, since this is a matter that concerns me somewhat closely, with your leave I also will accompany you.'

'In Typhon's name come then,' Carausius said, and strode out with the rest behind him.

The Guard-house seemed disturbed and excited. In the first cell a drunken legionary was singing.

> Oh why did I join the Eagles
> The Empire for to roam?
> Oh why did I leave me pumpkin patch
> And me little dun cow at home?

Their footsteps rang hollow down the flagged passage-way. The pale blur of a face appeared at the barred squint of a door, and hastily disappeared again as they went by. The voice of the singer fell more faintly behind them.

> They said I'd rise to Emperor
> As sure as sure could be,
> If I left me little pumpkin patch
> And sailed across the sea.

The door of the farthest cell was ajar, and a sentry who stood before it moved aside to make way for them. The cell was in darkness save for the reflection of the pharos beacon shining down through the high barred window, and the red square of light striped with shadows of the bars fell full across the figure of the Saxon lying face down of the floor.

'Bring a light, somebody,' Carausius said, without raising his voice.

Justin, the surgeon in him suddenly uppermost, had pushed through the rest, and was already kneeling beside the fallen man as the Centurion brought the Guard-room lantern. There was nothing to be done for the Saxon, and one look at him in the lantern light told Justin all he needed to know. 'Nightshade,' he said. 'He's been poisoned.'

'How?' Carausius snapped.

Justin did not answer at once, but picked up the pottery bowl that lay beside the man and sniffed the few thick drops of broth remaining in it. He tasted gingerly, and then spat. 'Probably in his supper broth. Quite simply.'

Away down the passage the singer had begun again, in a tone of deep melancholy.

> So I upped and joined the Eagles,
> And I left me little cow,

> And I may be Emperor one of these days,
> But Mother, just *look* at me now!

Justin had a sudden insane desire to laugh – to laugh and laugh until he was sick. But the sight of Flavius's face steadied him.

It was Allectus who spoke first. 'Then it must have been one of the prison guard. No one else could have been sure in which bowl to put the poison.'

'No, sir,' the Centurion contradicted respectfully. 'That isn't so, sir. There are only three other men in detention at this moment, and they are all on bread and water for their sins. Easy enough, 'twould be, for anyone to find that out and act according.'

Flavius cut in – Flavius with very bright eyes in a fierce white face. 'What matter for the moment how the poison came into the man's bowl? The thing that matters is *why*, and the answer to that is plain. Alive, he could tell who it was that he met on the marshes this morning, and what passed between them. Therefore he has died. Caesar, does the proof suffice?'

'It is both chilly and depressing in this place,' said Carausius. 'Shall we return to my quarters?'

And not until they were back in the lamplit office, and the door shut behind them, did he speak again, as though Flavius had but that moment asked his question. 'The Saxon you caught this morning in the marshes did indeed have dealings with *someone* in Rutupiae. For that, the proof suffices. No more.' Then as Flavius made a quick gesture of protest, 'Nay, hear me out. Had I, or the Camp Commandant or the bath-house sweeper had dealings with this Saxon, we should have had but two courses open to us after he was taken : to contrive his escape, or to kill him before he was questioned. And of the two, the second would be the surer and simpler method.'

Flavius spoke in a dead-level voice that somehow gave

all the more desperate earnestness to his words. 'Caesar, I beg you to listen to us. We were no more than a spear-throw from our men, it was more than half light, and neither of us is blind. We could not have been mistaken. If indeed the other man was not Allectus, then it must be that for some purpose of our own we deliberately bear false witness against him. Do you accuse us of that?'

Allectus himself answered first, with the quickness of anger. 'That is assuredly the most likely explanation of your behaviour. What you yourself have to gain by this I cannot imagine – it may be that your cousin has in-fluenced you in some way – but as for our Junior Surgeon,' he turned to Carausius, 'I remember that when first he was posted here, you yourself, Caesar, were not too sure of his good faith. This is surely some plot of Maximian's, to cast doubt and suspicion between the Emperor of Britain and the man who, however unworthily, serves him to the best of his ability as chief minister.'

Justin stepped forward, his hands clenched at his sides. 'That is a foul lie,' he said, for once without a trace of his stutter. 'And you know it, Allectus; none better.'

'Will you grant me also a space to speak?' Carausius said quietly, and silence fell like a blight on the lamplit chamber. He looked round at all three of them, taking his time.

'I remember my doubts, Allectus. I remember also that the dawn-light can be uncertain, and that there are in Rutupiae more tall, fair-haired men than one. – They will all be questioned in due course. – I believe that this has been an honest mistake.' He turned his attention to the two young men. 'However, I, Carausius, do not tolerate such mistakes, and I have no further use for the men who make them. Tomorrow you will receive fresh postings; and it may be that life on the Wall will keep you better occupied and save your over-active fancies from leading you into such mistakes again.' He picked up the scroll that he had been studying when they first entered. 'You may go now. I have no more to say.'

For one instant neither of the two made any move. Then Flavius drew himself rigidly to attention, and saluted. 'It is as Caesar commands,' he said, and opened the door and walked stiffly out.

Justin followed him, carefully closing the door at his back. On the far side of it, he heard Allectus's voice beginning, 'Caesar is too lenient –' and the rest was lost.

'Come to my sleeping-cell,' Flavius demanded, as they crossed the parade-ground under the great pharos.

'I will by and by,' Justin said dully. 'There are men needing me in the hospital. I must see to them first.'

Tomorrow they would be no affair of his, those men; but tonight he was the surgeon on duty, and it was not until he had made his round of the men in his care, that he went to join Flavius.

Flavius was sitting on the edge of his cot, staring straight before him; his red hair ruffled like the feathers of a bird with the wind behind it, his face, in the light of the wall lamp overhead, drawn and white and angry. He looked up as Justin entered, and jerked his head towards the clothes-chest.

Justin sat down, his arms across his knees, and for a while they looked at each other in silence. Then Flavius said, 'Well, so that is that.'

Justin nodded, and the silence settled again.

And again it was Flavius who broke it. 'I'd have staked all I possess that the Emperor would have given us a fair hearing,' he said moodily.

'I suppose coming out of a clear sky, it would be hard to believe that someone you trusted could betray you,' Justin said.

'Not for Carausius,' Flavius returned with certainty. 'He is not the blindly trusting kind.'

Justin said, 'If the *Sea Witch* puts in again to pick up

that Saxon, maybe our galleys will get her, and the truth will come out that way.'

The other shook his head. 'Allectus will find means to warn her not to come.' He stretched, with an angry and miserable laugh. 'Well, no good to yelp about it. He did *not* believe us, and that's all there is to it. We did our best, and there's nothing more that we can do – and if one day, in some stinking little Auxiliary outpost of the Wall, we hear that Allectus has led a Saxon invasion and made himself Emperor, I hope we both find that very comforting.' He got up, stretching still. 'The Emperor's done with us. We're broke, my lad, broke, and to no purpose. Get off that clothes-chest. I want to start packing.'

The sleeping-cell was looking as though it had been hit by a whirlwind, when a while later the tramp of feet came up the stair, and there was a rap on the door.

Justin, who was nearest, opened it, to find one of the Commandant's messengers standing there. 'For the Centurion Aquila,' said the man; and then, recognizing Justin, 'For you also, sir, if you will take it here.'

A few moments later he had disappeared into the night, and Flavius and Justin turned to look at each other, each with a sealed tablet in his hand.

'So he could not even wait for tomorrow to give us our marching orders,' Flavius said bitterly, snapping the crimson thread under the seal.

Justin broke the thread of his own, and opened out the two leaves of the tablet, hastily scanning the few lines of writing scored on the wax inside. A half-made exclamation from his cousin made him look up in inquiry. Flavius read out slowly, 'To proceed at once to Magnis on the Wall, to take over command of the Eighth Cohort of the Second Augustan Legion.'

'We are to be posted together, then,' Justin said. 'I am to report as Surgeon to the same Cohort.'

'The Eighth,' Flavius said, and sat down on his cot. 'I don't understand – I simply don't understand.'

Justin knew what he meant. It scarcely seemed a likely moment to be getting promotion; and yet it was promotion for both of them. Nothing spectacular, just the step up that should have come to them before long, in the normal way of things, but promotion, all the same.

Outside in the tawny half-light that was all Rutupiae ever knew of darkness, the trumpets sounded for the second watch of the night. Justin gave up the attempt to understand. 'I'm going to get some sleep,' he said. 'We must needs make an early start in the morning.' In the doorway he turned. 'C-could it be that Carausius knows he was there, that he was there by his orders, for some purpose best not brought into the daylight?'

Flavius shook his head. 'That wouldn't account for the Saxon's death.'

They were silent a moment, looking at each other. The terrible little Emperor would most certainly not allow one man's life – and he an enemy – to stand between him and his plans, but just as surely, he would have found another way, not poison. Justin would have staked his own life on that without hesitation.

'Maybe he is using Allectus for his own ends, without Allectus knowing,' he suggested. That would still leave the poisoning where he was convinced that it belonged, at Allectus's door.

'I simply – don't know,' Flavius said; and then suddenly explosive: 'I don't know and I don't care! Go to bed.'

6

Evicatos of the Spear

'You have come to the world's end,' said Centurion Posides. The three of them were in the Commander's quarters of Magnis on the Wall, where Flavius had just taken over from the man who would now be his Number Two. 'I hope you like it.'

'I don't very much,' Flavius said frankly. 'But that is beside the point. I also don't like the way the garrison bears itself on parade, Centurion Posides, and that is very much to the point.'

Centurion Posides shrugged; he was a big man with a little, crumpled, bitter face. 'You'll see no better anywhere else along the Wall. What can you expect from a mob of Auxiliaries, the sweepings of every breed and colour in the Empire?'

'The Eighth happens to be a legionary Cohort,' Flavius said.

'Aye, and here come you straight from your fine new fortress at Rutupiae, under the Emperor's eye, and think all legionary Cohorts are the same,' said Centurion Posides. 'Well, there was a time when I thought the like. You'll mend your ideas in time.'

'Either that, or the garrison of Magnis will mend its ideas,' Flavius said, standing with his feet apart and his hands behind his back. 'I rather think that it will be the garrison, Centurion Posides.'

But at first it seemed that he was mistaken in that.

Everything that could be wrong with Magnis, was wrong with Magnis. Fort and garrison alike were dirty and unkempt, the bathhouse smelt, the cooks were stealing the rations and selling them outside the walls. Even the catapults and skeins of the battery covering the North Gate were in ill repair.

'How often do you have catapult practice?' Flavius demanded when he came to the battery on his first inspection.

'Oh, not for a good while past,' said Posides carelessly.

'So I should judge. If you loosed off Number Three she'd fly to pieces, by the look of her.'

Posides grinned. 'So long as they look all right to the little painted devils. We don't need to use them these days, with the Emperor's fine treaty holding the Picts down.'

'That is no reason why we should not be able to use them if need arises,' Flavius said sharply. 'Look at this thing! The wood is rotten here, and the collar eaten up with rust. – Have Number Three taken down to the workshop for major repairs, Centurion, and let me know when the job is finished.'

'The work could be carried out just as well up here, without dismounting the thing.'

'And have every native hunter who passes Magnis see to what a shameful state our armament has fallen?' Flavius snapped. 'No, Centurion, we'll have her down to the repair shop.'

Number Three Catapult went down to the repair shop, the bath-house was scrubbed, and the fear of the gods put into the thieving cooks; and after the first three days the men no longer slouched on parade with their tunics dirty and their belts undone. But it was all no more than an unwilling gloss of saluting and heel-clicking under which the spirit of Magnis was not changed at all, and the new

Commander said wearily to his Cohort Surgeon at the end of the first week, 'I can make them stand up straight on parade, but that alone won't make them into a decent Cohort. If only I could reach them. There must be a way but I can't find it.'

Oddly enough, it was Number Three Catapult that was to find the way for him, a few days later.

Justin saw the whole thing happen. He was clearing up after morning Sick Parade when he heard a creaking and trundling outside, and strolling to the door of the little hospital block, saw that they were bringing the catapult back from the repair shop. From where he stood, he could see the battery by the North Gate, and he lingered a few moments, watching the great weapon being urged that way, trundling and lurching along on its rollers with its sweating team of legionaries hauling in front and pushing behind. He saw Flavius appear from the doorway of the Praetorium and walk forward to join the group about it, as it reached the foot of the temporary ramp that led up to the shoulder-high battery platform; saw the thing lurch like a ship in a gale as it began to climb. Its straining team were all around it, hauling, pushing, handling the rollers from either side. He heard the hollow rumble of it on the ramp, the orders of the Centurion in charge, 'Heave! – Heave! – Once more – he-eave!'

It was almost at the top when something happened; he never saw quite what, but he heard the creak of slipping timbers and a warning cry. There was a swift movement among the men, an order shouted by the Centurion, and a slithering clatter as one of the ramp-timbers went down. For a split moment of time the whole scene seemed frozen; and then, amid a splurge of shouting, the great catapult heeled over and side-slipped with a splintering crash, bringing down the rest of the ramp with it.

Justin saw men scattering outward, and heard a sharp,

agonized cry. He called back to his orderly behind him, and in the same instant was running toward the scene of the crash. The great engine lay like a dead locust on its side among the fallen ramp-timbers, partly on the ground and partly supported by the stone kerb of the battery platform. The dust of the crash still hung on the air, but already men were heaving at the wreckage beneath which one of their comrades lay trapped; and as Justin, thrusting through the rest, slithered in under the splintered framework to the man's side, he found someone before him, crouching braced under the weight of the beam which had come down across the legionary's leg, and saw without really looking that it was Flavius with the crest ripped from his helmet and blood trickling from a cut over one eye.

The injured man – it was Manlius, one of the hardest cases in all Magnis – was quite conscious, and the young surgeon heard him gasp, 'It's my leg, sir, I can't move – I –'

'Don't try,' Flavius said, breathing quickly; and there was an odd gentleness in his tone that Justin had never heard before. 'Hold still, old lad; we'll have you clear of this before you can sneeze ... Ah, here you are, Justin.'

Justin was already busy with the injured legionary, as hands appeared out of nowhere to help Flavius with the great beam. He called over his shoulder, 'Can you get this lot shifted away? I don't want to drag him out if I can help it.'

He was scarcely aware of the clatter of beams being dragged aside, and his own voice saying, 'Easy now, easy; you're all right,' and the straining, cursing moments as the framework of the great catapult was urged up and over, and toppled sideways away from them; until Flavius straightened, cherishing a bruised shoulder, and demanded, 'Is he going to be all right?'

And looking up from the work of his hands, he realized with surprise that it was all over, and the legionaries who had been straining at the wreckage were now standing round looking on, while his orderly knelt beside him steadying the injured man's leg. 'Yes, I think so, but he's got a bad break and he's bleeding like a pig, so the sooner we get him into the hospital and deal with it properly, the better.'

Flavius nodded, and remained squatting beside the man as he lay silent and sweating, until they were ready to move him, then helped to shift him on to the stretcher, and gripped his shoulder for a moment with a quick 'Good luck', before he turned away, wiping the blood from his eyes with the back of his hand, to see how bad was the damage to the catapult.

Number Three Catapult was almost past repair. But by evening word of what had happened had gone round the fort and along the Watch-towers and Mile Castles on either side, and the odd thing was that the new Commander of Magnis had very little more trouble with his garrison.

The weeks passed, and on an evening well into the spring, Justin was packing up after his day's work, when one of his orderlies appeared in the doorway with the news that a native hunter had come in with a wolf-bite to be dealt with.

'All right, I'll come,' Justin said, abandoning his hope of getting a bath before dinner. 'Where have you put him?'

'He's out in the parade-ground, sir; he wouldn't come any further,' said the orderly, with a grin.

Justin nodded. By this time he was growing used to the ways of the Painted People, for it was not the first time that wolf-bitten hunters had come up to the fort, wary and distrustful as wild animals, yet demanding that the Cohort Surgeon should make them well. He went out into the evening light, and there, leaning against the sun-washed wall, found a man naked save for a wolf-skin belted about his hips, and with a shoulder swathed in stained and bloody rags; a man much taller than was usual with his kind, with a mane of hair as thick and proudly tawny as a lion's, and eyes in his head like a pretty girl's. 'You are the Healer with a Knife?' he said, with the simple and direct dignity of wild places. 'I come to you that you may heal my shoulder.'

'Come you into the Healing-Place, and show it to me,' said Justin.

The man looked up at the low range of the hospital block beside him. 'I like not the smell of this place, but I will come, because you bid me,' he said, and followed Justin through the doorway. In the surgery, Justin made him sit down on a bench under the window, and began to undo the filthy rags about his arm and shoulder. When the last of them came away, he saw that the man had been only lightly mauled in the first place, but that with neglect the wounds had become sick, and now his whole shoulder was in a bad way.

'This was not done an hour ago,' Justin said.

The man looked up, '*Na*, half a moon since.'

'Why did you not come here when the harm was new?'

'Nay, I would not come for so small a matter as a wolf-bite; but the wolf was old and his teeth bad, and the bite does not heal.'

'*That* is a true word,' Justin said.

He brought fresh linen and salves, and a flask of the native barley spirit that burned like fire in an open wound. 'Now I am going to hurt you,' he said.

'I am ready.'

'Hold still, then; your arm like that – so.' He cleansed the wounds with searching thoroughness, while the hunter sat like a stone under his ruthless surgery; then salved them and bound the man's shoulder with strips of linen. 'That is done for today. Only for today, mind; you must come back tomorrow – every day for many days.'

In the doorway of the hospital block they parted. 'Come back at the same hour tomorrow, friend,' Justin said, and watched him go with the long, light step of the hunter across the parade-ground towards the gate, and scarcely expected to see him again. So often they did not come back.

But next evening at the same hour the man was once again leaning against the wall of the hospital block. And every day after that he appeared, sat like a stone to have his wounds dressed, and then disappeared until the same time next day.

On the seventh evening Justin had started to change the dressing as usual, when a shadow darkened the door and Flavius appeared on his way to look in, as he often did, on the legionary Manlius, who was still cot-bound with his broken leg. He looked in passing at the two under the window, and then checked, with his eyes on the man's shoulder, drawing in his breath in a hiss.

'It was looking worse than this a few days since,' Justin said.

Flavius peered more closely. 'It looks ugly enough now. Wolf?'

The hunter looked up at him. 'Wolf,' he agreed.

'How did it happen?'

'Nay, whoever knows how these things happen? They are too swift in the happening for any man to know. But it will be a while and a while before I hunt with the Painted People again.'

'The Painted People,' Flavius said. 'Are you not, then, one of the Painted People?'

'I? Am I blue from head to heel, that I should be one of the Painted People?'

That was true; painted he was, with blue warrior patterns on breast and arms, but not as the Picts with their close-set bands of tattooing all over their bodies. He was taller and fairer than most of the Picts, also, as Justin had thought when he first saw him leaning against the hospital wall.

'I am of the people of the firths and islands of the west coast up yonder, beyond the old Northern Wall; the people that were from Erin in the old times.'

'A Dalriad,' Flavius said.

The hunter seemed to draw himself together a little under Justin's hands. 'I was a Dalriad – a Scot of the tribe of . . . Nay, but I am a man without tribe or country now.'

There was a small stillness. Justin, to whom words never came easily in the things that mattered, went on salving the wolf-bites in the man's shoulder. Then Flavius said quietly, 'That is an ill thing to be. How does it come about, friend?'

· The hunter threw up his head. 'When I was in my sixteenth year, I all but slew a man at the Great Gathering, the three-yearly gathering of the Tribes. For that – even for carrying weapons upon the Hill of Gathering when the Council Circle is set up – the price is death or outlawry. Because I was but a boy who had taken Valour only that spring, and because the man had put an insult on my house, the King spoke the word for outlawry and not for slaying. Therefore these fifteen years and more I hunt among the Painted People, forgetting my own kind as much as may be.'

After that it became a habit with Flavius to stroll across to the hospital on his way to see Manlius, at about the time when he knew that Justin would be dressing the hunter's shoulder. And little by little there grew up a fellowship between the three of them, so that the hunter who had at first been so silent and withdrawn, came to speak more and more freely to the two young Romans; while little by little the wolf-wounds in his shoulder cleared and healed, until the day came when Justin said, 'See, it is finished. There is no more need for salves and linen.'

Squinting at the pinkish scars of the wolf's teeth that were all that was left, the hunter said, 'It would have been another story if I had met my wolf a year – a few moons ago.'

'Why so?' Justin asked. 'I am not the first healer here at Magnis on the Wall.'

'Na, and the Centurion is not the first Commander here at Magnis on the Wall. "Out dogs, to your dung-heap," that was the last Commander. *We* could never have come near the healer, even had we sought to.' He looked from Justin to Flavius lounging in the doorway. 'It is in my mind that Carausius your Emperor chooses his cubs well.'

Flavius said harshly, 'You are mistaken, my friend. It was not for our worth that Carausius posted us to this god-forsaken outpost.'

'So?' The hunter studied them thoughtfully. 'Yet it is not, I think, always that one may clearly see what lies behind the deeds of High Kings.' He rose, and turned to something that he had brought in with him half hidden under the plaid he had been wearing. '*Sa, sa*, that is as may be ... You were saying, a day since, that you had never seen one of our great war-spears; therefore I have brought mine, a queen among war-spears, that you may see what I would not show in peace to any other of your breed.'

He turned to the light of the high window. 'See now, is she not fair?'

The great spear which he laid in Justin's hands was the most beautiful weapon Justin had ever seen; the blade long and slender as a flame, a darkly silver flame in the cool evening light; the butt weighted by a bronze ball as big as an apple most wonderfully worked with blue-and-green enamel, and about its neck, just below the blade, a collar of wild-swan's feathers. Beautiful and deadly. He tested it in his hand, feeling it unusually heavy, but so perfectly balanced that one would scarcely notice the weight in use. 'It is indeed a queen among spears!' and gave it into the eager hand that Flavius was holding out for it.

'Ah, you beautiful!' Flavius said softly, testing it as Justin had done, running a finger along the blade. 'To carry this in battle would be to carry the lightning in one's hand.'

'Aye so. But I have not carried her in battle since I followed your little Emperor south, seven summers ago. Aye, aye, I keep her furbished, a fresh collar of wild swan's feathers every summer. But it is seven collars since the white feathers changed to red.' The hunter's tone was regretful, as he took back his treasure.

Flavius's head had gone up with a jerk, his fly-away brows twitching together. 'So? You have marched with Carausius? How came that to pass?'

'It was when he first landed. Over yonder among the mountains south and west, between Luguvalium and the Great Sands.' Leaning on his spear, the hunter all at once kindled to his story. 'A little man, a very great little man! He called together the Chieftains of the Painted People and the Chieftains of the Coastwise Dalriads, and the Chieftains out of Erin also; called them all together there among the mountains, and talked with them long and deeply. And at first the Chieftains and we who followed them listened to him because he was of our world, Curoi the Hound of the Plain, before ever he returned to his father's people and became Carausius and part of Rome; and then we listened to him because he was himself. So he made a treaty with the Kings of my people and the Kings of the Painted People. And when he turned south with the Sea Warriors from his fleet, many of us followed him. Even I followed him, among the Painted People. I was with him when he met with the man Quintus Bassianus who they said was Governor of Britain, at Eburacum of the Eagles. It was a great fight! *Aiee!* a most great fight; and when the day ended, Quintus Bassianus was food for the ravens and no more Governor of Britain, and Carausius marched on south, and those that were left of Quintus Bassianus's soldiers marched with him gladly enough; and I and most of my kind went back to our own hunting trails. But we heard from time to time – we hear most things among the heather – how Carausius was become Emperor of Britain, and then how he was become one with the Emperor Maximian and the Emperor Diocletian in the ruling of Rome – and we remembered that very great little man, among the mountains – and we did not wonder at these things.'

He broke off, and half turned towards the open doorway, then checked, looking from Justin to Flavius and back again, with a slow, grave inclination of the head. 'If you should wish to go hunting at any time, send word into the town for Evicatos of the Spear. It will reach me, and I will surely come.'

7

'To the Fates, that they may be Kind'

SEVERAL times that summer and autumn, Flavius and Justin hunted with Evicatos of the Spear; and on a morning in late autumn they took their hunting-spears and went out by the North Gate under the tall grasshopper heads of the catapults, and found him with his hounds and the three shaggy ponies waiting for them in their usual meeting-place at the foot of the steep northern scarp. It was a raw morning with the mist lying low and heavy like smoke among the brown heather, and the rooty tang of bog and the bitter-sweetness of sodden bracken hanging in the air.

'A good hunting day,' Flavius said, sniffing the morning with satisfaction, as they joined the waiting hunter.

'Aye, the scent will lie long and heavy in this mist,' Evicatos said; but as they mounted their ponies, Justin had a feeling that the hunter was thinking of something far removed from the day's hunting; and an odd chill of foreboding fell for an instant like a shadow across his path. But as they moved off down the burnside with the hounds loping about them, he forgot it in the promise of the day.

They got on the track of an old dog wolf almost at once, and after a wild chase, brought him to bay far up among the rolling border hills; and Flavius, dismounted now, slipped in low among the yelling hounds, with shortened spear, and made the kill.

By the time they had skinned the great grey brute

under Evicatos's direction, it was drawing on to noon, and they were ravenously hungry.

'Let's eat here. My stomach's flapping against my backbone,' Flavius said, stabbing his knife into the turf to clean it.

Evicatos was making the raw skin into a bundle, while the dogs snarled and tore at the flayed carcass. 'It is good to eat when the belly is empty,' he said, 'but first we will go a short way south from here.'

'Why?' Flavius demanded. 'We have made our kill, and I want to eat now.'

'So do I.' Justin seconded. 'It is as good a spot as any. Let's stay here, Evicatos.'

'I have a thing to show you, farther South,' Evicatos said, and rose to his feet with the bundled skin. 'Oh foolish one, have you never carried a baled wolf-skin before?' (This to the snorting and sidling pony.)

'Will it not keep till we are full?' Flavius demanded.

Evicatos got the wolf-skin settled to his entire satisfaction across the pony's withers before he answered. 'Did I not say to you when first we hunted together, that among the heather you should obey me in all things, because among the heather I am the hunter and the man who knows, and you are no more than children?'

Flavius touched palm to forehead in mock salute. 'You did – and we promised. So be it then, oh most wise of hunters. We will come.'

So they whipped the hounds off the carcass, and leaving it to the ravens that were already gathering, South they went, until, some while later, the hunter brought them dipping over a bare shoulder of the hills, to a burn of white water brawling down over shelving stones. Farther down, the glen narrowed in on itself, clothed in harsh willow-scrub, but here the hills rose bare on either side, clothed in short grass instead of heather; a great tawny bowl of hills running up to the tumbled autumn sky, empty save for a peregrine swinging to and fro along the farther slopes.

Evicatos checked his pony beside the burn, and the others with him, and as the sounds of their own movement ceased, it seemed to Justin that the silence and solitude of the high hills came flowing in on them.

'See,' said Evicatos. 'Here is the thing.'

The two young men followed the line of his pointing finger, and saw a dark lump of stone that rose stark and oddly defiant from the tawny burnside grass.

'What, that boulder?' Flavius said, puzzled.

'That boulder. Come closer now, and look, while I make ready the food.'

They dismounted and knee-hobbled the ponies, then made their way down the burn; and while Evicatos busied himself with the meal-bag, Flavius and Justin turned their attention to the thing that they have been brought to see. It seemed to be part of an outcrop of some kind, for small ledges and shelves of the same rock broke through the bank below it, half hidden in the grass; but looking more closely, they saw that it had been roughly squared, as though maybe it had always been rather square, and someone had decided to improve on nature. Also, as they examined it, there seemed to be carving of some sort on the stone. 'I believe it is an altar!' Justin said, dropping on one knee before it, while Flavius bent over him hands on knees. 'Look, here are three figures!'

'You're right,' Flavius said, with awakening interest. 'Furies – or Fates – or maybe it is the Great Mothers. The carving is so rough and weather-worn you can't really see. Scrape off some of this lichen down below, Justin. It looks as though there's something written there.'

A short space of work with Justin's hunting-knife and the ball of his thumb, and they were sure of it. 'Here's a name,' Justin said. ' "S-Y-L-V- Sylvanus Varus".' He worked on steadily, crumbling away the lichen from the rudely carved letters, while Flavius, squatting beside him now, brushed away fallen debris, until in a little, the thing was clear.

'To the Fates, Sylvanus Varus, standard-bearer of the fifth Tungrian Cohort with the Second Augustan Legion, raised this altar, that they may be kind,' Flavius read aloud.

'I wonder if they were,' Justin said after a pause, crumbling the golden lichen-dust from his fingers.

'I wonder what he wanted them to be kind *about*.'

'Maybe he just wanted them to be kind.'

Flavius shook his head with decision. 'You wouldn't make an altar just because you wanted the Fates to be kind in general, only if you needed their kindness badly, now, for some particular thing.'

'Well, whatever it was, it was all over a l-long time ago ... How long since we pulled out of Valentia the last time?'

'Not sure. About a hundred and fifty years, I think.'

They were silent again, looking down at those three crudely carved figures and the shallow ill-made letters beneath.

'So there are words there too. Was it worth seeing?' said Evicatos's voice behind them.

Flavius, still squatting before the stone, looked up at him smiling. 'Yes. But as worth seeing on a full stomach as an empty one.'

'The food is ready,' Evicatos said. 'Let you turn about and fill your bellies now.'

Clearly he had some reason in all this, but equally clearly he was not going to declare it save in his own good time. And it was not until the three of them were sitting round the pot of cold stir-about, and already well on with the buttered bannock and strips of smoked deer-meat, that he broke silence at last. 'As for this carved stone, one ex-

cuse serves as well as another. It was needful that I bring
you to this place and show reason for doing so, to – any
who might be interested.'

'Why?' Flavius demanded.

'Because even a Pict cannot hide in ankle-high grass, nor
hear across the distance from the willow-scrub yonder to
this stone. There are few places in Albu where one can be
sure that there is no little Painted Man behind a rock or
under the heather.'

'Meaning that you have something to tell us that must
not be overheard?'

'Meaning that I have this to tell you –' Evicatos cut a
gobbet from the dried meat and tossed it to his favourite
hound. 'Listen now, and hear. There are emissaries of the
man Allectus on the Wall and North of the Wall.'

Justin checked in the act of putting a piece of bannock
into his mouth, and dropped his hand back to his knee.
Flavius gave a startled exclamation. 'Here? – What do
you mean, Evicatos?'

'Go on eating; sight carries farther than sound, remember. I mean what I say; there are emissaries of the
man Allectus in Albu. They make talk of friendship with
the Picts; they make promises – and ask for promises in
return.'

'And these p-promises?' Justin said softly, cutting a
shaving from his dried meat.

'They promise that Allectus will help the Painted People
against us, the Dalriads, if first the Painted People will
help him to overthrow the Emperor Carausius.'

There was a long silence pin-pricked by the sharp cry
of the peregrine now high above the glen. Then Flavius
said with quiet, concentrated fury, 'So we were right
about Allectus. We were right, up to the very hilt, all
the time!'

'So?' Evicatos said. 'I know nothing of that. I know

only that if he succeeds in this thing, there will be death
for my people.' He checked as though to listen to what
he had just said, with a kind of half-wondering interest.
'My people – I that am a man without tribe or country.
But it seems that my faith reaches back to my own kind,
after all.'

'Will the Painted People agree?' Justin asked.

'It is in my heart that they will agree. Always there has
been distrust and ill blood between the Picts and my
people, until Carausius made his treaty. For seven years,
under the treaty, there has been peace. But the Painted
People fear us because we are different from them, and
because we begin to grow strong among the Western
islands and the coastwise mountains; and where the Pict
fears, there the Pict hates.'

'He fears and therefore hates the Eagles also,' Justin
said. 'And you say that he will make a promise with
Allectus?'

'Aye, he fears the Eagles and he fears the Dalriads,'
Evicatos agreed simply. 'He would as lief join with us
and drive the Eagles into the sea; but he knows that even
together, we are not strong enough. Therefore if he can,
he will join with the Eagles and drive us. Either way he
is rid of one enemy.'

'Allectus is not the Eagles,' Flavius said quickly.

'He will be, with Carausius dead.' Evicatos looked from
one to the other. 'You know the Wall, and the Cohorts of
the Wall; they will shout for whoever wears the Purple,
so that he pays them with wine enough. Can you be sure
that the Eagles elsewhere are of a different breed?'

No one answered for a moment; and then Flavius said,
'Your own people know of all this?'

'I do not speak with my own people, these fifteen years
past, but assuredly they know. Yet, knowing, what can
they do? If they make war on the Painted People while
there is still time, that is to break the treaty; and whether

Carausius or Allectus wears the Purple, we, the little
people, shall go down before the wrath of Rome.' Evicatos
leaned forward as though to dip into the stir-about. 'Warn
him! Warn this Emperor of yours; it is in my mind that
he may listen to you. (We hear things, among the heather.)
That is why I bring you to this place, and tell you these
things that are death to speak of – that you may warn
Carausius of the wind that blows!'

'Can a blackbeetle warn Almighty Jove? The blackbeetle tried it once, and was trodden on for his pains,'
Flavius said bitterly. His head was tilted back, and his
eyes gazing out beyond the far rim of hills that dropped
southward to the Wall. 'How are we going to get word
to him?'

'There isn't much sickness in the fort,' Justin heard his
own voice saying. 'And there's always the field surgeon
at L-Luguvalium if one should be needed. I'll go.'

Flavius looked round at him quickly, but before he
could speak, Evicatos cut in: '*Na, na*, if either one of you
go, it is deserting, and there will be questions asked. No
man will ask questions after me. Write him word of all
this that I have told you, and give me the writing.'

'You mean – you would carry it south yourself?' Flavius
said.

'Aye.'

'Why should you be running your head into a wolf-trap
on this trail?'

Evicatos, fondling the ears of the great hound beside
him, said: 'Not for the love of your Emperor, but that it
may not be death for my own people.'

'You would do so much – risk so much, for the people
that cast you out?'

'I broke the laws of my kind, and I paid the agreed
price,' Evicatos said. 'There is no more to it than that.'

Flavius looked at him a moment without speaking. Then
he said: 'So. It is your trail also.' And then, 'You know

what mercy there will be for you if you fall into the hands of Allectus's creatures with the writing on you?'

'I can guess,' said Evicatos with a small, grim smile. 'Yet since your names must be on the writing, clear for all to read, that will be a risk fairly shared among us, after all.'

Flavius said, 'So be it, then,' and leaned forward to the stir-about pot in his turn. 'But there is no time to lose. The letter must be on its way tonight.'

'That is a simple matter. Let one of you come down to-night to watch the cock-fighting in the Vallum ditch. One of your Optios has challenged all comers with his red cock; did you know? There will be many there, British and Roman, and if maybe you and I should speak together among the rest, none will think it strange.'

'Pray the gods he believes us this time!' Flavius said, softly and very soberly.

Justin swallowed his last mouthful of bannock with-out tasting it, and got to his feet, tightening his belt which he had slackened for ease when he sat down. His gaze fell again on the rough altar, on the worn figures and the uneven lettering from which they had scraped the moss.

Flavius, glancing up at him, caught the direction of his gaze, and turned his own the same way. Abruptly he took a silver sestercia from his belt, and pressed it into the turf before the altar. 'Surely we also have sore need that the Fates be kind,' he said.

Behind them, Evicatos was gathering up the remains of the food, tying up the neck of the meal-bag, as he had done after the other hunting meals that they had eaten together. On the fringe of the scrub, downstream, a feathering of vivid colour caught at Justin's eyes, where a tangle of dogwood had burst into its autumn flame. He walked down the burnside to the thicket, made careful selection, and broke off a long spray on which the leaves were scarlet as a trumpet-call. Something rustled among

the deeper shadows as he did so; something that might be
only a fox, but as he turned away he had a feeling of
watching eyes behind him that were not the eyes of fox or
wild cat.

The other two were waiting for him with the ponies,
when he rejoined them twisting the spray into a rough
garland; and he stopped on to one knee and laid it on the
weather-worn altar. Then they turned away and mounted,
whistling the dogs to heel, and rode with Evicatos of the
Spear down the burnside, leaving the bare bowl of the
hills empty once more, save for the wheeling peregrines
and the thing that had rustled in the shadows of the scrub.
And behind them Justin's dogwood garland was bright
as blood upon the lichened stone, where an unknown
soldier of their Legion had made his own desperate appeal
to the Fates, a hundred, two hundred years ago.

In the Commander's quarters that evening they wrote
the letter between them, their heads bent together in the
pool of lamplight, over the tablets open on the table.

It was just finished and the tablet sealed, when a knock
came at the door. Their eyes met for an instant, then Justin swept up the tablet into the flat of his hand, as
Flavius bade the visitor enter, and the Quartermaster
appeared. 'Sir,' said the Quartermaster, saluting, 'I have
brought the new supply lists. If you could spare me an
hour, we could get them settled.'

Justin had risen, also saluting. In public he kept up very
carefully the formalities between the Cohort Surgeon and
the Cohort Commander. 'I will not take up any more of
your time, sir. Have I your permission to leave camp for
an hour or so?'

Flavius looked up at him under red, fly-away brows. 'Ah
yes, the cocking main. Put something on our man's bird
for me, Justin.'

The great Vallum that had been the frontier before the

Wall was built, had become of late years a vast, unsavoury ditch choked with tattered and stinking hovels, small dirty shops and temples, garbage piles, and the dens of the legionaries' hunting dogs. The smell of it met Justin like a fog as he crossed the coast-to-coast road and dropped into it by the steps opposite the Praetorian Gate of Magnis. In an open space a spear-throw from the foot of the steps a crowd was already gathered, jostling round the makeshift arena and thronging the steep slopes of the Vallum on either side; shadowy in the autumn dusk save for the glow of a brazier here and there among them, and the splashing yellow light of one big lantern in their midst. Justin made his way towards it, shouldering through the noisy, shifting throng.

He could see no sign of Evicatos as yet; not that it would be easy to pick out one man from that shifting, shadowy crowd. But on the edge of the lantern light he found Manlius, who had returned to full duty only a few days before, and checked beside him. 'Well, Manlius, how is the leg?'

Manlius looked round, grinning in the lantern-light. 'Good as new, sir.'

Justin's heart warmed to him, because it had been a long fight and a hard one to mend that leg, and now it was as good as new. Anyone who had been hurt or ill under his hands always called out that humble and surprised warmth in Justin. It was one of the things, though he did not know it, that made him a good surgeon. 'So. That makes fine hearing,' he said, and the warmth was in his voice.

Manilus said rather gruffly, as though he were ashamed, 'If it hadn't been for you, sir, I'm thinking I'd be out of the Eagles now, with one leg to hobble on.'

'If it hadn't been for yourself also,' Justin said after a moment. 'It takes two, you know, Manlius.'

The legionary glanced at him sideways, then straight ahead again. 'I see what you mean, sir. None the less, I don't forget all you done for me; nor I don't forget the Commander with his face all over blood, hauling that cursed great beam off me when I thought I was about done for.'

They were silent then, among the noisy crowd, neither of them skilled in words, and neither with the least idea what to say next. Finally Justin said, 'Do you back our man and the red cock?'

'Of course, sir – and you?' Manlius replied with obvious relief.

'Assuredly. I have a wager with Evicatos of the Spear. Also I want to ask him about the skin of the wolf that the Commander killed today. Have you seen him anywhere in this crowd?'

'No, sir, can't say I have.'

'Ah well, he'll be somewhere about.' Justin nodded, friendly-wise, and side stepped between two legionaries, emerging on the lantern-lit edge of the arena. Somebody provided him with an upturned pail to sit on, and he sat, huddling his cloak around him for warmth. Before him stretched an open space covered with rush matting, in the centre of which a yard-wide ring daubed in chalk shone white in the light of the lantern rigged overhead. Above the lantern, the sky was still barred with the last fading fire-streaks of the sunset, but down here in the Vallum it was already almost dark, save where the light of the lantern fell on eager faces thronged about that shining chalk circle.

And now two men had pushed out from their fellows in the arena, each carrying a large leather bag which wriggled and bounced with the angry life inside it. And instantly a solid roar went up from the crowd. 'Come on, Sextus, show 'em what the red can do! – Ya-ah! Call that

dunghill rooster a fighting cock? – Two to one on the
tawny devil! – Give you three to one on the red!'

One of the men – it was the Magnis Optio – was undoing the neck of his bag now, bringing out his cock, and
there was a redoubled burst of voices as he handed it to a
third man who stood by to see fair play. The bird he held
up was indeed worth shouting for: red and black without
a pale feather anywhere, slim and powerful, very much
a warrior stripped for battle, with his close-cut comb,
clipped wings, and spare docked tail. Justin saw the
lantern-light play on his quivering wings, the fierce head in
which the black, dilating eyes were brilliant as jewels,
the deadly iron spurs strapped about his ankles.

The third man handed him back to his owner, and the
other cock was produced in his turn. But Justin took less
notice of him, for just as he was held up to view, Evicatos
appeared on the far side of the arena, while at the same
instant somebody edged through the crowd into the
vacant space at his side, and the voice of Centurion Posides
said, 'All the world is here, it seems, even to our Cohort
Surgeon. I did not know that you were one for the fighting
cocks, my Justin. – Nay, no need to shy like a startled
horse, or I shall think you have an unquiet conscience.'
For Justin had indeed jumped slightly at the sound of his
voice.

Centurion Posides was friendly enough, these days, but
Justin had never come to like him. He was a man with a
grudge against the world – a world that had denied him
the promotion he thought it owed him. Justin was sorry
for him; it must be hard to go through life bearing it a
grudge, but he certainly did not want him at his shoulder
just now. However, it would be a while yet before he
need do anything about passing on the letter under his
cloak. 'I am n-not, usually,' he said, 'but I have heard so
much about this red cock that I felt I must c-come and

judge his fighting p-powers for myself.' (Oh, curse that
stutter, it would have to betray him now, just when he
most needed to seem completely at ease!)

'We must be very healthy just now, up at the fort, that
our Surgeon can spend the evening at a cocking main after
a whole day's hunting,' said Posides in the faintly
aggrieved tone that was usual with him.

'We are,' Justin said quietly, mastering his stutter with
a supreme effort, 'or I should not be here.' He had meant
to add 'Centurion Posides', but he knew that the P would
be his undoing, so he left it, and turned his attention
firmly to what was passing on the matting before him.

The tawny cock had been returned to its owner, and to
the accompaniment of much advice from rival supporters,
the two men had taken their places and set their cocks
down at opposite sides of the chalk circle. Now, suddenly
as their owners loosed them, the birds streaked forward,
and the fight was on.

It did not last long, that first fight, though it was fierce
enough while it lasted. It ended with a lightning strike of
the red's spurs, and a few feathers drifting sideways on the
matting, and the tawny cock lying a small dead warrior,
where he had fallen.

His owner picked him up, shrugging philosophically,
while the other man took up his crowing and triumphant
property. Bets were being settled, and quarrels breaking
out in a score of places at once, as generally happened at a
cock-fight, and under cover of the noise and the shifting of
the crowd, Justin murmured something about speaking to
Evicatos of the Spear about the Commander's wolf-skin,
and getting up, made his way round to the far side of the
ring. Evicatos was waiting for him, and as they came together, close-jammed in the crowd, the sealed tablet passed
between them under cover of their cloaks.

The thing was done so easily that Justin, his ears full

of his own voice talking somewhat at random about the wolf-skin, could have laughed aloud in sheer relief.

The quarrels were sorting themselves out, and another cock had been brought in and set opposite to the red, as he turned back to the Arena. This time the fight was long drawn and uncertain, and before the end of it, both cocks were showing signs of distress: the open beak, the wing dragging on the blood-stained matting. Only one thing seemed quite unquenched in them, their desire to kill one another. That, and their courage. They were very like human gladiators, Justin thought, and suddenly he sickened, and did not want to see any more. The thing that he had come to do was done, and Evicatos of the Spear, when he looked for him, was already gone. He slipped away too, and made his way back to the fort.

But as he went, Centurion Posides, on the far side of the ring, looked after him with an odd gleam in his eyes. 'Now I wonder,' murmured Centurion Posides, 'I wonder, my very ill-at-ease young friend, if it really *was* only the wolf-skin? With your previous record, I think we will take no chances,' and he rose and slipped off also, but not in the direction of the fort.

8

The Feast of Samhain

Two evenings later, Justin was making ready to leave the hospital block after late rounds, when Manlius appeared in the surgery doorway with a bloody rag twisted round one hand. 'Sorry to trouble you, sir, but I hoped I might find you here. I've chopped my thumb and I can't stop it bleeding.'

Justin was about to call the orderly who was cleansing instruments nearby and bid him deal with it, when he caught the urgent message in the Legionary's eyes, and changed his mind. 'Come over to the lamp,' he said. 'What has happened this time? Another Catapult on top of you?'

'No, sir, I've been chopping wood for my woman. I was off duty – and I chopped it.'

The man moved after him, pulling off the crimson rag; and Justin saw a small but deepish gash in the base of his thumb from which the blood welled up as fast as he wiped it away. 'Orderly – a bowl of water and some bandage linen.'

The man dropped what he was doing and brought the water. 'Shall I take over, sir?'

'No, c-carry on cleaning those tools.'

And Justin set about bathing and dressing the cut, while Manlius stood staring woodenly into space. In a little, the orderly took the burnished instruments into an inner room, and instantly Manlius's eyes flew to the door after him, then back to Justin's face, and he muttered, 'Where's the Commander, sir?'

'The Commander? In the P-Praetorium, I imagine. Why?' Instinctively Justin kept his own voice down.

'Get him. Get all the money you have, anything of value, and go both of you to my woman's bothie in the town. It is the last bothie in the street of the Golden Grasshopper. Don't let any see you enter.'

'Why?' Justin whispered. 'You must tell me what you mean; I —'

'Don't ask questions, sir; do as I tell you, and in Mithras's name do it at once, or I've gashed my thumb to no purpose.'

Justin hesitated an instant longer. Then with the footsteps of the returning orderly already at the door, he nodded. 'Very well, I'll trust you.'

He finished his task, tied off the bandage, and with a 'Goodnight' to both men, strolled out into the autumn dusk, picking up in passing the slim, tube-shaped case that held his own instruments from the table on which it lay.

A few moments later he was closing the door of Flavius's office behind him. Flavius looked up from the table at which he was working late on the week's duty roster. 'Justin? You look very solemn.'

'I feel very solemn,' Justin said, and told him what had happened.

Flavius gave a soundless whistle when he had finished. 'One of the bothies of the town, and take all the money we have. What do you suppose lies behind this, brother?'

'I don't know,' Justin said. 'I'm horribly afraid it has to do with Evicatos. But I'd trust Manlius to the world's end.'

'Or *at* the world's end. Yes, so would I.' Flavius was on his feet as he spoke. He began to move quickly about the room, clearing the tablets and papyrus rolls from the table and laying them away in orderly fashion in the record chest. He locked the chest with the key which never left its chain about his neck, then turned to the small inner room that was his sleeping-cell.

Justin was already next door in his own cell, delving under the few garments in his clothes-chest for the leather bag containing most of his last month's pay. He hadn't anything else of value except his instrument-case. He picked that up again, stowed the small leather bag in his belt, and returned to the office just as Flavius came out from the inner room flinging on his cloak.

'Got your money?' Flavius said, stabbing home the brooch at his shoulder.

Justin nodded. 'In my belt.'

Flavius cast a look round to see that all was in order, and caught up his helmet. 'Come on, then,' he said.

They went down through the fort in the darkness and the mist that was creeping in from the high moors; and with a casual word to the sentries at the gate, passed through into the town.

The town that, though its name changed with every fort along its length – Vindobala, Aesica, Chilurnium – was in truth one town eighty miles long, strung out along the Wall and the coast-to-coast legionary road behind it. One long, teeming, stinking maze of wine-shops and baths and gaming-houses, stables and granaries, women's huts and small dirty temples to British and Egyptian, Greek and Gaulish gods.

The last bothie in the narrow, winding alley-way that took its name from the Golden Grasshopper wine-shop at the corner was in darkness as they drew near. A little squat black shape with the autumn mists creeping about the doorway. Almost as they reached it, the door opened silently into deeper blackness within, and the pale blur of a face showed in the opening. 'Who comes?' a woman's voice demanded softly.

'The two you wait for,' Flavius murmured back.

'Come, then.' She drew them into the houseplace, where the red embers of a fire shone like a scatter of rubies on the hearth but left the room in wolf darkness, and instantly closed the door behind them. 'There will be light in a moment. This way. Come.'

For the one moment it seemed very like a trap, and Justin's heart did undignified things in his throat. Then, as he moved forward after Flavius, the woman pulled aside a blanket over an inner doorway, and the faint gleam of a tallow dip came to meet them. Then they were in an inner room where the one tiny window-hole under the thatch had been shuttered close against prying eyes; and a man who had been sitting on the piled skins and native rugs of the bed-place against the far wall raised his head as they entered.

The woman let the heavy curtain fall again behind them, as Flavius whispered 'Evicatos! Ye gods, man! What does this mean?'

Evicatos's face was grey and haggard in the uncertain light, and the purple smudge of a great broken bruise showed on one temple. 'They caught and searched me,' he said.

'They found the letter?'

'They found the letter.'

'Then how do you come to be here?'

'I contrived to break free,' Evicatos said in a swift undertone. 'I laid them a trail that might serve – for a little – to make them think that I was still heading south. Then I doubled back to Magnis and slipped in at twilight, but I dared not come up to the fort after you, for all our sakes.'

'So he came here.' The woman took up the tale. 'Knowing Manlius was one he could trust, and I was Manlius's woman. And the gods so willed it that Manlius was at home – and the rest you know, or you would not be here.'

Justin and Flavius looked at each other in an utter silence that seemed to clamp down on the little back room. Then Flavius said, 'Well, the Cohort records are in good order for whoever takes them over.'

Justin nodded. There was only one thing to be done now. 'We must get to Carausius ourselves, and quickly.'

'It is going to be a race against time – and against Allectus – with the hunt up for the three of us,' Flavius said. 'Stirring days we live in.' His voice was hard, and his eyes very bright, and he was slipping free the great brooch at his shoulder as he spoke. He shook off the heavy folds of his military cloak, and stood forth in the bronze and leather of a Cohort commander. 'Manlius's wife, can you find us a couple of rough tunics, or cloaks to cover our own?'

'Surely,' the woman said. 'Food also you will need. Wait and you shall have both.'

Evicatos rose from the bed place. 'You have brought your money?'

'All that we had about us.'

'*Sa*. Money is good on a journey, especially if one would travel swiftly . . . I go now to fetch the ponies.'

'You ride with us?' Flavius said, as Justin took his sword from him and set it beside the crested helmet on the bed-place.

'Surely. Is not this my trail also?' Evicatos checked with a hand on the blanket over the door. 'When you leave this place, go out past the temple of Serapis, and make for the place of three standing stones, up the Red Burn. You know the spot. Wait for me there.' And he was gone.

The woman came back almost at the same instant, carrying a bundle of clothes, which she set down on the bed-place. 'See, here are two tunics of my man's, and one of them is his festival best, and rawhide shoes for the Commander – those mailed sandals will betray you a mile off; your dagger also, therefore I bring you a hunting-knife in its place. There is but one cloak, and the moth in the hood of that one; but take this rug from the bed; it is thick and warm, and will serve well enough with your brooch to hold it. Change quickly while I get the food.'

When she returned again, Justin was securing the chequered native rug at his shoulder with his own brooch; and Flavius, standing ready in the cloak with its moth-eaten hood pulled forward on his face, was thrusting the long hunting-knife into his belt. His military harness lay stacked on the bed-place, and he jerked his head toward it as she appeared. 'What of these? They must not be found in your keeping.'

'They will not be,' she said. 'They will be found – presently – in the Vallum ditch. Many things are found, and lost, in the Vallum ditch.'

'Be careful,' Flavius said. 'Don't bring yourself or Manlius to grief for our sakes. Tell us what we owe you for the clothes and food.'

'Nothing,' she said.

Flavius looked at her for a moment as though he were not sure whether to press the matter. Then he said, a little stiffly because he was very much in earnest, 'Then we can only thank you, both on our own behalf, and on behalf of the Emperor.'

'Emperor? What do we care for Emperors?' the woman said, with soft scornful laughter. '*Na na*, you saved my man in the spring, and we remember, he and I. Go now, quickly. Save this Emperor of yours if you can, and take care.' Suddenly she was almost crying as she pushed Flavius past her into the dark outer room. 'You're only boys, after all.'

Justin caught up the food bundle, and turned to follow him, but checked at the last moment on the edge of the dark, smitten with his usual inability to find the words he wanted when he wanted them badly. 'The gods be kind to you, Manlius's wife. Tell Manlius to k-keep his thumb clean,' he managed, and was gone.

A long while later – it seemed a long while later – they were squatting huddled together for warmth, with their backs against the tallest of the three standing stones by the Red Burn. Just before they reached it, Flavius had taken the key of the record chest from about his neck, and dropped it into the pool where the burn grew still and deep under the alders. 'They can get another key made when there is another Commander at Magnis,' he had said. And to Justin it seemed that the tiny splash, small as the sound of a fish leaping, was the most terribly final sound he had ever heard.

Up till now there had been no time for thinking; but now, crouching here in the solitude of the high moors with the mist thickening about them, the smell of it cold as death in their nostrils, and the slow moments dragging by without bringing Evicatos, there was too much time. Time to realize just how big and how bad the things that had happened were; and Justin was cold to the pit of his stomach and the depth of his soul. It was like the mist, he thought, the creeping, treacherous mist that made everything strange, so that you could not be sure of anything or anybody, so that you could not go to the Commander of the Wall and say 'It is thus and it is thus. Now therefore give me leave to go south with all speed.' Because the Commander himself might be one of Them.

The mist was creeping closer, wreathing like smoke through the sodden heather and around the standing stones. He shivered, stirred abruptly to cover it, and so felt the thing that he had carried out of Magnis along with the food-bundle under his cloak. His instrument-case. He had scarcely been aware of bringing it away with him, it was so much a part of himself; but here it was, and it belonged to the good things of life, the clean and the kindly things – something constant and unchanging to hold on to. He lifted the slim tube of metal and laid it across his knee.

Flavius glanced round. 'What is it?'

'Only my instrument-case,' Justin said, and then as the other gave a sudden splutter of laughter, 'Why is that funny?'

'Oh, I don't know. Here we are on the run, with the hunt up behind us and the world falling into shards around our ears, and you bring your instrument-case away with you.'

'I am still a surgeon, you see,' Justin said.

There was a moment's pause, and then Flavius said, 'Of course. That was stupid of me.'

Even as he spoke, from far down the burn came the unmistakable jink of a bridle bit, and as they listened with suddenly strained attention, it was followed by a shaken whistle that might well have been the call of some night bird.

'It is Evicatos!' Justin said, with a quick surge of relief, and threw up his head and whistled back.

The jinking came again, and with it the soft beat and brush of horses coming up through the heather; nearer and nearer yet, until a solid knot of darkness loomed suddenly through the mist, and Flavius and Justin rose to their feet as Evicatos rode up past the lowest of the standing stones, with the two led ponies behind him.

He reined in at sight of them, and the ponies stood with their breath smoking into the mist.

'All well?' Flavius said.

'Well enough so far, but I think that we are none too soon. There is a stirring in the fort, and the word runs already along the Wall that the Commander of Magnis and his healer are nowhere to be found. Mount now, and ride.'

*

It was just before dusk on the third day that they came down into the head of a widening dale, and saw before them a farm lost in the wilderness.

Until now they had kept clear of the haunts of men, but their meal-bag was empty, and since on this desperate forced march south they could not spend precious time in hunting, they must get more supplies from somewhere. It was a risk, but it had to be taken, and they turned the ponies' heads down into the dale, Evicatos reversing his great war-spear that he had brought with him, to show that they came in peace. In the lonely vastness of the surrounding hills, the cluster of bracken-thatched huts within the ring fence seemed no larger than a palmful of brown beans, but as they drew nearer they saw it was a big farm, as such places went, and that it was full of a great coming and going, both of men and cattle.

'Are they expecting an attack, that they drive all the cattle in among the steading huts?' Flavius said.

Evicatos shook his head. '*Na na*, it is the feast of Samhain, when they bring the sheep and cattle down from the summer pasture and pen them close for the winter. I had lost count of the days. Yet it will only make our welcome the more sure.'

And so indeed it proved, for at Samhain all doors stood open, and before it was full dusk the three strangers had been accepted without question, their ponies stabled, and they themselves brought in and given places on the men's side of the fire, among the others gathering there.

The fire burned on a raised hearth in the midst of the great houseplace, and at the four corners of the hearth four whole tree-trunks stood to uphold the crown of the bracken-thatched roof high overhead, and on every side the shadows ran away into the dark. The people gathering about the fire – he supposed that they were all one family – were roughly clad, the men for the most part in the skins of wolf and red deer, the women in rough woollen cloth, as though they were less skilled in spinning and weaving than the women of the South; but it seemed that they were prosperous in their way, and not cut off from the world, for among the pots in which the women were making ready the evening meal was some fine red Roman pottery; and the lord of the house himself, an immensely fat man clad in the skin of a wolf over his rough plaid breeks, had a necklace of yellow amber beads that shone here and there through the grey tangle of his beard. And when the woman of the house rose in her place, and brought the Guest Cup to the three strangers, it was an ox horn mounted in red Hibernian gold.

'It is good to have a stranger within the gates at Samhain,' said the woman, smiling.

'It is good to be the stranger who comes within such gates as these, at the day's end,' Flavius said, and took the cup, and drank, and gave it back to her.

There was much food and much drink, and the party waxed more and more uproarious as the heather-beer went round, and old stories were told and old songs chanted, for winter was the time for such things, and Samhain was the start of winter. But Justin noticed that through it all, the men kept a place empty among themselves, and no man touched the beer-cup that had been set before it.

Flavius it seemed had noticed it, too, for presently he turned to the Lord of the house, and asked, 'Are you expecting another guest tonight?'

'Why should we be expecting another guest?'

'Because you keep his place for him.'

The fat man glanced in the direction he had indicated. '*Na*, how should you know, being as I think Romans? Samhain is the feast of home-coming; we bring the cattle safe home out of the wild weather until spring comes

again, and should we deny a like shelter to the ghosts of
our own dead? For them also it is home-coming for the
winter, and we set their beer-cup by the hearth to bid
them welcome. Therefore Samhain is also the feast of the
dead. That place is for a son of mine that carried his spear
after the Emperor Curoi, and died down yonder at Eburacum of the Eagles, seven summers ago.'

'Curoi!' Flavius said swiftly, and then, 'I beg you forgive me. I should not have asked.'

'Nay, he was a fool that he went at all,' said the old
man grumblingly. 'I care not if he hears me say it now, for
I said it to him at the time.' He took a long pull at the
beer-pot and set it down, smacking his lips. Then he shook
his head. 'Yet it was a waste, for he was the best hunter
of all my sons. And now there is another Emperor in
Britain after all.'

Justin had an odd sensation, as though all the blood in
his body had leapt back to his heart; and suddenly everything seemed to go both still and slow. He shot one sideways glance at Flavius, and saw the hand that had been
hanging relaxed across his knee clench slowly, very
slowly, into a fist, and then relax again. Nothing else
moved. Then Evicatos said, '*Sa*, that is news indeed. Is it
the man they call Allectus?'

'Aye. Did you not know then?'

'We have been long away from men's tongues. How did
it come about?'

'I will tell you as it was told me by a Hibernian merchant that was here yester night. It was the Sea Wolves
that struck the blow. They slipped in past the ships of the
Romans that were against them, in the mist and darkness,
and ran their dragon keels ashore below Curoi's houseplace where Curoi was. They say that this Allectus gave
them the signal, and was with him that night and opened
the door to them; but that is a thing that matters little

either way, for all men know who stands behind the Sea
Wolves. They overcame his guards and slew them, and
cried to Curoi to come out to them from his great chamber
where he was; and he went out to them unarmed, and
they cut him down on the threshold.' He ended his tale
and reached again for his beer-pot, glancing sideways
under his brows at the three strangers, as though half
afraid that he had said too much.

Flavius said in a curious dead-level voice, 'Nay, we be
none of us Allectus's men ... When was this thing done?'

'Six nights since.'

'*Six nights?* Such news travels fast, but this must have
had the wings of the wind. Surely it can be no more than
some wild rumour?'

'Nay.' It was Evicatos who answered, with quiet certainty, his eyes on the lord of the house. 'It is no rumour.
It is news that runs by the old ways that you and your
people have forgotten.'

And something in his own heavy certainty made certainty for the other two also. No use, all this forced marching, Justin thought, no use pushing on. They were too late,
after all. Too late. Suddenly he was seeing that lamplit
room on the cliffs, just as he had seen it on a wild winter's
night nearly a year ago, with the logs burning on the
hearth, and the great window looking toward Gesoriacum
Light; and the terrible little Emperor who had held Britain
and the seaways of Britain safe in a ruthless yet loving
hand. He saw the red gleam of fire in the courtyard and
heard the cries and the clash of weapons; and the voices
shouting for Carausius. He saw the short, square-built
figure walk out by the courtyard door, unarmed, to meet
death. The drifting sea-mist gilded by the torches, and
the fierce barbarian faces; men who were seamen even as
the man who faced them was a seaman, and kin to him
in blood. He saw the wide-lipped, contemptuous smile on

the Emperor's face, and the flash of the saex blades as they cut him down . . .

But it was only a half-burned birch branch falling into the red heart of the fire; and the beer-jar was coming round again, and the talk had swung away from the change of Emperors to the prospects of the winter's hunting. A change of rulers, after all, meant little up here in the mountains. The deer were as fleet of foot and a cow carried her calf as many days, no matter who wore the Purple.

The three had no chance to speak to each other apart until far into the night, when, having been out to see that all was well with the ponies, they stood together in the thorn-closed doorway of the steading, looking away down the widening sweep of the dale toward the lopsided hunters' moon shaking clear of the dark fells.

Flavius was the first to break the silence. 'Six nights since. So it was already too late by a night and a day when we wrote that letter.' He looked round at the other two, and in the moonlight his eyes were like black holes in his face. 'But why should Allectus seek the help of the Painted People against the Emperor if he meant to murder him before their help could come? Why, why, why?'

'Maybe he did not mean it to happen so, when he sent his emissaries North,' Evicatos said. 'Then maybe Curoi began to suspect, and he dared wait no longer.'

Flavius said, 'If we could have made him believe us, back in the spring. If *only* we could have made him believe us!' And his voice was shaking. After a few moments he steadied it, and went on, 'Since Allectus has seized the Purple without aid of the Painted People, and will have, moreover, sundry other matters to attend to, it seems that at least for a while your people are saved, Evicatos of the Spear.'

'For a while, yes,' Evicatos said, smiling at the great

spear on which he leaned. A little chill wind ruffled the swan's feathers, and Justin noticed how white they shone in the moonlight. 'Presently, in a few years, if Allectus still wears the Purple, the danger will come back; but nevertheless, for this while, my people are saved.'

'And therefore this is your trail no longer.'

Evicatos looked at him. 'This is my trail no longer. So I will go North again, in the morning, to my hounds that I left with Cuscrid the smith and my own hunting runs; yet taking care, I think, that men do not see me on the Wall again. And maybe I shall watch a little, and listen a little, among the heather ... And you? What trail do you follow now?'

'Southward still,' Flavius said. 'There is one thing for us to do now – to make our way somehow across to Gaul, and thence to the Caesar Constantius.' He threw up his head. 'Maximian and Diocletian had no choice but to make peace with our little Emperor, but they'll not stomach his murderer in his place. Sooner or later they will send the Caesar Constantius to end the thing.'

Justin spoke for the first time, his eyes still on the wind-stirred swan's feathers about the neck of Evicatos's great war-spear. 'It is a strange thing – Carausius began to make of us something more and – and greater than a p-province among other provinces; and now, in the bare time that it takes to kill one man, that is undone, and all that we can hope for is that the Caesar Constantius will come and take back his own.'

'Better for Britain to take her chance with Rome than fall into ruin under Allectus's hand,' Flavius said.

9

The Sign of the Dolphin

WINTER had come, and a snow-wind was blowing up through the bare trees of Spinaii Forest, when at last Justin and Flavius entered Calleva with the market-cars as soon as the gates were open one morning.

They had made for Calleva because in spite of having sold the ponies, in spite of having lived lean all those weary weeks on the trail South, they had not as much money left as they would certainly need to get them across to Gaul. 'I do not want to go to the farm,' Flavius had said some days before, when they talked the thing over. 'Servius would raise the money somehow, but it would take time, and already most of the shipping will be beached for the winter. No, we'll go to Aunt Honoria – with any luck she won't have gone to Aqua Sulis yet. She'll lend us what we need, and Servius can pay her back how and when he can. Besides, it is in my mind that once we get to Gaul it may be a long time before we get back, and so I would not go without saying farewell.'

Just inside the East Gate, by which they had entered, Flavius said, 'This is where we turn off,' and leaving the trundling and lowing stream of market traffic, they plunged away to the left through a fringe of shops, into the gardens of some big houses, quiet save for the little hushing wind in the winter dawn; and presently, with many garden hedges behind them, emerged close to the back quarters of a house rather smaller than the rest.

'Round here,' Flavius whispered. 'Lie up behind the wood stack and spy out the land. Don't want to run into any of the slaves and have to explain ourselves.'

They circled the dark huddle of out-buildings, and a little later were lying up in the lee of the brushwood pile, while before them, across the narrow courtyard of the slaves' quarters, the house gradually awoke. A light showed in a window. A voice sounded scoldingly, and as the light broadened into a bar of cold daffodil behind the roof ridge a stringy little woman with her head tied up in a crimson kerchief began sweeping the dust and small refuse of the kitchen out into the yard, humming softly to herself the while.

It was full daylight when an immensely fat woman with a saffron-coloured mantle drawn forward over her grey hair appeared from the house doorway, and stood looking round her at the bleak morning. At sight of her, Flavius let out a soft breath of satisfaction. 'Ah, the Aunt is in residence.'

'Is that her?' Justin whispered. Somehow she was not what he expected.

Flavius shook his head, his face alight with laughter. 'That is Volumnia. But where Volumnia is, Aunt Honoria is also ... Now if I can catch her attention.'

The enormously fat woman had waddled out into the courtyard to get a better view of the weather; and as she halted, Flavius picked up a pebble and tossed it towards her. She glanced toward the tiny sound, and as she did so, he whistled very softly, an odd, low-pitched call on two notes, at sound of which she started as though a horse-fly had stung her. Justin saw her stand a moment, staring towards their hiding-place. Then she came waddling towards them. Flavius slithered back, swift as a snake, and Justin followed him, so that they were well out of sight of the house when she came panting round the brushwood pile and found them.

She had both hands to her enormous bosom, and she was
wheezing half under her breath as she came. 'Is it – is it
yourself then, my Flavius, my dearie?'

Flavius said softly, 'Don't tell me anyone else has ever
called you in just that way, Volumnia.'

'Nay – I knew it must be you the moment I heard it.
Many's the time you've called to me like that, and you
out when you should have been in your bed, and wishful
to be let in quiet like. But oh, my honey, what are you
doing here behind the woodstack when we thought you
was on the Wall? And you so ragged, and so lean as any
wolf in a famine winter – and this other with you – and –'

'Volumnia dear,' Flavius cut her short, 'we want to
speak with Aunt Honoria; can you get her for us? And
Volumnia, we don't want anyone else to know.'

Volumnia sat down on a pile of logs and clasped her
bosom as though it was trying to escape. 'Oh my dear, is it
as bad as that?'

Flavius grinned at her. 'It isn't bad in the way you
mean, at all. We haven't been stealing apples. But we do
need to speak with my aunt – can you contrive it?'

'Why, as to the Lady Honoria, that's easily done. Do
you go down to the arbour and wait there till I send her
to you. But my dearie dear what *is* all this? Can't you tell
your own Volumnia as used to bake you pastry-men, and
saved you many and many a smacking when you was
little?'

'Not now, 'Flavius said. 'There isn't time. If you bide
much longer round here we shall have one of the others
coming to see that you haven't been carried off by the
Sea Wolves. Aunt Honoria will tell you, I don't doubt.
And Volumnia' – he laughed, and slid an arm round where
her waist would have been if she had had one, and gave
her a kiss – 'that is for the pastry-men, and all those
smackings that you saved me.'

'Get along with you,' wheezed Volumnia. She surged to

her feet and stood an instant looking down at him and pulling her veil about her head. 'You're a bad boy, and you always were!' she said, 'and the gods alone know what you are up to this time. But I'll send My Lady down to the arbour to you.'

Justin, who had stood silent against the brushwood pile throughout, watched her waddle away, and heard her voice upraised distressfully from the house a few moments later. 'Something did ought to be done about those rats! There was one round by the woodpile just now; I heard it scuffling, and when I went to look, there it was – a big grey one, and sat up and stared at me so bold as a wolf – with all its teeth and whiskers –'

'We had one of that sort,' he said softly. 'My mother's old nurse. She was the best thing in my childhood, but she's d-dead now.'

A little later, working their way down through the dark tangle of privet and juniper that divided the garden from its neighbour, they had reached the arbour and settled themselves again to wait, seated very coldly on the grey marble bench within.

But they had not long to wait before they heard someone coming, and Flavius, peering through the screening ivy, said softly, 'It is her.'

Justin, doing the same, saw a woman muffled close in a mantle so deeply and brilliantly crimson that its colour seemed to warm the whole grey morning, coming across the grass from the house.

She came slowly, turning aside to look at this and that, as though she had no particular aim, only a stroll in the garden. And then she was round the tangle of bushes, shielded from sight of the house, and they rose to their feet as she appeared in the opening of the arbour.

A thin old woman with a proud beak of a nose and very bright eyes, brown and wrinkled as a walnut and painted like a dancing-girl – save that no dancing-girl would have put the paint on so badly. Yet even with the stibium smeared along her eyelids, and a valiant slash of mouth-paint sliding up towards one ear, she seemed to him more worth looking at than any other woman he had ever met, because her face was so much more alive.

She was looking from Flavius to him and back again, with her thin brows raised a little. 'I greet you, Great-Nephew Flavius. – And this? Who is this with you?' Her voice was husky, but clear-cut as a gem, and there was no surprise in it. Justin thought suddenly that she would never waste time in being surprised, whatever the emergency.

'Aunt Honoria, I salute you,' Flavius said. 'I think he's another great-nephew of yours – Justin. Tiberius Lucius Justinianus. I told you about him when I wrote from Rutupiae.'

'Ah yes, I know.' Great-Aunt Honoria turned to Justin, holding out a hand that felt dry and light in his when he took and bent over it. 'Yes, you have good manners, I am glad to see. I should intensely dislike to have an ill-mannered great-nephew.' She looked at him appraisingly. 'You must be Flavia's grandson. She married an extremely plain man, I remember.'

It was so obvious that she meant, though she did not say, 'That accounts for it,' that Justin felt himself reddening to the tips of his unfortunate ears. 'Yes, I – I am afraid she d-did,' he said ruefully, and became aware of the understanding and the glint of laughter in his great-aunt's eyes.

'Yes, that of course was very rude of me,' said Aunt Honoria. 'It's I who should be blushing, not you.' She turned back to Flavius, saying abruptly, 'Now what is it that brings you here when we all thought you were on the Wall?'

Flavius hesitated; Justin saw him hesitate, wondering just how much to tell her. Then, very briefly, he told her the whole story.

Half way through it Aunt Honoria seated herself composedly on the grey marble bench, setting down beside her something folded in a napkin that she had been carrying under her mantle; otherwise she made neither sound nor movement from beginning to end. When it was finished, she gave a small decisive nod. 'So. I wondered whether it had to do with this most sudden change of Emperors. It is an ill story, all of it a very ill story ... And now you would make your way overseas to join the Caesar Constantius.'

'There'll be a good few following that road in the next few months, I'm thinking,' Flavius said.

'So I suppose. These are evil days, and it is in my mind that they will grow more evil.' She looked up at him swiftly. 'And to join the Caesar Constantius you will need money, and so you come to me.'

Flavius grinned. 'We do need money. Also – once we get across the seas we may be gone a long time, therefore I come to take my leave, Aunt Honoria.'

Her face flashed up in a smile. 'I'm honoured, my dear Flavius. We will deal with the money question first. Now see – it was in my mind, when Volumnia came to me a while since, that if you were in trouble you would need money; but I have not much ready money in the house. So –' She laid a small silken purse on top of the napkin-covered bundle, 'I bring you what I can for your immediate needs, and also, I have dressed for the occasion.'

As she spoke she unclasped first one and then the other of a pair of bracelets from her thin brown wrists, and held them out to Flavius; narrow golden bracelets set with opals in which the fires came and went, rose and green and peacock blue in the wintry light.

Flavius took them into his own hands, and stood looking down at her. 'Aunt Honoria, you're wonderful,' he said. 'We'll give you another pair one day.'

'No,' said Aunt Honoria. 'They are not a loan, they are a gift.' She rose to her feet and stood looking at them. 'If I were a man, and a young man, I should be taking your road. As it is, my trinkets must serve instead.'

Flavius made her a little unconscious bow. 'Thank you for your gift then, Aunt Honoria.'

Aunt Honoria made a swift gesture with her hands, as though to dismiss the whole thing. 'Now – Volumnia is heart-stricken that we cannot bring you in and feast you; but short of that we have done what we can.' She touched the bundle in the napkin. 'Take it with you and eat on the road.'

'We will,' Flavius said. 'We will indeed; for we're both of us as empty as wine-skins after Saturnalia.'

'So. I think that is all that needs to be said; and now you must go. And in these ill and uncertain days, who shall say when you will come back – though indeed I believe with you that the Caesar Constantius will come one day. And so – the gods be with you, my nephew Flavius ... and you –' She turned to Justin and most unexpectedly put up her hands and took his face between them, and looked at him again. 'You are not at all like your grandfather – I never liked him over much. You're a surgeon, Flavius tells me, and, I *think*, a good one. The gods be with you, too, my silent other nephew Justin.'

She dropped her hands, and drawing the glowing folds of her mantle once more close about her, turned and walked away.

The two lean and ragged young men stood in silence a moment, looking after her. Then Justin said, 'You never told me she was like that.'

'I think I had forgotten myself until just now. Or maybe I didn't know,' Flavius said.

They walked out of Calleva by the South Gate, broke

their fast on the edge of the forest, and took the road
South through the forest and over the downs to Venta.
And the second day had scarcely turned towards evening
when they trudged into Portus Adurni, and saw the mass-
ive grey ramparts of just such another fortress as Rutupiae
standing four square among the marshes and the vast
maze of winding water that made up Portus Magnus, the
Great Harbour.

But it was not under the fortress walls that they were
likely to find their transport across to Gaul; and they
turned their steps towards the poorer part of the town,
where mean wine-shops mingled with fish-drying sheds,
and the hovels of seafaring folk straggled out along the
low shore, and the craft drawn up along the tide-line were
of all kinds from small trading-vessels to native dug-out
canoes.

That evening they got into conversation with several
owners of small, hopeful-looking vessels on the pretext
of looking for a kinsman who they thought was in the
wine trade in those parts. But everybody seemed either to
have just laid up for the winter or to be just going to do
so, while one little slim sea-captain with a blue faience
drop in one ear showed signs of knowing someone of the
name that Flavius had invented for the kinsman, which
might have been awkward if Flavius had not thought to
ask what colour the man's hair was, and on being told
red, said that in that case it could not be the same one because his kinsman was as bald as an egg. And they were
no further forward with their plans when, in the winter
dusk, cold, tired, and hungry, and both of them feeling
rather more desperate than they dared to admit, they
found themselves close by a wine-shop on the foreshore.
It was a wine-shop like any other – and there were many
in Portus Adurni – but daubed on a rough piece of board
over the doorway was something green, with an arched

back and a round rolling eye at sight of which Flavius said with a spurt of weary laughter, 'Look, it's the family dolphin! This is the place for us!'

The wind was rising, swinging the lantern before the doorway to and fro so that the painted dolphin seemed to dive and leap, and the shadows about the threshold ran like wild things. And in the confusion of wind and dusk and lantern-light, neither of them saw the little man with the blue faience ear-drop strolling by, who turned after they had gone in, and slipped away into the deepening shadows.

They found themselves in a place that would be a small open courtyard in summer, roofed in now with what looked like an old striped sail or ship's awning spread above the bare vine-trellis. A charcoal brazier glowed red at either end of the place, and though it was yet early, a good many men were gathered about them or lounging at the small tables round the walls, eating, drinking, or dicing. The babel of voices and the beat of the wind in the striped awning, the warmth of the braziers and the smell of broiling meat and crowding humanity made the whole place seem so bulging full that Justin thought the walls must be straining apart at the seams, like a garment too tight for the person inside it.

They found a corner well out of the way, gave their order for supper to a big man with the stamp of the legions clear upon him – half the wine-shops in the Empire, Justin thought, were kept by ex-legionaries – and settled down, stretching out their weary legs and slackening their belts.

Looking about them as they waited, Justin saw that the customers were for the most part seafarers of some sort, and a few traders, while about the nearest brazier a knot of Marines from the Fleet were playing dice. Then the master of the place dumped a bowl of steaming stew be-

tween Justin and Flavius, with a platter of little loaves
and a jug of watered wine. And for a while they were too
busy eating to spend much more attention on their surroundings.

But they had got over their first hunger when a newcomer ambled in through the foreshore doorway.

There had been a good deal of coming and going all
the while, but this man was of a different kind from the
others, and after one casual glance Justin put him down
as a government clerk or maybe a small tax-gatherer. He
hesitated, glancing about the crowded place, then came
drifting in their direction; and a few moments later was
standing beside them in their corner. 'The Dolphin is very
full tonight. Will you allow me to join you? It seems
that there is – ahem – nowhere else.'

'Sit, and welcome,' Justin said, and moved to make room
on the narrow horseshoe bench, and the man seated himself with a grunt of satisfaction, crooking a finger for the
shopkeeper.

He was a small man, not fat exactly, but flabby, running to paunch, as though he ate too much and too
quickly and didn't take enough exercise. 'My usual cup of
wine – your best wine,' he said to the shopkeeper; and
then, as the man went to fetch it, turned to the other two
with a smile. 'The best wine here is very good indeed.
That is why I come. It is – ahem – scarcely the kind of
place I should frequent otherwise.' The smile puckered his
plump, clean-shaven face rather pleasantly, and Justin
saw with sudden liking that he had the eyes of a small,
contented child.

'You come here often?' Flavius asked, clearly trying to
shake off his depression and be friendly.

'No, no, just sometimes, when I am in Portus Adurni.
My – ahem – my work takes me about a good deal.'

Flavius pointed to the wrought-iron pen-case and inkhorn that hung at the man's girdle. 'And your work is – that?'

'Not altogether, no. I was a government clerk at one time; now I have various interests. Oh yes indeed.' The wide, quiet gaze wandered from Justin to Flavius and back again. 'I buy a little here and sell a little there, and I play an – ahem – a small but I trust useful part in hand-ling of the Corn Tax.' He took up the wine cup which the master of the place had just set down at his elbow. 'Your health.'

Flavius raised his own cup, smiling, and echoed the toast, followed by Justin.

'And you?' said the little tax-gatherer. 'I think I have not seen you here before?'

'Nay, we come seeking a kinsman who was to have settled hereabouts, but it is in my mind that he must have moved on after all, for we can get no word of him.'

'So? – What is his name? Maybe I can help you.'

'Crispinius. He's in the wine trade,' said Flavius, keep-ing the question of his kinsman's hair in case it should be needed.

But the other shook his head regretfully. 'Nay, I fear I cannot call to mind anyone of that name.' His gaze seemed caught and held a moment by Flavius's left hand as it curved about his wine-cup on the table; and Justin, glanc-ing the same way, saw that it was the signet ring with the intaglio dolphin that had caught his interest. Flavius became aware of it at the same instant, and drew his hand back on to his knee under the table. But already the little tax-gatherer's gaze had drifted away to the knot of Marines round the brazier, who had wearied of dice and betaken themselves to loud-voiced argument.

'What's the odds?' a long, lean man with the white seam of an old sword-cut on his forehead was demand-ing. 'Any man who gives me free wine to drink his health

in and a fistful of sesterces can be Emperor for all I care.'
He spat juicily into the brazier. 'Ah, but it had better be a
big fistful this time, and it had better come quick.'

'Trouble is there's a sight too many Emperors all at the
same time,' said a sad-looking individual in the sea-green
tunic of the scouting galleys. 'And maybe the other two
aren't going to like the Divine Allectus in the Purple. How
if we have the Caesar Constantius a-top of us one of these
fine days?'

The first man took another drink, and wiped his mouth
with the back of his hand. 'The Caesar Constantius has got
plenty to keep him happy where he is. Every fool knows
the tribes are heaving like a maggoty cheese along the
Rhenus defences.'

'Maybe you're right at that, and maybe you're wrong,'
said the pessimist darkly. 'I've served under that lad, and
despite his wey face he's the best soldier in this tired old
Empire, and I'd not put it past him to settle the Germans
yet, and then come and settle *us*.'

'Let him come then!' roared the man with the sword-
cut in sudden defiance. 'Let him come; that's all *I* say!
We settled the Emperor Maximian when he tried that
game, and I reckon we can settle his pup if need be!' He
teetered backwards, recovered himself with a slight stag-
ger, and crooked a finger for the shopkeeper. 'Hi! Ulpius,
more wine.'

'When we settled the Emperor Maximian we had a
whole heart and a whole belly in the business.' It was a
third man who spoke, with a savagery that somehow
jarred like the clash of weapons in that crowded place.
'We haven't now.'

'Speak for your own belly,' somebody said, and there
was a general laugh.

'So I will then — I'm sick of all these brave doings, to
the pit of my own belly!'

The man with the scarred forehead, his wine-cup re-filled, swung round on him. 'You shouted loud enough with the rest of us when we swore allegiance to the new Emperor a while back.'

'Aye, I shouted loud enough with the rest of you curs. I swore my allegiance; by Jupiter I did, by Thundering Jove I did! And how much do you suppose my oath is worth if it comes to that? How much is *yours* worth, my friend?' He wagged a finger in the other's face, his eyes brilliant in the light of the swinging lantern. One of the other men tried to silence him, but he only raised his voice a little higher. 'If I were Allectus I wouldn't trust us a pilum's length, I wouldn't, Legion or Fleet, lest we shout for another Emperor tomorrow. — And what sort of use is an army and a fleet that you can't trust a pilum's length when it comes to fighting? Just about as much use as an Emperor you can't trust a pilum's length either!'

'Be quiet, you fool!' The wine shopkeeper had joined the group. 'You're too drunk to know what you're saying. Go back to barracks and sleep it off.'

'Yes, you want to get rid of me – you're afraid I'll get your wretched little dog-hole of a wine-shop into trouble.' The man's voice rose in reckless mockery. 'Phuh! What a country! Anybody give me a nice dark corner below decks in a ship making the crossing, and I'll go farther than back to barracks – I'll be off to Gaul tonight, and never once look back. Meanwhile I'll have another cup of wine.'

'You will not,' said the shopkeeper. 'You'll go back to barracks, and you'll go now.'

By this time the silence that had laid hold of the rest of the company was breaking up into an ugly splurge of voices, and men were on their feet, moving in on the group. A wine-cup fell with a clatter and rolled across the floor; and Justin, who had been listening with an almost painful attention to what went forward, for it was the first time that he had heard the Legions themselves on the change of Emperors, suddenly realized that the little tax-gatherer was leaning toward them with a murmured 'Best, I think, to get out of here.'

Flavius said uncompromisingly, 'Why?'

'Because,' said the tax-gatherer, 'the man nearest to the door has slipped out. At almost any moment now there is going to be trouble – and trouble spreads.' He smiled apologetically behind a plump hand. 'It is never wise to get mixed up in such things if one has oneself – ahem – anything that one does not wish the Watch to know.'

10

The *Berenice* Sails
for Gaul

JUSTIN'S eyes flew to the man's face, then to his
cousin's. Flavius had turned a little and was looking
at their new acquainance with a startled frown; then he
got up without a word, felt in his belt, and laid some
money on the table.

Justin rose also, his hand going instinctively to his instrument-case in the shoulder-sling he had made for it.
Their eyes met, questioningly, then Flavius gave a suspicion of a shrug, and turned toward the door on to the
foreshore. But the little tax-gatherer shook his head. 'No,
no, no, this way – much better,' and opened another door
close beside them but so lost in shadows that they had not
noticed it before. They followed him through, hearing behind them a sudden bellow of rage and the crash of a table
going over. Then Justin let the ramshackle door close
softly, and the swelling uproar fell away behind it.

They were in a passage-way of some sort, and a few
moments later, another door closing behind them, they
emerged into a narrow street with the harbour glimmering at one end of it; a street dark and empty, quiet save
for the wind that fretted the garbage to and fro.

'And now,' Flavius demanded in a swift undertone,
standing stock still in the deserted roadway, 'What makes
you think that we have anything we would not wish the
Watch to know?'

'My dear young man,' said their companion reasonably,

'do you think that the open street is quite the place to discuss that?'

'Where shall we discuss it, then?'

'I was about – ahem – to ask you to come home with me.'

There was a moment's surprised silence, and then Flavius asked, 'Can you give us any good reason why, supposing that we *had* something to hide, we should trust you?'

'No, I fear I cannot. It is most awkward – most awkward; but I assure you that you may.' The little man sounded so genuinely bothered that somehow they found themselves believing him.

Flavius said with a sudden breath of laughter, 'Well, of course, if you say so –'

They moved off up the street, the plump little tax-gatherer trotting in front, muffled so close in his cloak that Justin thought he looked like an enormous pale cocoon. Were they being complete fools? he wondered. No, somehow he was sure that they were not: this odd little man was to be trusted. Then, as they passed a narrow lane leading down to the foreshore, the wind swooping up it brought the quick tramp of mailed sandals as a patrol of the Watch hurried by in the direction of the wine-shop they had so lately left; and he said urgently, 'There they go. Isn't there anything we can do about that poor fool? It's d-dreadful to just abandon him.'

The cocoon looked over its plump shoulder as it scurried. 'Abandon him? Oh dear me, we haven't abandoned him. No need to worry. No, no; no need at all,' and dived into another dark alleyway.

Justin had lost all sense of direction by the time they came up a gash of a blind alley, and found at the end of it a door in a high wall. 'I ask your forgiveness for bringing you in the back way,' said the tax-gatherer, opening it. 'I generally come in this way myself because it isn't over-looked. My neighbours are, I fear, rather prone to – ahem – overlooking.' And so saying he led them through into a narrow courtyard.

It was not a dark night, and there was enough light in the courtyard, with its lime-washed walls, to show them the raised well-head in the centre, and the small tree growing beside it. The cocoon said bashfully, 'I call this my garden. It is just the one apple-tree, but it is the best little apart and his hands behind his back, said: 'And now an apple-tree that – ahem – to my mind no other tree possesses; "The apple-tree, the singing, and the gold" – you know your Euripides?'

Still burbling gently, he led the way across to a door on the far side, and opening it, ushered them through into a darkness that smelled pleasantly warm and lived in, with a suggestion of the last meal about it. 'Home again. I always like to get home at the day's end. This is the kitchen, if you will just come through here into my living-room. – Ah, Myron has left a nice bit of fire in the brazier; very nice, very nice indeed.' He was bustling about like a house-proud hen as he spoke, kindling a twig at the low red glow of the charcoal, lighting the lamp, putting fresh logs on the brazier. And as the light strengthened, Justin saw that they were in a small, cheerful room, with bands of colour on the walls, piles of gay native rugs on the two low couches by the fire, and a set of household gods in brightly painted plaster standing in niches round the walls. It was all so ordinary, so far away from the wild journey South and the scene in the wine-shop, that suddenly he wanted to laugh, and wasn't sure why. 'We shall not be disturbed,' said their host, testing the shutter over a high window to make sure that there was no chink. 'I don't keep slaves, I like to be quite free; and Myron goes out in the evenings.'

Flavius, standing in the middle of the floor, his feet a little apart and his hands behind his back, said: 'And now that we are no longer in the open street, will you tell us what lies behind all this?'

'Ah yes, you asked what made me think that you have anything to hide.' The little man held his fingers to the warmth. 'It is – ahem – difficult to explain. A good friend of mine, whom you spoke to on the foreshore this evening, was not quite sure that you were what you seemed. You – if I may say so – should try to slouch rather more. The Legionary carriage does not – ahem – altogether go with the rest of your appearance. He saw you into the Dolphin, and then came and reported to me. So I went down to the Dolphin to see for myself, feeling that you might be in trouble. And then of course I could scarcely help noticing that ring, which is also – ahem – somewhat out of keeping.'

'And then you made up your mind, with no more than that to go on?'

'Oh, no, no; I was not sure until I suggested to you that it would be as well to come away if one had anything to hide – and you came.'

Flavius looked at him blankly. 'Oh. Yes, it sounds quite simple when you put it like that.'

'Quite,' said their host. 'Now tell me what I can do for you.'

Justin's desire to laugh returned to him. Because he was so tired, his laughter did not seem under very good control, and nor did his legs. 'May I – may I sit down?' he asked.

The plump face of his host was instantly distressful. 'Of course; why, of course! What am I thinking of, that I leave my guests standing? See now, sit here, close to the brazier.' With the little man fussing round him like a hen, Justin smiled gratefully, and folded up on to the foot of the couch, holding out his hands to the warmth.

Flavius shook his head impatiently, and remained standing. He was frowning into the fire where the little new flames were beginning to lick up round the logs. Suddenly his brows quirked up to their most fly-away, and he laughed. 'Well, we have got to put our lives into somebody's hands, or we shall get no farther until the Greek Calends. – We want to get across to Gaul.'

'Ah, I thought it might be that.'

'Can you do anything about it, beyond thinking?'

'I – ahem – have arranged something of the kind before now.' The little tax-gatherer sat himself down, and fixed his wide, serene gaze on Flavius's face. 'But first I should require to know something more of your reasons. You must forgive me, but I dislike handling unknown cargoes.'

'Could you be sure of knowing more, however much we told you? We could tell you a string of lies.'

'You could try,' said their host limpidly.

Flavius looked at him very hard for a moment. Then he told him the whole story, much as he had told it yesterday to Great-Aunt Honoria.

When he had finished, the little man nodded. 'Under the circumstances your desire for foreign travel seems most reasonable. *Most* reasonable. Yes, I think we can help you, but it may not be for a few days yet. There are certain arrangements to be made, you see, arrangements and – ahem – and so on.'

'As to payment –' Flavius began.

'Oh, it isn't a matter of payment – no, no, no,' said their host cosily. 'In this kind of business, men who need buying are too dear at any price.'

There was a little silence, and then Flavius said, 'I ask your pardon.'

'No need, not the least need in the world, my dear young man. Now, as to present plans – you will of course accept my hospitality for the next few days. Though indeed I fear that the only quarters I can offer you are

somewhat close and primitive. You will understand that
I cannot safely keep you in the house.' He smiled apologetically, and rose to his feet. 'In fact, if you will not mind,
I will take you to your quarters now. There may be work
for me later in connection with – ahem – our rash friend
of the Dolphin; and I should like to see you safely bestowed before I go forth again.'

'We are under your orders,' Flavius said, with a smile.

Back they went across the kitchen, and into what
seemed to be a storeroom beyond. They heard the little
tax-gatherer moving boxes and baskets in the darkness,
and sensed rather than saw, that a hole had opened in the
opposite wall. 'Through here. There was a larger door
once, filled in long ago. I – er – adapted it, oh quite a
while since. Mind your heads.'

The warning seemed scarcely necessary, as the hole
was about half man high, and they followed him through
on all fours. Beyond the hole there was a steep and much-
worn flight of steps leading up into the darkness, and at
the head of it a space of some kind smelling strongly of
dust and mildew.

'What is this place?' Flavius said.

'It is part of the old theatre. Alas, no one ever thinks of
going to a play now, and there are no more actors left;
and the place has become a veritable slum since it fell
from its original use, and the populace moved in.' Their
host was panting slightly from the stairs. 'I fear I cannot give you a light; there are too many chinks for it to
shine through. But there are plenty of rugs here in the
corner – clean and dry – yes, yes : and I suggest that you
go to sleep. When there is nothing else to do, go to sleep;
it passes the time.'

They heard him pause at the stairhead. 'I shall be back
in the morning. Oh, there are some loose boards in the
wall just to the right of the stairway here : I would sug-

gest that you do not take them out and crawl through to
see what is on the other side. The floor is quite rotten beyond them, and if you go through it, you will not only
break your own necks, but – ahem – betray this very useful little hiding-place of mine.'

They heard his footsteps on the steep stair, and then the
baskets and boxes being stacked over the entrance hole
again.

They did not discuss the situation when they were
alone; somehow there did not really seem anything to
say; and they were too blind weary to say it, even
if there had been. They simply took their host's advice,
and groping their way over to the pile of rugs in the
corner, crawled in and fell asleep like a couple of tired
dogs.

Justin woke with a crash to find the first greyness of the
morning filtering in through a chink of a window high
above his head, and the sound of footsteps on the stair,
and for a moment he could not remember where he was.
Then he tumbled out after Flavius from among the rugs,
shaking the sleep out of his eyes, as their host loomed
into the doorway.

'I do trust I did not disturb you,' he said, ambling forward to set something he was carrying on the bench below the window. 'I have brought you your morning meal
– only bread and cheese and eggs, I am afraid.' He gave
that little apologetic cough that they were coming to
know. 'Also my library, to help you pass the time; just
the first roll of my "Hippolytus", you know. – I think I
mentioned Euripides to you last night; and I fancied from
your manner that neither of you had read him ... I always
think one values a thing more if one has had to make –
ahem – a certain amount of sacrifice for it. The "Hippolytus" cost me a great many meals and visits to the Games
when I was one of Carausius's Under-Secretaries, and –

ahem – not over well paid. I know that I need not ask you
to treat it gently.'

'Thank you for trusting it to us,' Justin said.

And at the same instant Flavius said quickly, 'You were
one of Carausius's Secretaries, then?'

'Yes – oh, a long time ago, when he was first – ahem –
raised to the Purple. Quite a temporary measure, but it
suited both of us at the time.'

Flavius nodded, and asked after a moment, 'What happened to that fool at the Dolphin?'

'Our rash friend? We – picked him up before the Watch
Patrol could do so, the wine shopkeeper being somewhat
of a friend of mine – which was as well for him; Allectus
does not encourage wild talk of that kind.' They heard
him smile. 'Our friend is a sober and a very scared man
this morning, and more than ever eager to be away to
Gaul.'

'Where is he now?' Flavius asked.

'Quite safe. There are more hiding-places than one in
Portus Adurni; so we did not put him in here. You have
all you want? Until this evening, then.'

They were very hungry, and they cleared the food to the
last crumb, while slowly the daylight grew, and around
and below them Portus Adurni woke to life. The cold light
filtering in through the chink of window showed them
that they were in a narrow slip of a room, whose sloping
rafters, high on the side where the window was, came
down on the other side almost to the level of the uneven
floor. And when they investigated, they found that from
the window, by standing on the bench to reach it, they
could look down through the withering leaves of a creeper
into the trim, lime-washed courtyard where grew the best
little apple-tree in the Empire. And by lying on the floor
opposite, and shutting one eye to squint down through a
gap where some tiles had fallen, they could catch a glimpse

of the old, elegant ruins of the theatre, and the squalid turf roofs of the slum bothies that had come crowding in among the fallen columns.

They seemed perched between two worlds; and the odd-shaped chamber was as fantastic as its situation, derelict, half ruined, the uneven planks of the floor blotched with livid fungus where the rain had beaten in, the corners grey with cobwebs that hung down, swaying in the wind that rustled the dead creeper leaves to and fro along the floor. Yet with one wall still showing traces of the frescoes it had once worn, faded ghosts of garlands hanging on painted columns that had long since flaked away, even a little Eros hovering on azure wings.

Justin spent that day in trying to read Euripides, mainly because he felt that if he lent someone a thing that he loved as their plump host loved his Euripides, and they did not use it, he should be hurt. But he made poor progress with it. He had always hated and feared being shut up in any place from which he could not get out at will – that was from the day when the wine-shed door had swung to on him, when he was very small, and held him prisoner in the dark for many hours before anyone heard him. Last night he had been so drugged with weariness that nothing could have come between him and sleep. But now his consciousness of being caged in the narrow secret chamber, as surely as though the piled baskets over the entrance hole were a locked door, came between him and the story of Hippolytus, and took all the power and the beauty out of what he read.

At evening their host returned, and remarked that as it was now dark and they were not likely to be disturbed, it might be that they would give him the pleasure of their company at supper. And after that, each night save once, when their supper was brought to them early by a boy with a sharply eager face and two front teeth missing, who introduced himself as 'Myron that saw to everything', they supped with the tax-gatherer behind closed shutters in the little house that backed on to the wall of the old theatre.

Those winter evenings in the bright commonplace room, with Paulinus, as they found their host to be called, were completely unreal, but very pleasant. And for Justin they were a respite from the cage.

For the small secret chamber was increasingly hard to bear. He began to be always listening, listening for voices in the courtyard and blows against the house door; even at night, when Flavius slept quietly with his head on his arm, he lay awake, staring with hot eyes into the darkness, listening, feeling the walls closing in on him like a trap...

The only thing that made it bearable was knowing that one day quite soon – surely very soon now – Gaul lay at the end of it, like daylight and familiar things at the end of a strange dark tunnel.

And then at last, on the fifth evening, when they were gathered as usual in the pleasant room behind its closed shutters, Paulinus said, 'Well now, I am happy to tell you that moon and the tide both serving, everything is settled for your journey.'

They seemed to have waited for it so long that just at first it did not sink in. Then Flavius said, 'When do we go?'

'Tonight. When we have eaten we shall walk out of here, and at a certain place we shall take up our friend of the Dolphin. The *Berenice*, bound for Gaul with a cargo of wool, will be waiting for us two miles westward along the coast, at moonset.'

'So simple as that,' Flavius said, with a smile. 'We are very grateful, Paulinus. There doesn't seem much that we can say beyond that.'

'Hum?' Paulinus picked up a little loaf from the bowl at the table, looked at it as though he had never seen such a thing before, and put it back again. 'There is – ahem – a thing that I should very much like to ask you.'

'If there is a thing – anything – that we can do, we will,' Flavius said.

'Anything? Will you, both of you – for I think that you count as one in this – let the *Berenice* sail for Gaul with only our friend of the Dolphin on board?'

For a moment Justin did not believe that he had really heard the words; then he heard Flavius say, 'You mean – stay behind, here in Britain? But why?'

'To work with me,' Paulinus said.

'*Us*? But Roma Dea! what use should we be?'

'I think that you would have your uses,' Paulinus said. 'I have taken my time, to be sure, and it is because of that that I can leave you so little time to decide ... I need someone who can take command if anything happens to me. There are none of those linked with me in this – ahem – business whom I feel could do that.' He was smiling into the red glow of the brazier. 'We are doing really very good business. We have sent more than one hunted man out of Britain in these past few weeks; we can send word out of the enemy camp of such things as Rome needs to know; and when the Caesar Constantius comes, as I believe most assuredly he will, we may have our uses as – ahem – a friend within the gates. It would be sad if all that went down the wind because one man died and there was no one to come after him.'

To Justin, staring at the flame of the lamp, it seemed bitterly hard. Gaul was so near now, so very near, and the clean daylight and familiar things; and this little fat man was asking him to turn back into the dark. The silence lengthened, began to drag. Far off in the night-time hush he heard the beat of mailed sandals coming up the street,

nearer, nearer: the Watch patrol coming by. Every evening at about this time it came; and every evening at its
coming, something tightened in his stomach. It tightened
now, the whole bright room seemed to tighten, and he was
aware, without looking at them, of the same tension in
the other two – tightening and tightening and then going
out of them like a sigh, as the marching feet passed by
without a check. And it would always be like that, always,
day and night; the hand that might fall on one's shoulder
at any moment, the footsteps that might come up the
street – and stop. And he couldn't face it.

He heard Flavius saying, 'Look for somebody else, sir;
somebody better suited to the task. Justin is a surgeon and
I am a soldier; we have our worth in our own world. We
haven't the right kind of make-up for this business of
yours. We haven't the right kind of courage, if you like
that better.'

'I judge otherwise,' Paulinus said; and then, after a little
pause, 'It is in my mind that when the Caesar Constantius
comes, you may be of greater worth in this business than
you would had you gone back to the Legions.'

'Judge? How can you judge?' Flavius said desperately.
'You have talked with us a little, on four or five evenings.
No more.'

'I have – ahem – something of a knack in such things. I
find I am very seldom mistaken in my judgements.'

Justin shook his head, miserably. 'I'm sorry.'

And Flavius's voice cut across his in the same instant.
'It's no good, sir. We – must go.'

The tax-gatherer made a small gesture with both hands,
as one accepting defeat; but his plump pink face lost none
of its kindliness. 'I also am sorry ... Nay then, think no
more of it; it was unfair to put you to such a choice. Now
eat; see now, time passes, and you must eat before you
go.'

But to Justin, at all events, the food which should have had the taste of freedom in it tasted like ashes, and every mouthful stuck in his throat and nearly choked him.

Some two hours later they were standing, Justin and Flavius, the tax-gatherer and the Marine from the Dolphin, on the edge of a clump of wind-twisted thorn-trees, their faces turned seaward toward the small vessel that was nosing in under oars. The moon was almost down, but the water was still bright beyond the darkness of the sand dunes; and the little bitter wind came soughing across the dark miles of the marshes and low coast-wise grasslands, making a faint Aeolian hum through the bare and twisted branches of the thorn-trees. A gleam of light pricked out low down on the vessel's hull, marigold light in a world of black and silver and smoky grey; and the tension of waiting snapped in all of them.

'Ah, it is the *Berenice*, safe enough,' said Paulinus.

And the time for going was upon them.

The Marine, who had been subdued and completely silent since they took him up at the agreed meeting-place, turned for a moment, saying ruefully, 'I know not why you should have taken so great pains on my account; but I'm grateful. I – I don't know what to say –'

'Then don't waste time trying to say it. Get along, man. Now get along, do,' said Paulinus.

'Thank you, sir.' The other flung up his hand in leave-taking, and, turning, strode away down the shore.

Flavius said abruptly. 'May I ask you something, sir?'

'If you ask it quickly.'

'Do you do this for adventure?'

'Adventure?' Paulinus sounded quite scandalized in the darkness. 'Oh dear me, no, no, no! I'm not at all the adventurous kind; too – ahem – much too timid, for one thing. Now go quickly; you must not keep your transport waiting, with the tide already on the turn.'

'No. Good-bye, then, sir; and thank you again.'

Justin, a hand on his instrument-case, as usual, murmured something that sounded completely unintelligible,
even in his own ears, and turned in behind Flavius, setting his face down to the shore.

They overtook the Marine from the Dolphin, and together made their way down between the sand dunes to
the smooth, wave-patterned beach below. The boat was
waiting, quiet as a sea-bird at rest. At the water's edge,
Justin checked, and looked back. He knew that he was lost
if he looked back, yet he could not help himself. In the
very last of the moonlight he saw the stout little figure of
Paulinus standing solitary among the thorn-trees, with all
the emptiness of the marshes behind him.

'Flavius,' he said desperately, 'I am not going.'

There was a little pause, and then Flavius said, 'No,
nor I, of course.' Then, with a breath of a laugh, 'Did not
Paulinus say that we counted as one in this?'

The Marine from the Dolphin, already foot-wet looked
back. 'Best hurry.'

'Look,' said Flavius. 'It is all right. We are not coming.
Tell them on board that the other two are not coming. I
think they'll understand.'

'Well, it's your own affair —' began the other.

'Yes, it's our own affair. Good luck, and — best hurry.'
Flavius echoed him his own words.

In the silence the tide made small, stealthy noises
around their feet. They watched him take to the water,
wading deeper and deeper until he was almost out of his
depth as he reached the waiting vessel. They saw by the
light of the lantern that he had been pulled on board. Then
the lantern was quenched, and in complete silence the
sails were set and the little vessel gathered way and slipped
seaward, like a ghost.

Justin was suddenly very much aware of the lap and

hush of the ebbing tide, and the wind-haunted, empty darkness of the marshes behind him. He felt very small and defenceless, and rather cold in the pit of his stomach. They could have been slipping out to sea now, he and Flavius; by dawn they would have been at Gesoriacum; back once more to the daylight and the life they knew, and the fellowship of their own kind. And instead . . .

Flavius shifted abruptly beside him, and they turned without a word and went trudging back through the soft dune-sand toward the figure waiting by the thorn-trees.

11

The Shadow

THEY handed one of Great-Aunt Honoria's opal bracelets over to Paulinus for use, as it might be needed. They would have given him both, but he bade them keep the other against a rainy day; and Flavius took off the battered signet ring which was out of keeping with the sort of characters that they would be henceforth, and hung it on a thong round his neck, inside his tunic. And a night or two later, Justin asked Paulinus for leave to write to his father. 'If I might write, once, to warn him that he will hear no more of me for a while. – I will g-give you the letter to read, that you may be sure I have betrayed nothing.'

Paulinus considered a moment, and then gave a brisk nod. 'Yes, there is wisdom in that; it may well save – ahem – awkward inquiries.'

So Justin wrote his letter, and found it unexpectedly hard to do. He knew that it might quite likely be the last letter that ever he would write to his father, and so there were many things that he wanted to say. But he did not know how to say them. 'If it should come to your ears that I left my post at Magnis,' he wrote finally, after the bare warning, 'and if that, and this letter, should be the last that ever you hear of me, please do not be ashamed of me, father. I have done nothing to be ashamed of, I swear it.' And that was almost all.

He gave the open tablet to Paulinus, according to his

word, and Paulinus cast one vague glance in its direction and handed it back to him. And in due course it went off by a certain trader making the crossing in the dark; and Justin, feeling as though he had cut the last strand that held him to familiar things, turned himself, with Flavius, full face to this other, stranger life in which they found themselves.

A strange life if proved to be, and full of strangely assorted company. There was Cerdic the boat-builder, and the boy Myron who had originally been caught by Paulinus trying to steal his purse; and Phaedrus of the *Berenice*, with his blue faience ear-drop; there was a government clerk in the Corn Office at Regnum, and an old woman who sold flowers outside the temple of Mars Toutate at Clausentium, and many others. They were linked together by nothing more definite than a snatch of tune whistled in the dark, or a sprig of common rye-grass tucked into a brooch or girdle-knot. Many of them, even those who lived in Portus Adurni, did not know the secret of the hole behind the lumber in Paulinus's store-room, nor that other way – 'the Sparrow's Way' Paulinus called it when he showed it to Justin and Flavius – that started behind a low wall near the main entrance to the old theatre, and ended at those loose boards in the wall of the room where the painted Eros was. Yet in their odd way they were a brotherhood, none the less.

Justin and Flavius lodged with Cerdic the boat-builder, earning their living at any kind of job that they could pick up around the town and the repair yards. That is, they did so when they were at Portus Adurni; but often, that winter, they were at Regnum, at Venta, at Clausentium. Justin, though not Flavius, who would have been too easily recognized even in his present guise, pushed as far north as Calleva more than once. Five great roads met at Calleva, and the Cohorts of the Eagles were forever passing and re-passing through the transit camp outside the walls; and in all the province of Britain there could have been no better place for keeping one's eyes and ears open.

Winter wore away, and Paulinus's apple-tree was in bud. And upward of a score of men had been sent safely overseas; men who came to the Dolphin or to one or other of the meeting-places, wearing a sprig of rye-grass somewhere about themselves, saying, 'One sent me.'

Spring turned to summer, and the best apple-tree in the Empire shed its pink-tipped petals into the dark water of the courtyard well. And from his chief city of Londinium, the Emperor Allectus was making his hand felt. Those corn and land taxes, heavy but just in Carausius's day, which men had expected would be lightened under Allectus, became heavier than ever, and were levied without mercy for the Emperor's private gain. And before midsummer news was running from end to end of Britain that Allectus was bringing in Saxon and Frankish Mercenaries, bringing in the brothers of the Sea Wolves, to hold his kingdom down for him. Britain was betrayed indeed! Men said little – it was dangerous to say much – but they looked at each other with hot and angry eyes; and the trickle of those who brought their sprig of rye-grass to the Dolphin increased as the weeks went by.

The first time Portus Adurni saw anything of the hated Mercenaries was on a day in July when Allectus himself came to inspect the troops and defences of the great fortress.

All the town of Adurni turned out to throng the broad, paved street to the Praetorium Gate, drawn by curiosity and the exciting prospect of seeing an Emperor, even an Emperor they were coming to hate, and by the fear of Imperial displeasure if they did not make enough show of rejoicing.

Justin and Flavius had found good places for themselves right against the steps of the little temple of Jupiter, where the Emperor was to sacrifice before entering the fortress. In the July sunlight the heat danced like a cloud of midges above the heads of the crowd, – a great crowd, all in their best clothes and brightest colours. The shops had hung out rich stuffs and gilded branches for a sign of rejoicing, and the columns of the temple were wreathed with garlands of oak and meadow-sweet, whose foam of blossom, already beginning to wilt, mingled its honey sweetness with the tang of garden marigolds and the sour smell that rose from the close-packed crowd. But over the whole scene, despite the festival garments, the bright colours and the garlands, there was a joylessness that made it all hollow.

The two cousins were close against the Legionaries on street-lining duty; so close to the young Centurion in charge that when he turned his head they could hear the crimson horsehairs of his helmet-crest rasp against his mailed shoulders. He was a dark, raw-boned lad with a jutting galley-prow of a nose, and a wide, uncompromising mouth; and for some reason, perhaps because he was someone very much of their own kind, Justin took particular note of him.

But now, far off up the Venta road, a stir arose, and expectancy rippled through the crowd before the temple. Nearer and nearer, a slow, hoarse swell of sound rolled toward them like a wave. All heads were turned one way. Justin, crushed against a particularly craggy Legionary, with a fat woman breathing down his neck, saw the cavalcade in the distance, swelling larger and clearer moment by moment. Saw the tall, gracious figure of the new Emperor riding in the van, with his ministers and staff about him, and the Senior Officers of the fortress garrison; and, behind him, the Saxons of his bodyguard.

Allectus the Traitor was within a few feet of them now, riding up between the swaying crowd; a still, white man, whose eyes and skin seemed all the paler in the sunlight by contrast with the glowing folds of the Imperial Purple that fell from his shoulders over the gilded bronze of his armour. He turned with the old charming smile to speak to the Camp Commandant at his side; he looked about him with interest, acknowledging the acclamation of the crowd with a bend of the head and a gesture of one big white hand, seeming unaware of the hollow ring to the cheering. And after him crowded the Saxons of his bodyguard; big, blue-eyed, yellow-haired tribesmen out of barbarian Germany, sweating under their back-flung wolf-skin cloaks, with gold and coral at their throats and serpents of red gold above the elbows, who laughed and made their guttural talk among themselves as they rode.

Now they were dismounting before the temple portico, the horses wheeling out in all directions to spread confusion among the close-jammed crowd. Over the Legionary's shoulder, Justin saw the tall figure in the Purple turn on the flower-strewn steps, with an actor's gesture to the populace; and was seized with such a blinding rage that he scarcely saw what happened next until the thing was half over.

An old woman had somehow slipped under the guard of the Legionaries, and ran forward with hands outstretched to cast herself at the Emperor's feet with some plea, some petition. What it was, nobody ever heard. One of the Saxons stooped and caught her by the hair and hurled her backward. She went over with a scream, and they were all round her. They pricked her to her feet with the tips of their saexes, laughing, for the sport of seeing her scuttle. A stupefied hush had descended on the crowd; and then, as the old woman stumbled and all but fell again, the Centurion strode forward, sword in hand, and

stepped between her and her tormentors. Quite clearly in
the sudden hush Justin heard him say, 'Get back quickly,
old mother.' Then he turned to face the Saxons, who
seemed momentarily quelled by his air of authority, and
said, 'The game is finished.'

Allectus, who had turned again on the steps to see what
was happening, gestured to one of his staff officers. Somehow the thing was sorted out; the Saxons were whistled
off like hounds, and the old woman had gathered herself together and scuttled weeping back into the crowd,
the Legionaries parting their crossed pilums to let her
through.

When Justin, who had been watching her, looked round
again, the young Centurion was standing on the temple
steps before Allectus. Justin was within a spear's length
of them, half shielded by a garland-hung column; and he
heard Allectus say very gently, 'Centurion, no man in-
terferes with my bodyguard.'

The Centurion's hands clenched at his sides. He was
very white, and breathing rather quickly. He said in a tone
as gentle as Allectus's own. 'Not even when they turn
their dirks on an old woman for amusement, Caesar?'

'No,' said Allectus, still more gently. 'Not even then. Go
back to your duties, Centurion, and another time remember not to step beyond them.'

The Centurion drew himself up and saluted, then turned
and marched back to his place, with a face that might
have been cut from stone. And Allectus, smiling his very
charming smile, turned and went, with the senior officers
about him, into the temple.

The whole thing had passed so swiftly that it was over
before half the crowd had realized what was happening.
But Justin and Flavius were to remember it afterward; to
remember – of all unexpected things – the narrow,
pointed face of Serapion the Egyptian, starting out of the

ranks of those in attendance on the Emperor, his dark, darting gaze fixed on the young Centurion.

In the great fortress that night, the Commandant's quarters, made over to the Emperor for his visit, bore a very different aspect from their usual one. Soft Eastern rugs and embroideries of delicate colours from the Emperor's baggage-train had made the place more like a suite of chambers for a queen; and the air was heavy with the sweetness of the perfumed oil burning in a silver lamp beside the couch on which Allectus reclined. The evening garland of white roses which he had just taken off lay wilting beside him, and he was amusing himself by delicately pulling the flowers to pieces. His rather heavy face was satisfied as a great white cat's, as he smiled at the Egyptian seated on a stool at his feet.

'Ceasar should have a care to that young Centurion,' Serapion was saying. 'He looked as though he would have knifed Caesar for a denarius this morning, and this evening he excused himself from attending the banquet in Caesar's honour.'

'Bah! He was angry at being called to account before the world, no more.'

'Nay, I think that it was more than that. It was a pity that Caesar's bodyguard thought fit to amuse themselves as they did this morning.'

Allectus shrugged indifferently. 'They are barbarians, and they behave as such; but they are loyal, so long as I pay them.'

'Nevertheless, it was a pity.'

Allectus's smile faded a little. 'Since when has Serapion the Egyptian been Caesar's counsellor?'

'Since Serapion the Egyptian furnished Caesar with enough nightshade to kill a man,' said the other smoothly.

'Hell and the Furies! Am I never to hear the last of

that? Have I not paid you well enough? Have I not made you one of my personal staff?'

'And am I not a good servant?' Serapion cringed, his dark eyes downcast. 'Nay, but I did not seek to remind Caesar of – unpleasant things ... Yet I served Caesar well in that matter. It would have been better had Caesar used my services again – for a greater occasion.'

The other laughed softly. 'Nay, man, you set too much store by secrecy and the dark. In these days no Emperor troubles overmuch to hide the hand that slew the Emperor before him. Besides, it was politic to get the Saxons deeply involved, that I might be sure of a good supply of Saxon Mercenaries thereafter.'

Serapion cast up his eyes. 'Caesar thinks of everything! None the less, it is in my mind that while we are here at least, I will have an eye to that young Centurion and his affairs.'

The big, pale man on the couch turned to look at him more closely. 'What is in that crooked mind of yours, little poison-toad?'

'One was telling me that of late months on this part of the coast more than one man who had no cause to love Caesar has – disappeared from under the noses of Caesar's Authorities. And it is in my mind that by watching that young Centurion one might just possibly – find out how.'

At about the same time next night, Justin was sitting in the shadowy corner at the Dolphin. It was a still, close summer evening, and the old striped awning had been rolled back, so that the narrow, lantern-lit courtyard was roofed with a luminous darkness of night sky above the leafy interlacings of the trellised vine. The wine-shop was not very full tonight, and he had the dark corner to himself and his thoughts.

He had got the news that he had come for, and when he had finished his cup of wine – not too quickly, lest any-

one should be watching – he would be on his way back to
Paulinus with word that the latest man to be shipped to
Gaul had been safely landed. Flavius would be there, and
Phaedrus coming later when he had finished unloading a
cargo of wine from the *Berenice*. They had some plans to
discuss for shortening the time that it took to get a man
out of the province; plans that needed a good deal of
thought. Justin tried to think about them, but for the most
part his mind was taken up with that startling glimpse of
Serapion the Egyptian among Allectus's personal atten-
dants yesterday. Why should Allectus take the little per-
fume-seller into his train? Something in the back of his
mind whispered that there was, there always had been, a
strong link between such things as Serapion sold, and
poison. The Sea Wolf who could have told too much had
died of poison ... Well, whatever the truth of the matter,
there could be no menace for them in the man's reappearance, for, thank the gods, he had not seen them. And yet
Justin could not clear his mind of an odd uneasiness; something that was almost foreboding.

Someone strolled in from the dark foreshore; and Justin
glanced up to see a young man in a shaggy homespun
cloak, with ruffled dark hair above a pock-marked forehead, and a great bony beak of a nose, who hesitated an
instant in the doorway, glancing about him. Lacking harness and helmet, he looked very different from the last
time Justin had seen him, but with his thoughts already
hovering around yesterday's scene on the temple steps, he
knew him instantly.

The man seemed to make up his mind, and crooking a
finger for the keeper of the place, came to sit not far from
where Justin was watching. As he did so, a shadow moved
in the darkness beyond the doorway; but there was nothing unusual in that, many people came and went along
the foreshore. Justin went on watching the young Cen-

turion. The wine came, but he did not drink it, only sat forward, his hands across his knees, playing with something between his fingers. And Justin saw that it was a sprig of rye-grass.

He picked up his own wine-cup, rose, and crossed over to the newcomer. 'Why, this is a pleasant and unexpected thing. I greet you, friend,' he said in the manner of one joining a chance-found acquaintance, and placing his wine-cup on the table, sat down. The other had looked up quickly at his coming, and was watching him guardedly, his face carefully non-committal, as Justin studied it in his turn. There was always a risk about this moment, always the chance that the sprig of rye-grass had found its way into the wrong hands. But he was sure enough of this man, remembering that scene yesterday on the steps of the Temple of Jupiter; besides, his pleasant, craggy face was not the face of an informer, and had in it something strained and a little desperate.

'It is very hot tonight,' Justin said, and loosed the folds of his light cloak, revealing the sprig of rye-grass thrust through the bronze clasp at the neck of his tunic.

The other saw it, and there was a kind of flicker in his face, instantly stilled. He leaned a little towards Justin, saying in a quick undertone, 'It was told me by – someone – that if I came to this wine-shop wearing a certain token, it might be that I should find those who would help me.'

'So? That depends on the help,' Justin murmured, watching lantern-light and leaf-shadows mingle in his cup.

'The same help as others have found before me,' said the man, with a quick, strained smile that barely touched his eyes. 'Let us lay aside the foils. See, I set myself in your hands. I do not wish to serve longer under such an Emperor as Allectus.'

'That is since yesterday?'

'You know about yesterday?'

'I was c-close by, among the crowd before the Temple of Jupiter.'

'Yesterday,' murmured the young man, 'was the last straw that breaks the camel's back. What do we do now?'

'Drink our wine slowly, and try to look a little less like c-conspirators,' said Justin, with a flicker of laughter.

They sat on for a while, quietly drinking their wine, and talking of the prospect of fair weather for the harvest, and kindred subjects, until presently Justin crooked a finger for the wine shopkeeper. 'Now I think that it is time we were moving.'

The other nodded without a word, pushing away his empty cup. They paid each their own score, and rising together, passed out, Justin leading and the other at his shoulder, into the still summer night.

None of those who came and went after dark to the little house or the secret chamber in the old theatre ever travelled straight, lest they should be followed; and to-night, because of the uneasiness that the sight of Serapion had left with him, Justin led his companion by ways even more roundabout than usual. Yet when at last they came down the narrow gash of darkness to the courtyard door, a shadow that had been behind them all the way from the Dolphin was still behind them. Justin paused by the courtyard door, listening, as always, for any sound of their being followed. But there was no sound, nothing moving in the crowding gloom of the alleyway. Yet as he lifted the latch and slipped through with the young Centurion, letting the latch fall silently again behind them, one of the shadows shook free of the rest, and darted lizard-swift across the door.

The little courtyard was in darkness, but the light of a late-rising moon just past the full was whitening the crest of the old theatre wall above them, and the upper branches of the little apple-tree by the well were touched with silver, so that the half-grown apples were like the apples on Cullen's beloved Silver Branch. Justin paused again, listening with strained intensity born of that odd uneasiness that he could not shake off. But the shadow in the alleyway made no more sound than a shadow makes, and with a murmured 'This way' he drew his companion across to the house door.

It was unbolted as the courtyard door had been, ready for Phaedrus coming later, and he opened it and led the way through.

The courtyard door opened a crack behind them, then closed again as silently as it had opened. Nothing moved in the courtyard but a silver night-moth among the silver branches of the apple-tree.

12

A Sprig of Broom

A CRACK of light showed primrose pale under the door ahead of them, and the little room seemed very bright as Justin raised the latch and went in. Flavius was there with Paulinus, and a chess-board set out on the table between them showed how they had been whiling away the time as they waited for Phaedrus of the *Berenice*.

'Ah, you are back,' Paulinus greeted him, and then, seeing the figure behind him, 'And who is this that you bring with you?'

'Another to go by the usual road,' Justin said.

'So? Well, we must see what can be done.' Paulinus moved his piece a little absent-mindedly. 'What news of the last one?'

'Safely landed.'

Flavius was watching the newcomers. 'It was you who fell foul of the Divine Allectus outside the Temple of Jupiter yesterday,' he said suddenly, and rose to his feet, rocking the chess-board so that a pained expression flitted for a moment across Paulinus's face.

The newcomer smiled, that quick, strained smile. 'You also were among the crowd?'

'I was,' Flavius said. 'I hope I'd have had the courage to do the same, if it had been my Cohort on street-lining duty yesterday.'

For a moment they stood looking at each other across the lamp on the table; Flavius in his rough workman's clothes, hairy and none too clean. And yet the newcomer said with only half a question in his tone, 'You speak, I think, as one of the brotherhood.'

'This time last year I commanded a Cohort on the Wall.'

Paulinus, who had been watching the newcomer, gave a little grunt of approval. 'I have heard the story of this falling foul of the Emperor. Unwise, my dear young man; but on the whole – ahem – creditable, very creditable indeed. And so now you feel Gaul to be a fitter place for you than Britain?'

'Can you arrange that for me?'

'I can arrange it,' said Paulinus tranquilly, 'if you will have patience for a few days, during which you will be my guest in – ahem – slightly close quarters, I fear.' And so saying he heaved himself to his feet and began one of his soft, hen-like fusses. 'But why do I keep you all standing here? Sit down, do sit down. There will be one more of us presently, and when he comes, if you will forgive me, I will show you up to those same close quarters. In this business it is best for no one to know more than they need. No, no, no. Meanwhile, have you supped? A cup of wine, then? – and do pray sit down.'

The newcomer wanted neither wine nor supper, but he sat down. They all sat down round the table, and after a moment's pause he said, 'I feel that the thing to do is to ask no questions, and therefore I will ask none ... Will you not go on with your game?'

Paulinus beamed at him. 'Well, well, if you are sure you will not think it discourteous. There will be no more time for chess when our – ahem – friend arrives, and I confess I do hate to leave a game unfinished, especially when I am winning. Flavius, I believe that it is your move.'

It was very hot in the small bright room with the shutters closed, very quiet behind the buzzing of a bluebottle among the rafters, and the faint click of the pieces as they moved on the board. The young Centurion sat with his arms across his knees, staring soberly before him. Justin, watching the game, began to be very sleepy, so that the pieces danced a little on the blurred black-and-white chequer, and the click as they were moved seemed to be going further and further away ...

But that game of chess was never to be finished, after all.

Suddenly Justin was broad awake again, to the sound of lumber being thrust aside in the storeroom, and next instant Phaedrus the ship-master burst in upon them, bringing with him a desperate urgency, a smell of deadly danger that had them all on their feet even before he gasped out his warning.

'The Barbarian Guard are all round the house. In the street – and the courtyard is full of them! I all but blundered into them, but by the grace of the gods I saw them in time and cast back for the Sparrow's Way.'

The little silence that followed could have lasted no more than a heart-beat, but it seemed to Justin to swell out and out like a gigantic bubble; a bubble of utter stillness. And from the midst of the stillness, Paulinus said quietly, 'Justin and Flavius, will you oblige me by barring the outer doors?'

They sprang to do his bidding; only just in time, for even as Justin dropped the bar of the courtyard door – an unusually strong bar for a private house – into place, a crash of blows came against it, making the timbers jar and vibrate under his hand, and a roar of guttural voices arose outside. 'Open up! Open up, or we break the doors down! Open up, man who harbours traitors, or we fire the roof and smoke you out!'

Well, the bar would hold for a little while, though the end was sure. He swung back into the living-room, still bright and commonplace, with its half-played game of chess on the table and its painted household gods in their niches on the walls, just in time to hear the Centurion saying, 'This is my doing. Someone must have followed me. I'll go out to them, sir.'

And Paulinus answered, 'No, no, it was liable to happen at any time, and as for going out to them: my good boy, do you think they would be content with you?'

Justin shut the living-room door and stood with his back to it. Flavius was standing in the same way against the door that led directly into the street, and behind him also the wolf-pack uproar rose. Paulinus glanced quickly at one after another of his companions and gave a little brisk nod. 'Yes, you're all of you slight and active – a mercy it's you, Phaedrus, and not that giant Cerdic. Out by the Sparrow's Way, all four of you, and make for Cerdic's boat-yard.'

'And you?' Flavius snapped.

'Have I the figure for the Sparrow's Way? Go now; wait for me at the boat-yard, and I'll join you when I can.'

'How?' Justin demanded bluntly, standing his ground, his hand on the dagger in his belt. 'I think we'll stay with you, sir, and fight it out t-together.'

The blows had spread to the high, shuttered window now, and from street and courtyard the wolf-pack yelling rose. 'I have another way out,' Paulinus said quickly; 'one that I have always kept for myself because I am too fat and too old for the other. But it can only be used alone. Will you waste all our lives?'

'Is that the truth?' Flavius said.

'The truth. Listen; the door will go any moment now. *Get out!* That's an order.'

'Very well, sir,' Flavius saluted, as to a superior officer, and turned towards the door into the kitchen before which Justin stood.

Justin, the last of the four to go, looked back once, and

saw Paulinus standing beside his unfinished game of chess.
His face was very pink in the heat, and he looked, as
always, faintly ridiculous; a plump, commonplace little
man in a plump, commonplace little room, looking after
them. Remembering that moment afterward, it always
seemed to him odd that Paulinus should still have looked
ridiculous. He should have looked – Justin was not sure
how, but not ridiculous; and there should have been a
shiningness about him that did not come from the lamp.

With the thunder of blows and the guttural voices in
their ears, they made for the crowded darkness of the
storeroom. 'You go first; you know the way best of all of
us,' Flavius whispered to the little seaman. 'I'll do rearguard.'

'Right.' The whisper came back out of the blackness,
and one after another they ducked through into the stairway. Justin heard Flavius draw a couple of store-baskets
over the hole behind them – not that that would be much
use when the tide of barbarians broke in. In the dark well
of the stairway the menacing uproar was muffled, but as
they gained the upper chamber it came bursting up to
them full force, and Justin saw the red glare of torches
reflected up from below mingled with the white light of
the moon as he dropped on his stomach and wormed
after the young Centurion through the gap in the wall.

There was a halt, while Flavius replaced the loose
boards, which were so worked that they could be dealt
with from either side; and then they set out in good earnest. The Sparrow's Way was never pleasant, and to Justin,
who had no head for heights, it was very unpleasant indeed, even when it did not have to be negotiated above
the heads of a mob of yelling Saxon Mercenaries, along
ledges flickering with reflected torch-light, where an un-
wary handhold or the slip of a foot on a sloping roof might
bring the hunt all round them at any moment.

But they made it safely; and a very long while later, as it seemed, swung themselves over the last low ledge, and landed soft in a garbage pile behind the tumbledown entrance of the theatre.

Later still, with Cerdic the boat-builder in their midst, the four of them were gathered in a waiting knot about the doorway of the turf-roofed bothie just outside the town, where Justin and Flavius had lodged all these months.

They were quite silent, stunned by the suddenness of what had happened, their strained gaze going out to a red glow that had sprung up in the sky over Portus Adurni. Justin shivered a little in the cool marsh air. Had the Saxons fired the place? Or was it something to do with Paulinus's way of escape? How long would it be before Paulinus came? – or – would he ever come? No, he must not think like that; he pushed the thought away in a hurry. Paulinus had sworn that there was another way out . . .

Flavius, frowning into the moonlight, said abruptly, 'Phaedrus, have you ever heard of this other way out before? This way that can only be taken alone?'

The seaman shook his head. 'Nay – but he said that it was one that he had kept for himself. Happen we should none of us have heard of it.'

'I hope you're right,' Flavius said. 'I hope to the gods you're right.'

Almost as he spoke, something moved in the shadow of the dunes, and Justin's heart gave a little lurch of relief. 'Here he comes now!'

And then, as the moving thing swayed out into the moonlight, stumbling in the soft, drifted sand, they saw that it was not Paulinus, but the boy Myron.

Flavius whistled softly, and the boy looked up and saw them and came on at an increased speed; and as he drew nearer they could hear him gasping, half sobbing as he ran.

'Name of Thunder! What's happened?' Flavius said under his breath, starting to meet him.

And somehow they were all down into the soft sand, and in their midst the boy Myron was gasping out in a broken jumble that at first they could scarcely understand. 'Oh, thank the gods you are here! The whole town's full of those devils, and I couldn't do nothing – I – I –' And he fell to gusty weeping.

Flavius caught him by both shoulders. 'Time enough for that later, if need be. Tell us what has happened.'

'Paulinus!' The boy drew a shuddering breath. 'They've killed Paulinus – I see them do it.'

Justin couldn't speak; he heard Phaedrus make a harsh sound in his throat, and then Flavius said in a hard, level voice, 'What have you seen?'

'I went back early because I'd forgot to fill the lamps, and he hated to have them run dry in the middle of the evening. And I was almost there when I heard the shouting and saw the flames. And I crept closer to look – right up to the courtyard door – and the courtyard was full of those Saxon devils with firebrands, and the roof was on fire and all – and just as I got there, the house door opened and – Paulinus walked out – just walked out into the middle of them, and they killed him – like killing a badger.'

There was a long, long silence. No sound in all the world but the sighing, singing, air-haunted stillness of the marsh under the moon. Not even a bird calling. Then Flavius said, 'So there wasn't another way out, after all – or, if there was, something went wrong and he couldn't use it.'

'There was another way out – and that was it,' Justin said slowly.

The young Centurion, who had been completely still throughout, said very softly, as though to himself, 'Greater love hath no man —' and Justin thought it sounded as though he were quoting someone else.

The boy Myron was crying desolately, repeating in a snuffling whisper over and over again, 'I couldn't do nothing — I couldn't —'

'Of course you couldn't.' Justin put an arm round his shoulders. And then, 'It was we who left him.'

Flavius made a harsh gesture of denial. 'We did not leave him. He ordered us out, that we might carry on the work after him. It was for that that he took us in the first place. So now we carry on the work.' Then, seeming for the first time to remember the stranger among them, he turned to him saying, 'I am sorry, but your jaunt to Gaul will have to wait awhile.'

The young Centurion had turned seaward, his head up into the faint breath of night wind. 'May I change my mind about Gaul?'

'It is too late to go back,' Flavius said.

'I do not ask to go back. I ask to join this team of yours.'

'Why?' Flavius demanded bluntly, after a small, startled pause.

'I — do not speak of paying my debts: there are debts that cannot be paid. I ask to join it because it seems to me worth joining.'

By dawn, Paulinus's neat little house was a gutted ruin, the secret chamber torn open to the sky, the apple-tree in the courtyard hacked to pieces in the sheer wanton joy of destruction; and Allectus's barbarians were questing like hounds into every corner of Portus Adurni, in search of they did not quite know what.

And crouching in the lee of Cerdic's boat-shed, with the faint mist rising about them as the night drew towards

dawn, Flavius spoke straightly to those of the band whom
they had been able to gather, with an arm over Justin's
shoulder as he spoke, as though to make it clear that the
two of them were one in the leadership that had fallen
upon them with Paulinus's death. 'You all know the thing
that has happened; talking won't mend it. Now we have
to make plans for carrying on the work in the future.'

There was a ragged murmur of agreement from the
dark, huddled shapes, and the keeper of the Dolphin said,
'Aye, and the first thing we'll be wanting is a new headquarters. And I'd suggest that after tonight's work, Portus
Adurni will be no place for it for a while and a while
to come.'

'Somewhere inland a bit,' said another man briefly.

Flavius glanced over them in the low moonlight. 'That
same thing is in my mind also,' he said.

'Anywhere to suggest?' That was Phaedrus, leaning forward with his arms round his up-drawn knees.

'Yes,' Flavius said, and Justin felt the arm across his
shoulders tighten a little. 'As Paulinus used his own home
for the purpose, so I have it in mind – unless any among
you find reason against the plan – to use mine.'

It was the first Justin had heard of it, but he knew instantly that it was right; the whole feel of the plan was
right, and fitting.

'And whereabouts might your home be?' Cerdic the
boat-builder asked in the deep rumble that seemed always
to come from somewhere far down in his barrel chest.

'Up into the Chalk, north-east of here, ten or twelve
miles. It's a good strategic position, as near to Clausentium as we are now, nearer to both Regnum and Venta.
Easy of access over the Downs or by the old track from
Venta; and the forest for cover in case of trouble.'

There was a certain amount of urgent and low-voiced
talk before the thing was settled, but none of the men

gathered there had any particular fault to find with the plan, and indeed after some discussion and argument they found it good. The house by the theatre had never really been a meeting-place, rather it had been the spot where the threads were gathered together. And so long as they were gathered together somewhere reasonably near to the centre of the web, it made very little difference exactly where.

'So: it is a good plan, and we will abide by it,' Phaedrus said at last. 'Show us now how we may find this place.'

And so, in the misty moonlight and the first cobweb greyness of the dawn, Flavius made them a relief map in the sand, that they might know how to find it. The great curved ridge of the Downs, rising a handspan high among the marsh grasses, with the soft moon-shadows in its tiny valleys; and the furrow of a finger trailed through the sand for the great roads and the tracks that had been old before the roads were new. And for the farm itself, a sprig of broom with the sand between its leaves, and one spark of blossom.

And when each of them had carefully memorized the map, he smoothed it all away. 'So. That is all. Justin and I go inland now to make arrangements, but we shall be back in two days at the latest. The newest recruit comes with us, I think. He will be too well known in these parts.'

Justin glanced towards a small desolate figure, huddled against the boat-shed wall, and said quickly, half under his breath, 'Myron, too. He has nowhere and no one belonging to him in Portus Adurni — and he's in no fit state to be seen by our enemies.'

Flavius nodded. 'Yes, you're right. We can't leave him here. Myron too, then.'

The light was growing, and it was time to break up, but at the last moment he stayed them. 'Wait; there's one thing more. Better after this that we change the token. There may be others now besides ourselves on the look-out for sprigs of rye-grass.'

'What shall it be, then?' said Phaedrus.

It was Justin, in the act of turning away to fetch his beloved instrument-case from the bothie, who picked up the sprig of broom that had been used to mark the position of the farm and shook the sand out of it. 'How about this? It is easily come by, and all men know it.'

'So : that will serve,' Flavius said. 'Pass the word along the coast, Phaedrus.'

At noon, far up on the crest of the downs, Flavius halted them for a few hours, not wishing to walk into the farm, where doubtless he and Justin were thought to be in Gaul, unheralded and in broad daylight.

There were harebells in the tawny downland grass, and the blue butterflies of chalk country dancing in the sun-shine, the turf was warm to the touch, and thyme-scented; and it seemed to Justin unbearable that it should be like that after last night – after Paulinus. Paulinus was in all their thoughts, he knew – that timid little man who had made sure of the safety of his followers, and then walked quietly out to his own death – but they did not speak of what had happened. It was as Flavius had said, 'You all know what has happened. Talking won't mend it.' They did not talk of anything. They had not known while they were on the march that they were tired; but now that they were halted, they were suddenly weary to the bone. The boy Myron, who seemed completely dazed, simply pitched down where he stood, and was asleep almost before he touched the ground; and the other three, taking turns to keep watch, followed his example.

Justin had the last watch, and by the time it came the warm noontide was long past, and the sunlight was thick-ening into an amber glow over the hills. Now that he had

slept, the crowding beastliness of last night had drawn
back a little, and he could say to something accusing
within himself, 'No, I took all the care that anyone could
take, to be sure that none followed me. Whoever it was,
was cleverer than I am. That is all.' And he could know
that it was true. But the thing within him went on accusing, all the same, so that he had to go over it all in his
mind round and round, until his head ached almost as
much as his heart. At last, desperate for something to do
with his hands that might stop him thinking, he slipped
free the worn shoulder-sling of his instrument-case, ranged
the contents on the grass beside him, and with the soft
cloth in which they had been muffled, fell to burnishing
the tools of his trade. Not that they needed burnishing, for
he had kept them bright as glass all these long months, as
though by doing so he was keeping faith with something
in himself – something that was for healing and creating
and making whole again, in a world that seemed to be all
destroying.

Presently he became aware that Anthonius the young
Centurion was no longer asleep, but had turned his head
on his arms to watch him. 'Is it a rust spot, that you rub
– and rub – and rub so desperately?' the Centurion asked,
as their eyes met.

Justin said slowly, 'I think I try to rub away the knowing that – it was I who led the wolves to P-Paulinus's door
last night.'

'Far more likely it was I. I found that little Egyptian
shadow of Allectus's watching me more than once, after
that business on the temple steps. It should have put me
more on my guard.'

The Egyptian shadow, Justin thought; yes, that fitted
Serapion perfectly. He had been right to smell danger at
the sight of the creature in Allectus's train. Danger and
death; it had come swiftly. 'Yet, whichever one of us it

was they followed, it was still I who led the way,' he said miserably, unable to slip out so easily from under the blame and leave it on the other's shoulders.

'Paulinus blamed neither of us,' Anthonius said quietly. 'He knew that it was a thing that might happen any day, through no fault of any man within the team. It was a risk he was prepared to run, just as – you run it, from now on.'

And somehow those last most uncomforting words comforted Justin a little, as nothing else could have done. He laid down the instrument he had been burnishing, and took up another.

The young Centurion watched him in silence for a while, then he said: 'I wondered what was in that case that you carry with such care.'

'The tools of my trade.'

'Ah. So you're a surgeon?'

Justin looked at his hands, seeing them hardened and calloused after nine months in the shipyards and rope-walks of Adurni, cut to pieces and ingrained with pitch; feeling the finger-tips no longer sensitive as they had used to be. 'I – was a surgeon, when Flavius was a C-Cohort Commander,' he said.

Anthonius took up one of the little bright instruments and looked at it, then laid it down again among the dwarf thyme. 'You're lucky,' he said. 'You're wonderfully lucky. Most of us can only break things.'

Presently Flavius woke up also, and with the sun sinking low behind Vectis, roused Myron, who had not stirred since he first fell asleep, and got them all to their feet again. 'If we start now, we shall just about make the farm at dusk ... Look how the Island is rearing up out of the sea. It's going to rain at last.'

Rain it did, and that night in the Atrium of the old farmhouse, they could hear it hushing and pattering on the roof and among the broad leaves of the fig-tree outside; and the little breath of air from the open door that scarcely stirred the flame of the lamp on the table bore with it that most wonderful of all smells, the throat-catching heart-catching scent of rain on a hot and thirsty earth.

They had stayed their empty stomachs with curds and bannock and fried downland mutton, and left Myron asleep once more before the low fire in the steward's quarters, and now here they were in the old Atrium, with the folk of the farm about them in obedience to Flavius's summons. Justin, looking about him at the men gathered in the faint lamplight, found them little changed since that leave he had spent among them a year and a half ago. Servius himself, seated on the one stool by right of his position as steward; Kyndylan with his broad pleasant face half lost in a fuzz of golden beard; Buic the old shepherd, crinkle-eyed from a long lifetime of looking into the distance after his sheep, with his crook beside him and his wall-eyed sheep-dog against his knee; Flann the ploughman, and the rest, all seated comfortably on the store-chests and the baled wool yet remaining of the last clip. Two or three women also, gathered about Cutha near the door. The first startled excitement of their arrival had died down, and the company sat looking to the master of the place with no more than mild inquiry; a quiet attention that seemed somehow one with the unchanging quietness of the Downs themselves.

Flavius sat sideways on the table by the lamp, swinging a muddy foot as he looked round on them. He said, 'You'll be wondering what all this is about, and why Justin and I are not in Gaul, and I can't tell you. At least, I'm not going to tell you – for the present, anyway. But I need your help. You've none of you ever failed me before, and I'm trusting you not to fail me now, so you've got to trust

me. There'll be odd things happening, strangers coming
and going about the farm. Mostly they'll be wearing a
sprig of broom somewhere about them, like this –' He
shook back the fold of his rough cloak, and showed the
little green sprig with its one spark of blossom still clinging to it, stuck in the shoulder-pin. 'Justin and I will be
coming and going too; and there must be no word of all
this outside the farm – not one word. That is life and
death. I am depending on your loyalty to me, and to
Justin, who is one with me in this.' He looked round on
them with a grin. 'That is really all I wanted to say.'

There was a long silence while the company thought
this over; and the sound of the rain came into the room.
Justin had expected Servius to speak for the rest, by the
same right as he sat on the one stool; but it was Buic the
shepherd, by right of age, who spoke up for his fellows,
in the soft speech of his own people that came to his
tongue more readily than the Latin did. 'We've knowed
your father, my dear, and we've knowed you since the
third day after you was born, and I knowed your grandfather pretty well, too. So I reckon we'll trust you, and
no questions asked; and I reckon we won't fail you.'

When steward and farm-folk were all gone, and the
three of them were alone in the smoke-darkened Atrium,
they gathered to the small fire that Cutha had lit for them
on the hearthplace, for with the rain the evening was
turning chilly. Anthonius, who stood by, watching the
scene in silence, said suddenly, 'You are fortunate to be
able to trust your people so completely.' And after a
moment, 'They are none of them, I think, slaves?'

Flavius looked at him in surprise. 'Slaves? Oh no, there
are no slaves on the farm; there never have been. Those
were all free men and women and – rather dear friends.'

'So? It is in my mind that this must be a happy place,'
Anthonius said. He looked from one to the other, leaning

a little sideways, his right hand moving idly across his knee to trace something in the white ash on the hearth-stone.

And Justin, watching, saw that the thing he drew was a fish.

He had seen that sign before, in Judea. It was something to do with a man called the Christos – a man who had been executed more than two hundred years ago : but it seemed that he still had followers. You would need to be a good leader, Justin thought suddenly, for people to follow you still, two hundred years afterward : not just priests out for what they could get, or silly women; but men like Anthonius.

The young Centurion's eyes caught and held his for a moment, with a shadow of a question in them; then moved to Flavius, who was making some adjustments to his shoulder-pin and did not seem even to have noticed. Then he brushed his hand across the hearth, and the fish was gone again.

13

The Silver Branch

THAT summer the Sea Wolves, slipping past the slackened guard of the Galleys, came raiding far up the south-coast rivers, burning and harrying far into the Downs and the Weald. It was as it had been before Carausius came; worse, for now Allectus's Saxon Mercenaries were loose in the land. Pirates and Mercenaries fought to the death when they met, like two wolf-packs hunting the same territory. But for the hunted there was often enough little difference between one pack and the other.

The farm, lost in its downland valley, somehow escaped. Summer passed, and they harvested the cornland below the Downs, and the work that Paulinus had died for went on. But as summer turned to autumn, the sprig of broom was coming to mean something wider than it had done at first.

It began with three young brothers from the Otter's Ford, their farm burned over their heads by a band of drunken Mercenaries, who came to Flavius for refuge and a chance by and by to repay their debt to Allectus.

'If you take them,' Servius said on a note of warning, 'you'll have a legion before you know where you are.'

And Flavius, with his red brows at their most fly-away, replied : 'So be it, then. We'll have a legion !'

By the time it was the season for salting down the winter's meat supply, the legion numbered upward of a score, including the boy Myron; men dispossessed, men with wrongs to avenge, fugitives of all kinds, with a couple of legionaries gone wilful-missing to toughen the whole, who made their hide-outs in the forest for miles around – the forest that was ever the friend of wanted men. Later, Kyndylan came to Flavius with three of the younger farm-hands behind him, and said : 'Sir, my father, your steward, is old now, and too stiff from old wounds to be of use to you; but we four, who are the young men of the farm, we would have you know that our spears are sharp and ready, and when you have need of us, we also are your hounds.'

And only a few days after that, Justin added a derelict gladiator to the growing band.

He found him at Venta on the day of the Games, standing in the shadow of the main entrance to the amphi-theatre; a gaunt and tattered creature, pressed back from the rest of the throng, with his head turned toward the distant glimpse of the arena, and on his face a look of absolute despair that seemed to Justin to take all the shine out of the gleamy autumn day.

His first instinct had been to say, 'What is it? Is there anything – anything at all – that I can do to help?' but something about the man warned him against that. 'There's a good bill today,' he said after a while. 'A Libian tiger isn't to be seen every day in these parts. Going in?'

The man started and glanced round. 'No,' he said, and defiance came up like a shield over the naked despair in his face.

From somewhere below them, beyond the barred gates of the wild beasts' den, a wolf began to howl, the wild and mournful note rising above the uproar of the crowded benches. The man said, 'Aye, even the wolves feel it.'

'Feel it?'

'The thing that's running through the dens down there. But what should you know of that?' The man glanced contemptuously at Justin again. 'How should you know what it's like, the last moments of waiting before the trumpets sound? You test your weapons again, though you tested them not a hundred heart-beats ago; and maybe your sword-hand grows a little sticky, so you rub it in the sand to give you a better chance of life. You take your place in the file that's forming up, ready to march into the arena; and you hear the crowd gathering, a thousand, twenty thousand strong, it makes no matter – as many as the place will hold – and you know that they've come to watch *you*. And the bread and onions you ate this morning tasted better than any feast to a man who expects to eat again. And the sun through the grills overhead is brighter for you than for any man who thinks to see it rise tomorrow; because you know that, like as not, you're going to die, out there in the sand with twenty thousand people looking on ... If not this fight, then the next, or the hundredth after that. But there's always the chance that you'll gain your wooden foil.'

'Ave Caesar, those about to die salute you,' Justin said quietly. 'B-but for you, it was the wooden foil.'

The man looked at him quickly, clearly startled to realize how completely he had betrayed himself. 'Aye, they gave me my wooden foil last winter, at the Games in honour of the new Emperor – up yonder at Londinium,' he said after a moment.

'And so now you are free.'

'Free?' said the other. 'Aye, I'm free. Free of all that, free to starve in a ditch, free to follow my own road. And all roads are flat and grey.'

Justin was silent, borne down by that terrible 'All roads are flat and grey', and his own inability to do anything about it.

The other looked at him, and broke into a jeering laugh. 'That's it. Now make helpful suggestions. Here's a denarius; go and buy myself something to eat. They want men at the dye-works, why don't I go there and ask for work? I don't want your denarius, and I'm not the sort for steady work. Can you give me the sort of work I'm good for? Can you give me a risk to run? A gamble with life and death hanging on the fall of the dice? If so –'

And suddenly Justin saw light; 'I am not sure,' he said. 'But I think it may be that I can.'

As spring wore on, the rumours that had been rife in Britain all winter gathered substance and certainty. The Caesar Constantius had begun building transports at Gesoriacum. The Emperor Maximian himself was coming north to take over the Rhenus defences! The transports were ready to sail – a great fleet of transports and escort galleys waiting at Gesoriacum and in the mouth of the Sequana! And then, a little after sheep-shearing, the news came down by the ways of the wilderness that Allectus, who was massing his forces along the south-east coast, with his headquarters at Rutupiae, had withdrawn more than half the troops from the Wall.

It was a few nights later that the next news came. They were in Calleva, Justin and this time Flavius too, in search of weapons for their tattered legion. There had been many recruits in the past few weeks, and though some had weapons of their own, others had come in with nothing but a light hunting-spear that would be little use in battle. An ambushed Saxon here and there had done something to increase their stock of war-gear, but they were still badly under-armed, and so the second of Great-Aunt Honoria's opal bracelets, carefully saved against a sudden need, had been sold to a jeweller in Clausentium; and in the past few days several swordsmiths and armourers in that town, in Regnum and Venta, and now in Calleva, had received visits from a couple of strangers who bought here a plain but serviceable sword, there a heavy spear-

head. Now the thing was finished, and earlier that evening Justin and Flavius had seen the last of their purchases
packed in lamp-oil jars, ready for loading on to a pair of
pack-mules lent them by a good friend near the South
Gate. They had had a hasty meal in an eating-house just
behind the Forum kept by an ex-legionary with one eye,
and were actually setting out to pick up the mules, when
a man passed them half running, who called out to them
in passing, 'Have you heard? – Constantius's sails have
been seen off Tanatus!' and hurried on to spread the news
elsewhere.

'It looks as though we have got our lamp-oil none too
soon,' Flavius said when he had gone, and then, 'I'm glad
Aunt Honoria is safe in Aqua Sulis – whatever happens,
they should be well out of it down there.' For they had
passed the Aquila house earlier that day, and seen it shuttered close, and obviously empty of life.

In the wide street that ran straight as a pilum-shaft
from the Forum to the South Gate, a few people were
abroad, despite the lateness of the hour, and the mizzle
rain that had begun to fall, standing in little half-anxious,
half-eager groups in shop doorways and at street corners,
with an air of waiting, like people waiting for a storm to
break.

They were half way down the street, when, with a
sudden hubbub of shouts and flying feet, out from a dark
side-street just ahead of them bounded a small fantastic
figure with a knot of howling Saxons on its heels. The
fugitive was swift and light as a cat, but the hunters were
almost upon him, and even as he gained the street, with
a yell of triumph, the foremost of them had him round the
neck, bringing him half down, and instantly they were
all around him. For an instant, as they pulled him down,
Justin caught the little man's desperate upturned face in
the light of a lantern over a shop doorway; a narrow,

beardless face with enormous eyes. And in the same instant he heard Flavius cry, 'Ye gods! It's Cullen!'

Then they were running. 'Hold on, Cullen; we're coming!' Flavius shouted, and next instant they were into the fight. There were four of the Saxons, but surprise was on the side of the rescuers, and Cullen himself fought like a mountain cat. Flavius threw one man across his hip – a gymnasium throw – and he came down with a stunning crash, bringing another with him. A knife flashed in the lantern light, and Justin felt the wind of it on his cheek as he side-stepped and sprang in under the Saxon's guard ... And then somehow – quite how the break-away came, he never knew – the three of them were running for their lives down the dark side-street, with the pounding feet of their pursuers hard behind.

'Round here,' Flavius panted, and they swung left into a gash of darkness that opened between the houses. Up one narrow way and down another they dived, bursting through the hedges of quiet gardens, doubling and turning in their tracks, with always the clamour of pursuit swelling behind them. Flavius was trying to make for the northern part of the town, in the hope of shaking off their pursuers and being able to get down to the mules and the precious oil-jars again from the other side. But when they came upon a street leading in the right direction, there were more Saxons with torches a little way up it, and as they swerved back into the dark gap between the two shops, a redoubled yelling told them that they had been seen.

It was not so much that they were being chased now, as hunted. From all quarters of Calleva, it seemed, the Saxons were up and hunting, part in deadly earnest, part in sport that would be just as deadly, closing in on them, driving them farther and farther into the south-east angle of the old ramparts. And, to make matters worse, poor little Cullen, who had been hard hunted before they came upon him, was almost done. The dark shape of a temple loomed ahead of them, and they rounded it and dived into the thick shadows under the colonnade, crouching frozen for a few tingling moments, as the hunt came yowling by; then they were up again, and running, almost carrying Cullen between them, heading for the dark mass of evergreens and neglected roses behind the place. Into it they dived, worming their way forward into the deepest heart of the tangle, and lay still.

At any moment the hunt would be back on its tracks, but now, for this little space of time, there was respite; the clamour of the hunt dying into the distance, only the hushing of the wind through the evergreen branches all around them, and the dark brown smell of old dry leaves and exposed roots, even the mizzle rain shut out. Little Cullen lay flat on his belly, his flanks heaving like the flanks of some small hunted animal. Justin lay straining his ears to catch any sound of the hunt returning, above the sickening drub of his own heart. Any moment now ... Well, the cover was dense enough, anyway; they might stand a chance.

And then suddenly the hounds were giving tongue again, ahead of them now as well as behind, from a score of places at once; and Justin, tensing under the holly tangle, caught the red flare of a torch, and then another; and heard Flavius draw a harsh breath. 'Fiends and Furies! They've called in all their friends to beat us out!'

So that was that. Justin thought quite calmly, 'I suppose this is the end. It will be for us as it was for Paulinus – as it was for the Emperor himself; the torch-light and the naked saex blades, I wonder what it will really be like.'

But Flavius was crouching over them, whispering urgently, 'Come – we've one more chance. Up, Cullen; it's the last lap – you can do it, you've got to!' And beside him Cullen was drawing his legs under him again, with a hoarse sob of sheer exhaustion. And somehow they were on the move once more, belly-snaking down through the bushes towards the old ramparts.

'Where?' whispered Justin urgently.

'Our house – empty –' he caught, and the rest was lost in the wind through the holly branches and the cries of the hunt behind.

Torches were flaring in the street beyond the houses, and the hunt was closing in through the gardens of the temple of Sul Minerva, as they gained the shelter of the thick-growing things at the foot of the Aquila garden and headed for the house.

A few moments later they were into the colonnade, and the wing of the dark and silent house was between them and the distant torches, reaching out like a protecting arm to hold back the danger and gain them a little time. 'There's a way in – through the bath-house if they haven't – had the shutter mended,' Flavius panted, starting along the colonnade.

'If they're beating – this cover for us – they'll beat the house too,' Justin objected swiftly.

'The odds are they'll miss the hypocaust – they don't warm their houses in that way beyond the Rhenus. Come on.'

And then the Atrium door opened, letting out into the courtyard a soft flood of lamplight to set the white roses of the colonnade shining, and Aunt Honoria appeared, evidently drawn by the nearing uproar, and prepared if need be to do something about it, for she held in one hand a small flower-shaped lamp, and in the other an old uniform dagger.

Her gaze fell with the lamplight on the three tattered and panting fugitives, and she stiffened, her eyes widening a little. But Justin had been right in his judgement of her at their first meeting. She would never waste time in surprise or useless questions. She said in that husky, jewel-cut voice of hers, 'So, my Great-Nephews – and another.' Then, with a flick of her dagger-hand towards the clamour that rose with the unmistakable note of a hunt giving tongue, 'Is that for you?'

Justin nodded dumbly, his breath too thick in his throat for speech. Flavius said, 'Yes, Saxons.'

'Inside with you.' She stepped back, and next instant they were in the Atrium, and the door shut and barred behind them. 'The hypocaust,' said Aunt Honoria. 'Thank the gods it is summer and there's no fire.'

'You and I always thought alike,' said Flavius, with a breathless croak of laughter, his back against the door, 'but we thought the house was empty. Better put us out again through the slaves' quarters and let us run for it. We shall bring danger on you if we stay.'

'Flavius dear, there isn't time to be noble,' said Aunt Honoria, and her bright glance flicked to the little Fool drooping between the other two. 'Besides, one of you at least is past running. Quick now.' And somehow while she was yet speaking, without any of them but herself quite knowing how it happened, she had swept them after her through the door at the end of the Atrium into a passage-way beyond, then by an outer door, down three steps into the narrow, windowless stoke-house. The light of the little lamp showed logs and charcoal stacked against the lime-washed wall, and the square iron door of the stoke-hole. The clamour of the hunt sounded no nearer; probably they were still beating the temple gardens or had turned to one of the other houses. Flavius stooped and pulled open the little iron doors.

'You first, Justin.'

And suddenly Justin's old horror of enclosed places, places from which he could not get out again at will, had him by the throat, and it was all he could do to force

himself down on hands and knees and through that square
of darkness that was like the mouth of a trap, the mouth
of a tomb.

'You next,' Flavius said, and he heard little Cullen coming after him, and then Flavius's voice again, in a hurried
undertone, 'Aunt Honoria, I'll stay outside where I can
come to your help if need be – and take my chance.'

'Do you really want to kill us all?' said Aunt Honoria
crisply. 'Get in after the others, and don't any of you try
to get out again until I come for you.'

And then the three of them were together in the enclosed space. The iron door shut behind them, and they
were in darkness such as Justin had never known existed.
Black darkness that pressed against one's eyeballs like a
pad. Faintly they heard Aunt Honoria piling logs against
the door. 'Get forward a bit,' Flavius whispered.

Justin could sense that they had come out into a wider
space. They must be right under the floor of the Atrium,
here. He put out a hand and felt one of the fire-brick
pillars on which the floor rested, strong pillars so short
that if one tried to sit up, the floor would be against one's
shoulders. Justin tried not to think of that. He tried listening instead. He heard Aunt Honoria's footsteps overhead,
and women's voices somewhere. He could hear the hunt
too, very close now. It was odd to hear so much, when one
seemed to be miles down below the world of living men.
The sounds must come down the wall-flues, he supposed,
like the air. Plenty of air coming down the wall-flues; no
need to feel as though one couldn't breathe. 'Don't be such
a fool,' he told himself angrily. 'You can breathe perfectly
well; you're just a bit winded with the running, that's all;
and the Atrium floor isn't sinking down on top of you
either. Breathe slowly – *slowly*. You can't panic in here,
Justin, you miserable coward; it's bad enough for the
other two without that.'

How long he lay sweating, with the darkness turned

soft and loathsome and suffocating about him, he had no idea; but it could not have been long, because little Cullen's exhausted panting had scarcely quieted away when there was a furious pounding on one or other of the Atrium doors, and a crash, and then the tramp of feet almost overhead and a ragged splurge of voices, so many and so guttural that it came down to the three in hiding only as a confused roar. Then Aunt Honoria's voice, raised a little from its usual quietness, clear-cut and imperious. 'Will someone among you tell me what is the meaning of this?'

A deep voice, almost unintelligible in its thickness, answered her. 'Ja, we seek three men that ran this way. Maybe you hide them here?'

'Three men?' said Aunt Honoria coolly. 'There are none here but myself and these my slaves, four old women, as you see.'

'So you say, old woman – old thin cow! Now we look.'

It was at that moment Justin realized that Cullen was no longer beside him. Well, there was nothing to be done about that now save pray that the little man was not doing anything foolish.

Aunt Honoria's voice sounded again, cool as ever. 'Look then, but I tell you beforehand that if you would find these men, whoever they be, then you must search elsewhere.'

There was a growl of voices and rough laughter, and the swift tramp of feet overhead again. And in the same instant, from somewhere before him in the darkness of the hypocaust itself, came a faint grating sound, a sound that Justin could give no name to save that it was like something shifting. What in the name of Esculapius was Cullen doing? He tensed, waiting for the next thing, but no other sound came out of the darkness. A woman squealed shrilly; and then suddenly the footsteps were everywhere, and a guttural snarl of voices calling to each other, laughing, savage. And after a while Justin felt little Cullen slipping back to his side.

The steps went to and fro across the Atrium floor, dulled and muffled into a kind of thunderous padding in the enclosed space underneath, dying away and pounding back again as the Saxons scattered questing through the house, like hounds drawing a dense cover. There was a crash somewhere, and a roar of laughter; and a rising babble of other voices, shrill and scared, that must be the household slaves. Once again Aunt Honoria's voice sounded. But the three listening with straining ears in the dark could make out little of what was passing.

And then, quite suddenly, it seemed that it was over.

The distant distressful babble of women's voices still reached them faintly, but the guttural tones of the Saxons had blurred into the night, and the padding footsteps sounded no more overhead. The scared voices of the slaves sank away little by little into quiet; and again they waited.

And then, faintly through the iron door, they heard the logs being shifted. The iron door opened; lamplight burst in upon them in a dazzling beam, and Aunt Honoria's voice said, 'I'm sorry to have left you here so long. It has taken me all this while to soothe my silly women and get them safely back to their own quarters.'

A few moments later the three of them, covered with ash and charred brick-dust, were standing in the stoke-house; and in the blessed sense of space above his head and air to breathe, Justin stood drawing in great gasps of breath as though he had been running. Flavius said quickly, 'You are not scathed, Aunt Honoria?'

'I am not scathed. I have had a somewhat anxious time; no more.'

The Atrium, when they were back in it a few moments later, bore testimony to the Saxons' passing, in broken furniture and hangings torn down, mud trampled across the tesserae, and the painted plaster of one wall scored across and across as with a dagger, in the sheer wanton pleasure of breaking and marring. Aunt Honoria wasted no look on the damage, as she crossed to the shrine of the household gods and set the flower-shaped lamp on the altar.

'What a good thing our household gods are only bronze,' she said. 'The altar lamp was silver.' Then she turned to the tattered and grimy figures behind her. 'When did you return from Gaul?'

'We have not been in Gaul,' Flavius said. 'We put your bracelets to a better use this side of the water, Aunt Honoria.'

She searched his face with those beautiful eyes, so bright under the wrinkled lids and the eye-paint. 'So you have been in Britain all this while? A year and the half of a year? And could you not have found means to send me word, just once, or twice, in all that time?'

Flavius shook his head. 'We have been busy, Justin and I and some others; busy on the sort of work you do not risk dragging your family into.'

'So,' Aunt Honoria said, and her gaze went to little Cullen in his tattered motley on the edge of the lamplight. 'And here is one of those others?'

Justin and Flavius turned to look at the little Fool as though becoming truly aware of him for the first time. Somehow, after that first startled moment of unbelief when the lantern-light showed them his face as he struggled with his captors, there had been nothing to spare for surprise. But now all at once they realized the astonishing thing that had happened. That this was Cullen the Fool of Carausius, whom they had never once thought of as among the living, since his lord was dead.

It was Cullen himself who answered first. '*Na*, Lady, I am Cullen that was hound to Curoi the Emperor. And though for long and long I have been seeking these two, it was not until tonight, by all the wheeling stars of the sky, that I found them again in my need.'

'You have been seeking us?' Flavius said.

The little man nodded vehemently. 'Seeking and seeking, because my Lord Curoi bade me.'

'The Emperor bade you? When – what is it that you mean?'

'Two years ago last seed-time he wrote a letter, and when it was written, he gave it to me, and bade me take it to you if he should – die. He gave it to me because he knew that he could trust me; he said I was the most faithful of hunting dogs. But when he was slain' – Cullen showed his teeth as a hound shows them – 'they caught and held me captive a while and a long while to make them laugh. And when at last I broke free, I went North – my Lord said I should find you on the Wall.' He sounded reproachful. 'But you were gone, and I could get no word of you for another long while, until a woman in the street of the Golden Grasshopper at Magnis told me you were gone South on the road to Gaul. Then South I came – and this evening, those who held me captive aforetime knew me again in the streets of Calleva.'

Flavius nodded. 'And the letter? Have you the letter yet?'

'Should I have come without it?' Cullen said. From the breast of his tattered motley he brought out something long and curved, muffled close in rags, and unwinding it gently as a woman loosing her babe from its swaddling bands, laid bare his Silver Branch.

Justin wondered at its silence in his hands until he saw the wisp of sheep's wool sticking through the opening of the largest apple, and realized that, as well as the outer wrappings, each apple had been packed with wool to silence it. 'Other things I have carried for Curoi my Lord in this hiding-place. It is a good hiding-place,' Cullen was saying. He did something to the end of the enamelled hand-piece, and drew out from it a roll of papyrus not much thicker than a man's finger. 'Sa, here it is, safe where it has lain these more than two years past.'

Flavius took and unrolled it with great care, turning to the little lamp on the altar. The papyrus was so thin that the flame shone through it pinkish until he tipped it to catch the light on the surface. Justin, looking over his shoulder, saw Carausius's bold writing flash up blackly from the fragile sheet.

'To Centurion Marcelus Flavius Aquila, and to Tiberius Lucius Justinianus, Cohort Surgeon, from Marcus Aurelius Carausius, Emperor of Britain, Greeting,' he read. 'If ever you read this it will be that the man of whom you sought to warn me has slipped beneath my guard in the end. And – as though it mattered – if I should have no more speech with you in this world, I would not have you think I sent you from me in anger. You young fools, if I had not sent you to the Wall as being of no further use to me, you would have been dead men within three days. I salute you, my children. Farewell.'

The was a long silence. Only the faint whisper of the rain and the distant night-time sounds of the city. The noise of the hunt had quite died away. Flavius let the thin papyrus roll up on itself, very gently. Justin was staring at the flame of the lamp; a slender, spear shaped flame, blue at the heart, exquisite. There was a small aching lump in his throat, and somewhere below it, a small aching joy.

'So he d-did believe us,' he said at last. 'He knew, all the time.'

'A great man, our little Emperor,' Flavius said huskily, and slipped the roll into the breast of his ragged tunic.

14

An Ancient Ensign

As he did so, from somewhere just beneath their feet came a thud, followed by a rustle as of falling plaster.

'What is that?' Flavius said, after a moment's startled hush.

Little Cullen squirmed slightly, as a dog squirms in apology when he knows he has been doing what he should not. 'Maybe it is the stone that moved in one of the pillars that hold up the floor. When we were down there I crept forward to hear better what went on, and it moved under my hand as I felt before me in the dark. It might be that I disturbed something.'

So that was what the sound in the darkness of the hypocaust had been.

'Ah well, better the house falling down than more Saxons,' Flavius said, and put out a hand to the lamp on the altar. 'Aunt Honoria, may I take this? Better perhaps that I go see what *has* happened. Cullen, come you and show me.'

Aunt Honoria, who had seated herself in the one unbroken chair, rose. 'While you are gone I'll see to some food for you.'

Justin went with neither his Great-Aunt nor Flavius. There was no point in his going with either, and he was possessed suddenly of an odd stillness, a certainty that something very strange was coming. And he stood beside the little altar, waiting for it to come. With the lamp gone, it was almost as dark as it had been in the hypocaust. He heard the wind and the rain, and the waiting silence of the poor scarred house. He heard the other two moving below the floor, a grunt that was unmistakably Flavius, the soft, formless sound of something being shifted, followed by a muffled exclamation; and in a little the sounds of movement drawing away towards the door.

And then the other two were back, the shadows circling and racing before the lamp in Cullen's hand. Flavius carried something else, a shapeless bundle of some sort, and as Cullen set the lamp once more on the altar, and the light steadied, Justin, casting a questioning glance at his cousin, was struck by the look of hushed excitement on his face.

'All's well?' he asked.

Flavius nodded. 'The house isn't falling down. The side had come out of an old hiding-place in one of the hypocaust pillars – the plaster must have crumbled away. And inside was – this.'

'What is it?'

'I – do not know yet.' Flavius turned to the lamp, and began very carefully to turn back the dark, musty-smelling folds of cloth in which the thing was wrapped. 'The wool is rotten as tinder,' he said. 'But look at these inner folds, where the lamplight falls. Look, Justin, you can see that it has been scarlet!'

Justin looked; and then put out his hands to take the mass of tindery cloth as the last folds fell away – scarlet : scarlet for a military cloak.

Flavius was holding an eagle of gilded bronze. Green-stained with verdigris where the gilding was gone, battered, mutilated – for where the great back-swept silver wings should have sprung from its shoulders were only empty socket-holes staring like blind eyes; but defiant in its furious pride, unmistakably an Eagle still.

Justin drew a long breath. 'But it is an Eagle!' he whispered unbelievingly. 'I mean – it is the Eagle of a Legion.'

'Sa, it is the Eagle of a Legion,' Flavius said.

'But – only one such Eagle was ever lost in Britain.'

They looked at the thing in silence, while Little Cullen, with an air of being very well pleased with himself, after all, stood swinging his hound's tail behind him with little flicks of his rump, and looking on. The lost Ninth Legion, the lost Hispana that had marched into the Northern mists and never returned ... 'But how could it be that one?' Justin whispered at last. 'Who could have brought it South again? None of them ever got back.'

'I don't know,' Flavius said. 'But Marcus's father disappeared with the Ninth, remember, and there was always that story in the family about an adventure in the North ... Maybe he went to find out the truth and bring back the Eagle. A Roman Eagle in the hands of the Painted People would be a powerful rallying point. Justin, do you remember once – one evening at the farm, we were wondering how it all started; why he got that gratuity and land-grant from the Senate? Don't you see it all fits?'

'But – but if he brought it back, why should it have been hidden here? Why was the L-legion never re-formed?'

'It wasn't exactly hidden, it was buried before the Altar,' Flavius said. 'Maybe it was disgraced. We shall never know. But there could have been reasons.' In the circle of lamplight, a soft yellow rose of lamplight in the darkened house, they looked at each other with growing excitement and certainty; while little Cullen stood by, swinging his hound's tail behind him. 'And I'd wager all I have that this is the Ninth's lost Eagle!'

Aunt Honoria, who, unnoticed by any of them, had returned a little before, set down the bundle of food on a nearby table, and said, 'So, you have found a lost Eagle, under the floor. At another time I will wonder and care and be amazed, but now it seems to me that it is not the time to be discovering lost Eagles. Here is food – the hunt may rouse up again at any moment, it will be dawn in an hour, and after this disturbance the Fates alone know how soon Volumnia and the rest will be stirring – let you take it, and go.'

Flavius did not seem to hear the last part of this speech. His head was up and his eyes suddenly blazing bright under the red fly-away brows. He held the battered thing against his breast. 'But it is the time of all others to be discovering lost Eagles! We have our dunghill legion – and now the gods send us a standard to follow, and who are we to refuse a gift of the gods?'

'So, take it with you. Only take it now, and go!'

Flavius had turned from her to the shrine, the Eagle still held against his breast, looking to the tiny crocus-flame of the lamp, or to the little bronze figures of the household gods in their niches, Justin was not sure which; or through them to something beyond. 'I take it for the old Service again,' he said.

And as though in answer, far off and faintly down the wind came the long-drawn, haunting notes of Cockcrow sounding from the transit camp without the Walls.

'Flavius dear,' said Aunt Honoria very gently, 'I have had a rather trying night, and I feel my temper none too sure within me. Will you please go, before I lose it and box all your ears?'

And so a few moments later they stood ready to depart; Flavius with the Eagle once more wrapped in the remains of what had once been a military cloak, Justin with the food-bundle under his arm. Aunt Honoria had taken the lamp into another room, that it might not outline them in the doorway, and slipped out first herself to see that all was quiet, before she beckoned them after her. At the last moment, as they stood in the Atrium doorway with the soft rain blowing in their faces, Flavius said, 'You have heard the news, that Constantius's sails have been sighted off Tanatis?'

'Yes, I have heard. Who has not?'

'We thought you were at Aqua Sulis, safely out of the way.'

'But, then, I have always hated to be out of the way when things happen.'

'Well, there's likely to be plenty happening soon,' Flavius said, and kissed her gravely on the cheek. 'The gods keep you when they start happening, you and Volumnia.'

Justin, going out last of all, hesitated, then bent also, and gave her a kiss that was clumsy with shyness, and at which she laughed on an unexpectedly soft and young note, as she closed the door behind them.

They found their friend who lived near the South Gate waiting anxiously with the mules ready loaded up, and when the gates opened at first light, passed out without any trouble, leading the beasts, little Cullen between them with his head coyly down-bent and the folds of a woman's mantle drawn close over his motley rags which he had refused to change.

And two evenings later they stood on the crest of the Downs, where their way turned down to the farm. The wind that had been blowing off and on for several days had strengthened and was blowing hard from the South-West, driving before it the mist-scurries and low cloud as a dog drives sheep. Soft rain blew in their faces – rain that tasted faintly salt on their lips – and already the light was fading; but Justin, straining his eyes into the blurred and drifting distance, could make out no sign of Vectis Light.

His gaze going out in the same direction, Flavius said, 'Dirty weather out round the Island. The Vectis fleet would have its work cut out to intercept anything that tries to get through on this part of the coast tonight, I'm thinking.'

And they turned their backs on the sea and went on down the last home stretch, urging the tired mules ahead of them. Anthonius met them at the lower end of the vine-terraces, followed by the boy Myron, who was seldom willingly apart from him. 'All well?' he asked.

'All well, though there were exciting moments. And here?'

'We've had nine new recruits in the past few days, and several of the old lot from Regnum and Adurni have come in. More than ever the "lamp-oil" will be welcome, especially if half the rumours flying through the forest be true.'

Young Myron had come forward to take charge of the mules, and as he led them away, Flavius said, 'Here is another for the brotherhood. One that was Carausius's hound and has no love for Allectus.'

'So. We grow more to a full Legion every hour,' Anthonius said. And then, 'Pandarus and I have already called the band in and camped them about the farm. We thought it best not to wait for your orders, lest there be too little time to spare for mustering them later.'

Flavius nodded. 'Good. Then let's go and eat. I've forgotten what food looks like.'

Anthonius turned back beside them. 'There's a man waiting for you up at the houseplace – been there since yesterday, and won't tell his errand to anyone.'

'What sort of man?'

'A hunter. Big, rather splendid-looking fellow with a great spear.'

Justin and Flavius glanced at each other in the dusk, with one swift unspoken thought between them. Then Flavius said, 'Sa, we will go up and see this hunter. Anthonius, take Cullen and feed him; we'll be down for some food ourselves by and by.'

'We'll keep you some deer-meat,' said Anthonius. 'Come, Cullen, hound of Carausius.'

And so while Anthonius and the little Fool turned off toward the farm-garth below the terrace, where a deer shot by Kyndylan was being baked, Flavius and Justin made their way up to the houseplace in search of the stranger with the spear.

A dark figure squatting on the terrace before the house-place shook clear of the shadows as they drew near, and stood out into the faint glow of a doorway that shone coppery on his lion's mane of hair and touched with palest moony gold the collar of white swan's feathers about the neck of the great spear on which he leaned.

'It *is* Evicatos!' Flavius said, voicing the thing that had been unspoken in both their minds. 'Evicatos, by the gods!' And he started forward. 'In the name of all that is most wonderful, what brings you down here?'

Justin did not feel any particular surprise. After Cullen, it seemed natural and fitting, somehow; a gathering to-gether of those who had been caught up in the thing at the outset, now that the end of it was in sight.

'Allectus has withdrawn half the garrison from the Wall, and there is talk, much talk, among the heather,' Evicatos said. 'So I left my hounds again with Cuscrid the Smith, and came south with my spear, to share the last fight, that nothing may be left of Allectus to join with the Picts one day against my people.'

'So. But how did you know where to find us? How did you know that we were not in Gaul?'

'One hears things,' said Evicatos vaguely. 'One hears things, among the heather.'

'Well, however you found the trail, glad we are to see you!' Flavius said, with a hand on the hunter's shoulder. 'You and your great spear. But you had an over-long wait after a long trail, and they are baking a deer down yonder.

Afterward we will talk of many things; but now – come you and eat.'

But before he himself sat down to eat with the rest of the band, Flavius fetched a new white-ash spear-shaft from the store; and after the meal was over he went and routed out old Tuan the shoesmith and bade him blow up the forge fire and make him a cross-bar of iron with a socket to fit on to the head of the spear-shaft, and four bronze pegs. And later that night, when all the rest of the band had lain down to sleep in the byres and barns and the wing-rooms of the houseplace, he took all these things into the Atrium. And there, crouching over the low fire, with Little Cullen, who had refused to be parted from them, curled hound-wise in a corner, his Silver Branch, freed now of its muffling sheep's wool, shining in his hand, Flavius and Justin mounted the battered bronze Eagle on its spear-shaft, driving home the bronze pegs through the peg-holes in the gripping talons to make all secure.

Justin had had complete faith from the first that the Eagle was what Flavius had guessed it to be, but if he had had doubts, they would have left him that night as he worked in the sinking firelight with the soft sou'wester filling the night outside. The thing was strangely potent under his hands. What things it must have seen – bitter and dark and glorious things – this maimed bird of gilded bronze that was the life and the honour of a lost Legion. And now, he thought, it must feel that the old days were back. Again there came to him as he worked that sense of kinship with the young soldier who had made a home in this downland valley, the young soldier who surely had brought the lost Eagle of a lost Legion home to its own people, so that Eagle and farm were linked, and it was fitting that the ancient standard should go out from here to its last fight. The feeling of kinship was so strong that when, just as they had finished their task, someone loomed into the open doorway, he looked up almost expecting to see the other Marcus standing there with the windy dark behind him.

But it was Anthonius who came in, shaking the rain from his rough, dark hair.

'There's a light – a fire of some kind, burning up on the Chalk,' Anthonius said. 'Come and have a look.'

The night was clearer than it had been, and from the corner of the sheep-fold above the steading, when they reached it, they could see a red petal of fire on the crest of the Chalk far over toward the South-East.

'Yes,' Flavius said. 'Chance fire, or signal beacon? That's the question.' He put up his hand and thrust the hair back from his eyes. 'Well, there's nothing we can do to find out; that blaze is upward of a day's march away.'

Justin, straining his eyes eastward, caught another spark, away beyond the first, infinitely small and faint, but surely there. 'Signal beacon,' he said. 'There's another. It's a chain of beacons.'

The fire had sunk to red embers and the Atrium was almost in darkness when they returned, but the faint glow from the hearth was enough to show the Eagle on its spear shaft, as Flavius took it up and held it for Anthonius to see.

Anthonius looked closely and in silence. Then he said : 'A standard for tomorrow?'

'A standard for tomorrow.' Flavius was smiling a little.

The other looked from him to the thing he held, and back again. 'And one, I think, that comes out of yesterday – out of a long-ago yesterday,' he said at last. 'Nay, then, I will ask no questions, and nor shall the others, though I think – some of us may guess ... We have a standard to follow, and that is good. That is always good.'

Turning to go, he flung up a hand in salute, as a soldier in the presence of his Eagle.

In the grey of the dawn, Justin woke with a crash to hear the flying hoof-beats of a horse coming at full gallop down from the Chalk towards the farm. He tossed off the rug and scrambled to his feet. Flavius was before him at the door, and others were already at their heels as they plunged out into the mizzle rain. A moment later a rider on a lathered pony swung into the farmyard and, reining his mount back on its haunches, dropped to the ground.

The pony stood where it had slithered to a stop, with hanging head and heaving flanks; and Phaedrus of the *Berenice* was calling out to them almost before his feet touched the ground. 'It's come, lads! It's come at last!'

Men were starting out of the half-light in all directions, to throng around him. He turned to Flavius and Justin, breathing hard. 'Constantius and his legionaries are here! They must have slipped in past the Vectis Fleet in last night's murk. I watched them run the transports aground at the head of Regnum Harbour about midnight, with a screen of galleys to cover them!'

Justin remembered the beacons in the night. Signal beacons they had been, all right. Sails off Tanatis, and now a landing in Regnum Harbour. What did that mean? An attack from two points? Maybe from many points? Well, they would know soon.

There was a moment's silence; men looked at each other almost uncertainly. The years of waiting were over. Not merely drawing to a close, but *over*, finished. And just for the first few moments they could not quite take it in.

Then they went wild. They were all round Phaedrus, round Flavius, giving tongue like a hound-pack. 'The Caesar Constantius! Caesar is come! What are we waiting for? Lead us out to join him, Flavius Aquila!' Bucklers were shaken, spears were tossed in the grey dawn-light. Suddenly Justin turned and shouldered out of the throng,

back to the houseplace. He caught up the Wingless Eagle
from its corner among the storechests and stacked farm
implements, laughing, almost weeping, and strode out
again, holding it high above his head. 'See now, my hearts!
M-march we shall, and here's a standard for our following!'

He stood above them on the edge of the terrace steps,
holding high the battered Eagle on its spear-shaft. He was
aware of Flavius and Anthonius suddenly beside him, of
faces looking up; a wild sea of faces. Men who had
marched too long with the Eagles not to recognize the
standard for what it was, to whom it meant lost honour
and old habits of service; men to whom, without understanding, it was a thing to rally round and shout for. A
reckless, tatterdemalion throng, of legionaries gone wilful-
missing, farmers and hunters with wrongs to right; a
sneak thief, a ship-master, a gladiator, an Emperor's Fool
. . . The roar of voices beat up to him in a solid wave of
sound, crashing about him so that he seemed engulfed
in it.

But Flavius had flung up his arm and was shouting down
the uproar. '*Sa, sa, sa!* The waiting is over, and we go to
join the Caesar Constantius; but first we will eat. I want
to eat, if you don't! Softly! Softly, lads! We march in an
hour.'

Gradually the tumult sank, and men began to break
away, making for the food-store. Pandarus the gladiator
checked to break a small yellow rose from the bush below
the terrace, grinning up at them. 'When I was a sword-
fighter before my wooden foil, I ever liked to have a rose
for the Arena!' and stuck it in the shoulder-pin of his cloak
as he swaggered after the rest.

Flavius watched them go with suspiciously bright eyes.
'Ye gods, what a rabble!' he said. 'A lost Legion, sure
enough! A Legion of broken men. It is fitting that we

should follow a wingless Eagle!' And his laughter cracked
a little.

Anthonius said very gently, 'Would you change them
for the finest Cohort of the Praetorian Guard, if you
could?'

'No,' Flavius said. 'No, by the gods I wouldn't. But that
does not explain why I should want to cry like a girl-
child.' He flung a heavy arm across Justin's shoulder. 'That
was nobly done, old lad. You brought the Eagle out at the
one perfect moment, and they'll follow it through Tophet
fires now, if need be ... Come on, let's get some food.'

15

Return to the Legions

THE mizzle rain had finally cleared, and the wind fallen; and the skies were breaking up as the tatter-demalion war-band crossed the coast road and set their faces to the last low wooded ridge between them and the sea. At the crest of the ridge the wind-shaped oaks and thorn-trees ceased abruptly, and before them the land fell gently away to the seaward marshes; and far to the west-ward, where the ground rose a little clear of the saltings, uncompromisingly square among the blurred and flow-ing lines of the marsh, the outline of a Roman Camp, with beyond it, like a school of stranded sea-beasts along the tide-line, dark shapes of the transports, and beyond again, anchored well out into the harbour, the screening galleys. Justin, scanning the oily sea that still heaved uneasily off-shore, could just make out, away, beyond the harbour mouth, the dark flecks of two patrol galleys on guard, he supposed, against the fleet of Allectus.

'There they are,' Flavius said. 'There – they – are!' And a deep murmur ran through the tattered band behind him.

About a hundred paces from the Dexter Gate of the camp they were halted by pickets with levelled pilums. 'Who comes?'

'Friends, in Caesar's name,' Flavius shouted back.

'Two of you may advance.'

'Wait here,' Flavius said to the rest of the band, and he and Justin went forward together.

By the turf horseshoe of the picket post the Optio met them, demanding their business.

'We are reinforcements,' Flavius said, with superb assurance. 'And must speak with the Caesar Constantius.'

The Optio looked past him and goggled slightly. 'Reinforcements, are you? Then we're sure of victory.' He brought his gaze back to Flavius's face. 'But as to the Caesar Constantius – you've got the wrong army. We're the Western Force.'

'So? Who commands here, then?'

'Asklepiodotus, his Praetorian Prefect.'

'Then we must speak with Asklepiodotus.'

'Must you?' said the Optio. 'Well, I don't know so much about that,' and then, after studying them both again, and taking another long stare at the men behind them, 'Well, you can take that robber band of yours up to the Gate, anyway. I'll send one of my men with you.'

At the Gate they were confronted by the Optio of the Gate guard, who goggled in his turn, and sent for his Centurion, who sent for one of the Tribunes; and at last they were passed through under the raised locust heads of the catapult battery covering the gateway.

Within the strongly manned stockade – clearly the camp was prepared to withstand an attack at any moment – was an ordered activity that seemed actually to throb. Bands of men working under their Optios were stacking rations and war supplies; field armourers were at work, and horses still groggy from the voyage were being got up from the stranded galleys and picketed within the seaward gate, and the smoke of many cooking-fires rose into the morning air; while here, there, and everywhere came and went the crimson crests of the Centurions overseeing all. But amidst all this, the Via Principia was almost empty

as they marched up it. A broad, straight street of trampled
turf, along which, supported in stands of lashed spears,
stood the Cohort and Century standards, blue and violet,
green and crimson, stirring a little in the light wind that
still sighed across the marshes. And close beside the tent
of the Commander himself, as they halted before it, the
spread-winged Eagle of the Legion.

The Tribune spoke to the staring sentry at the tent-
opening, and passed within; and they were left to wait.
Justin looked up at the great gilded Eagle, reading the
number and titles of the Legion. The Thirtieth, Ulpia Victrix; a Lower Rhenus Legion that had come under Carausius's influence at one time, and closely flanking it – this
was evidently a mixed force, drawn from more Legions
than one – a Vexhilation standard bearing the number
and Centaur badge of a Gaulish legion that had followed
the little Emperor in the early days. Somehow that seemed
fitting.

The Tribune had returned now. 'The two leaders may
enter.'

Flavius glanced quickly at Anthonius, saying very much
in earnest beneath the laughter, 'Keep them in good order
for the gods' sakes!' And to Justin, 'Now for it!'

They advanced together, past the sentry into the brown-
shadowed interior of the tent, and halted with drilled
precision, head up and heels together, just within the entrance. A large pink-and-gold man seated at a camp table,
with a papyrus list in one hand and a half-eaten radish in
the other, looked up as they did so, and said in a tone of
mild inquiry that reminded Justin a little of Paulinus, 'You
wish to speak with me?'

The two young men came to attention and saluted; and
Flavius, the spokesman as usual, said, 'Sir, in the first
place we would bring you word, if you have it not already, that the Caesar Constantius's sails were sighted

several days since, off Tanatis; and that last night beacon-fires were burning along the Chalk.'

'As signalling the news of our landing, you mean?' said the large man, with gentle interest.

'I think so, yes.'

The large man nodded once, deeply. 'The first of these things we have heard; the second we have not heard. What else is there that you would say to me?'

'We have brought in a band of' – Flavius hesitated for a flicker of time over the word – 'of allies, sir, to serve with you in this campaign.'

'So?' Asklepiodotus considered them quietly. He was a very large man, tall and stooping and beginning to be fat, with an air of gentle sloth about him which they learned later was deceptive. 'Supposing – just as a start to negotiations – that you tell me who and what in Typhon's name you are – beginning with you.'

'Marcelus Flavius Aquila,' Flavius said. 'A year and a half ago I was Cohort Centurion of the Eighth Cohort of the Second Augustan, stationed at Magnis on the Wall.'

'H'mm,' said the Commander, and his heavy-lidded eyes moved to Justin.

'Tiberius Lucius Justinianus, Surgeon to the same C-Cohort at the same time, sir.'

Asklepiodotus raised his brows. 'So? This is all very surprising. And this past year and a half?'

Briefly and levelly, with the air of one making a formal report, Flavius accounted for the past year and a half, while the Praetorian Prefect sat and gazed at him as one lost in a gentle reverie, the radish still in his hand.

'So the occasional intelligence and – reinforcements – that have reached us from time to time from this province were of your providing?'

'Some of them, anyway, sir.'

'Most interesting. And this band – how many does it number, and what is it made up of?'

'Something over sixty. Tribesmen for the most part, with a stiffening of legionaries gone wilful-missing.' Suddenly Flavius was grinning. 'Another Cohort Centurion, and an ex-gladiator and Carausius's tame Fool for good measure ... Oh, it's a thundering fine Legion, sir. But we all know how to fight, and most of us have something to fight for.'

'So. Show it to me.'

'If you come to the tent opening you will see it in all its glory.'

Asklepiodotus laid his half-eaten radish back in the dish of little loaves and cheese from which he had been making a belated morning meal when they arrived, laid the papyrus sheet neatly and exactly on top of another, and got up. His bulk almost completely filled the tent-opening, but Justin, peering anxiously from behind him, could catch a wedge-shaped glimpse of the band drawn up outside. Anthonius rigidly erect as any Cohort Centurion of the Empire on parade; Pandarus with his yellow rose and the desperado swagger of his old calling in every line of him; little Cullen with his Silver Branch in the girdle of his tattered motley, holding the wingless Eagle proudly upright, but standing himself on one leg like a heron, which somewhat spoiled the effect; Evicatos beside him, leaning on his great war-spear, whose collar of white swan's feathers stirred and ruffled in the light wind. And behind them, the rest – the whole tattered, reckless, disreputable crew.

Asklepiodotus looked them over, seemed to ruminate for a few moments on the battered Eagle, and turned back to the mule-pack on which he had been sitting. 'Yes, I see what you mean.' He took up the radish again, looked at it for a moment as though he were going on with his breakfast, and then seemed to change his mind. Suddenly he opened both eyes wide upon the two young men before him, and it was as though for an instant the bare blade glinted through the furry sheath. 'Now, give me proof that you are what you claim to be. Give me proof that there is so much as a mustard seed of truth in this story that you have been telling me.'

Flavius said a little blankly, 'What proof can we give you? What else could we be?'

'For all that I know, you may be no more than a band of robbers and renegades in search of easy plunder. Or – you may even be a Trojan horse.'

Complete silence descended on the brown shadowed tent; and around it even the great camp was silent with one of those odd hushes that fall sometimes for no reason on a busy place. Justin could hear the faint, uneasy sounding of the sea, and the mocking ripple of bells beyond the tent-flap, as Cullen changed from one weary leg to the other. 'There must be a right thing to say or do,' he was thinking. 'There must be *some* answer. But if Flavius can't think of it, there's not much chance for me.'

And then footsteps sounded outside, and someone loomed into the opening of the hut. A thin, brown man in the uniform of a Senior Cohort Centurion entered and saluted, laying some tablets on the table before the Commander. 'List complete, sir. I suppose you are aware that there's some kind of comic war-band with what looks remarkably like the remains of a Roman Eagle tied to a spear-shaft paraded in the Forum?' Then, as his quick glance took in the two young men standing in the deeper shadows, he gave a startled exclamation. 'Light of the Sun! Justin!'

Justin's gaze had been fixed on the newcomer from the first instant of his appearing. 'That makes three –' he was thinking. 'Cullen and Evicatos and now ... Things always go in threes – things and people. Oh, but this is wonderful; most wonderful all the same!'

'Yes, sir!' he said.

'Do you know these two, Centurion Licinius?' interposed the Commander.

Licinius had already caught Justin's hand. 'I know this one, anyway, though he does seem to have grown into a hairy barbarian. He was cub to my Cohort Surgeon at Beersheba. Roma Dea! Boy, are you one of that band of cut-throats outside?'

Justin's wide mouth was curling up at the corners, and his deplorable ears were bright pink with pleasure. 'I am, sir. And this my k-kinsman also.'

'So?' Licinius looked Flavius over, and nodded brusquely as he saluted.

'When you have finished your reunion,' said Asklepiodotus, 'tell me this, Primus Pilus: would you trust these two?'

The lean brown Centurion looked down at his Commander with a faint smile in his eyes. 'The one I know, I would trust anywhere, and in any circumstances. If he vouched for the other, as seems to be the case, then I would trust him too.'

'So be it, then,' said Asklepiodotus. 'We could do with scouts who know the countryside; also with more cavalry. Was there ever a time when the Legions could not do with more cavalry?' He drew tablets and stylus towards him, and scratched a few words on the soft wax. 'March this cut-throat band of yours down to the horse-lines, and take over the mounts and equipment of the two squadrons of Dacian horse that came in last night from the Portus Adurni garrison; here is your authorization. Then hold yourselves ready for orders.'

'Sir.' Flavius took the tablets, but stood his ground.

'Something more?'

'Leave to lodge our Eagle in the Via Principia with the rest, sir.'

'Ah yes, this Eagle,' said Asklepiodotus reflectively.
'How did you come by it?'

'It was found in a hiding-place beneath the shrine of
my family's house in Calleva.'

'So? You know, of course, what it is?'

'It is what remains of a Legionary Eagle, sir.'

Asklepiodotus picked up the list which his Senior Centurion had laid on the table. 'Only one such Eagle has ever
been lost in this province.'

'That also I know. One of my line was lost with it. I
– think the Senate knew about its coming back, at the
time.'

They looked at each other steadily. Then Asklepiodotus
nodded. 'The sudden reappearance of a lost Eagle is a
serious matter, so serious that I propose to know nothing
about it ... Permission granted, on condition that the thing
is – shall we say "missing" again when all be over.'

'Agreed, and thank you, sir,' Flavius said, saluting.

They had turned to the opening of the tent when the
Commander halted them again. 'Oh, and Centurion Aquila,
I have called a Council to meet here at noon. As men who
know the country, and as – er – leaders of an allied force,
I shall expect you both to attend.'

'At noon, sir,' Flavius said.

They found the Decurian in charge at the horse-lines,
showed him the Commander's authorization, and duly
took over the fine little part-arab cavalry mounts of the
Dacian Horse. The bow-legged Auxiliary who was told
off to show them the equipment stores and fodder stacks
was a friendly soul, fortunately more interested in talking
himself than in asking questions. In common with about
half the camp, he was not yet over the rough crossing.

'My *head*!' said the bow-legged Auxiliary. 'Like an
armourer's shop. Bang – bang – bang! And the ground
heaving almost as bad as the deck of that cursed transport.

It would be my luck to be in the Western force, with the long crossing all up from the Sequana – and me the worst sailor in the Empire!'

Flavius, more interested in troop movements than in the bow-legged Auxiliary's sufferings, said, 'I suppose the Caesar Constantius and the Eastern force sailed direct from Gesoriacum?'

'Aye – Constantius sailed before we did, so they say; and the galleys with him to scout ahead and cover the transports coming on after; so I do suppose *he'll* have been at sea as long as us or longer – but his transports will have had maybe only a few hours of it, and it's transports I'm interested in...'

Altogether, Justin and Flavius were a good deal wiser as to the general situation when, at noon, they found themselves in the exalted company of half a dozen staff Tribunes, several Senior Centurions, and the Legate of the Ulpia Victrix, gathered round the makeshift table before the Commander's tent.

Asklepiodotus opened the proceedings sitting with his hands clasped peacefully on his stomach. 'I believe you know, all of you, that Constantius's sails were seen off Tanatis several days ago. You will not, I believe, know that in all probability Allectus has already been warned of our landing by beacon chain. You will agree that this makes it imperative that we march on Londinium without delay.' He turned to the Senior Centurion. 'Primus Pilus, how soon can you have us in marching order?'

'You must give us two days, sir,' said Licinius. 'We've had a foul crossing and both men and horses are in poor shape.'

'I had a feeling you were going to say that,' said Asklepiodotus plaintively. 'I can't think *why* people will be seasick.' (Here the Legate of the Ulpia Victrix, still faintly green, shuddered visibly.) '*I* never am.'

'The rest of us have not your strength of mind, sir,' said Licinius, with a quirk of laughter in his hard face. 'We need two days.'

'Every hour's delay adds to the danger, amongst other things, of our being attacked while still in camp. I'll give you one day.'

There was a moment's silence, and then Licinius said, 'Very good, sir.'

The Council went on, following the usual way of such Councils, while the short noontide shadow of the Ulpia Victrix's Eagle crept slowly across the group before the Commander's tent. And Justin and Flavius had no part in it until Asklepiodotus brought up the question of routes. 'There are two roads possible for our advance; and the choice of them we have left until now, since it is a matter depending on circumstances. Now it is time that we considered the matter; but before we make choice of either road, I feel that we should hear what one who knows the country well has to say,' and he crooked a plump finger at Flavius, who with Justin stood silent on the outskirts of the group.

Flavius's head went up with a jerk. 'Me, sir?'

'Yes, you. Come here and give us your counsel.'

Flavius moved forward into the circle, to stand beside the makeshift table; suddenly very much the Cohort Centurion under his barbarian outer-seeming, suddenly very sober and rather white as he looked round him at the grave-faced men in the bronze and crimson of the higher command. It was one thing to lead the kind of outlaw band that he had brought in that day to serve in the ranks of Rome; quite another to be called on suddenly to give advice which, if it were taken and proved wrong, might lead an army to destruction.

'There are, as the Prefect says, two roads from here to Londinium,' Flavius said, after that one moment's pause.

'One from Regnum about two miles east of here, one through Venta and Calleva. I would choose the Venta and Calleva road, though it may be a few miles longer.'

Licinius nodded. 'Why?'

'For this reason, sir: that after the first day's march, over the Chalk, the road from Regnum runs into the Forest of Anderida. Dense wild country, ideal for ambush, especially for such as Allectus's mercenaries, used to forest warfare in their own land. And you'll have that with you right up to where the scarp of the North Chalk rises like a rampart only a day's march before Londinium. The Venta road, on the other hand, runs into wooded downland almost at once, and the chief danger of ambush lies in the first forty miles – the part farthest from Allectus's main force, and therefore least open to attack.'

'And after that first forty miles?' asked Asklepiodotus.

'Calleva,' Flavius said. 'And once half a march past Calleva, you are well down into the Thamesis Valley. That is forest too, in part, but open forest; big trees, not damp-oak scrub – and open cornland. And you will be in the very heart of the province, where it will be hard indeed for any defence to stand against you.'

'Yes, you have a good eye for country,' Asklepiodotus said, and there was silence. One or two of the men about the table nodded as though in agreement. Then the Commander spoke again. 'Thank you, Centurion; that is all for now. If we have further need of you, I will send for you again.'

And there the thing rested.

But when the Western Force marched out for Londinium next morning, it was by the Venta and Calleva road.

Flavius, knowing the country as he did, had been sent for to ride with Asklepiodotus, leaving Justin and Anthonius to command the two squadrons of ragged cavalry that the band had now become; and looking round at them, Justin felt that, all things considered, tattered and disreputable as they were, they made a good showing, finely mounted, properly armed now with long cavalry swords – all save Evicatos, who had refused any weapon but his beloved spear, and little Cullen, who was their Eagle-bearer. His glance rested for a moment on the Fool riding in the forefront of their company, managing his mount one-handed with surprising ease, while with the other he steadied aloft the wingless Eagle, its spear-shaft now adorned with a wreath of yellow broom hung there by Pandarus in a mood of reckless mockery, to imitate the gold wreaths and medallions of the Ulpia Victrix.

Gradually the ground began to rise, and they were clear of the marsh when an exclamation from Anthonius, riding knee to knee with him, made Justin glance back over his shoulder toward the deserted camp behind them. Fire met his gaze; red, hungry fire leaping heavenward from the stranded transports, and dark smoke drifting aside on the sea-wind.

It was as though the Prefect Asklepiodotus said to his Legions, 'Forward now, to victory. Victory it must be, for there's no sounding the Retreat in *this* campaign.'

16

'Carausius! Carausius!'

NEWS met them on the march, news brought in by the scouts, by native hunters, by deserters from the usurper's army; and some of it was not good. The transports of the Eastern Force had failed to make contact with Constantius in the foul weather; and knowing that the young Caesar could not force a landing without his troops, Allectus was staking everything on a wild attempt to finish with Asklepiodotus before the moment came to turn at bay against the other. He was hurrying westward along the ancient track from Durovernum under the scarp of the North Chalk, straining every nerve to reach the pass in the downs before the avenging forces of Rome could do so, and with him every fighting man that he could lay hands on. Twelve thousand men or more, said the reports: mercenaries and marines for the most part. Not more than six or seven Cohorts of the regular Legions. The Cohorts of the Wall had not reached him yet, and even if they did so in time, there was so much disaffection among the Legions that it seemed very doubtful if he would dare to use them.

That was to the good, anyway, Justin was thinking, casting up good and bad as he sat two nights later looking out over the camp-fires of the army massed in the shallow downland pass where the old track came up to cross the Calleva road. He did not really doubt the outcome of to-morrow's battle, he had faith in Asklepiodotus and the power of the Legions. But the fact remained that since Constantius had failed to land, they were going to have only half their forces tomorrow, to handle everything that Allectus could bring against them; and he realized soberly that they would have no easy victory.

The army had come up at full pace, covering the fifteen miles from Venta in three hours, a gruelling business in June, for men in heavy marching order. But they had done it, and now they waited – a long flat waiting – around their bivouac fires, while Allectus, beaten in that desperate race for the strategic pass, had made camp also, a couple of miles away, to rest his weary host, and maybe also in the hope of tempting the forces of Rome from their strong position.

Asklepiodotus, not finding himself tempted, had used the time to make strong defence works of felled thorn-trees across the mouth of the pass from which to base tomorrow's operations. And now the camp was complete; the bivouac fires glowed red in the moon-washed darkness, and around them the men took their ease, each with his sword buckled on and his shield and pilum to his hand, waiting for tomorrow. From where he sat with the rest of the Lost Legion round their own fire a little above the main camp, Justin could look out to the silver snail-trail that was the moon on the metalled road to Calleva, six miles away. But that other, more ancient way, coming up from the lower ground, was hidden by the rising mist – mist which already lay like the ghost of a forgotten sea over the low ground of the Thamesis Valley; over the great camp where Allectus waited with his host.

Figures came and went like shadows between him and the fires, low voices exchanged a password. The horses stamped and shifted from time to time, and once he heard the scream of an angry mule. But the night itself was very still, behind the sounds of the camp. A wonderful night,

up here above the mist; the bracken of the hillside frozen
into silver stillness below the dark fleece of thorn-scrub
that covered the higher slopes on either side, the moon
still low in a glimmering sky that seemed brushed over
with a kind of moth-wing dust of gold. Somewhere far
down the widening valley a vixen called to her mate, and
somehow the sound left the silence empty.

Justin thought, 'If we are killed tomorrow, the vixen
will still call across the valley to her mate. Maybe she has
cubs somewhere among the root-tangle of the woods. Life
goes on.' And the thought was somehow comforting.
Flavius had gone down to the Praetorium to get the new
watchword and tomorrow's battle-cry; and the rest of the
band sprawled about their fire, waiting for his return.
Cullen sat beneath the battered Eagle, which they had
driven upright into the turf, his face absorbed and happy
as he touched almost soundlessly the apples of his beloved Silver Branch; and beside him – an unlikely couple,
but drawn together by the bond of their Hibernian blood,
as fellow countrymen in a strange land – Evicatos sat
with his hands round one updrawn knee, his face turned
to the North and West of North, as though he looked
away to his own lost hills. Kyndylan and one of the legionaries were playing knuckle-bones. Pandarus, with the
dried wisp of yesterday's yellow rose in his cloak-pin,
had found a suitable stone and was sharpening his dagger,
smiling to himself a small, grimly joyous smile. 'The
bread and onions you ate this morning tasted better than
any feast to a man who expects to eat again, and the sun
through the grills overhead is brighter for you than for
any man who thinks to see it rise tomorrow,' Pandarus
had said once. For himself, Justin found that the know-
ledge that he was quite likely going to be killed tomorrow
was rather a heavy price to pay for his own sudden and
piercing awareness of the moonlit world and the faint

scent of honeysuckle on the night air, and the vixen calling to her mate. 'But then I suppose I've always been a
coward – maybe that was the real reason I never wanted
to be a soldier. It really isn't any wonder father was so
disappointed in me,' thought poor Justin.

Somebody came by on his way back from visiting out-
posts, whistling a tune half under his breath, and checked
beside them. Justin glanced up and saw a crested helmet
outlined against the moon and was on his feet in an instant, as Licinius's voice said, 'It is pleasant up here above
the camp; may I join you for a while?'

'Surely, sir. Sit here.' Justin indicated the sheepskin
riding-rug on which he had been sitting, and with a word
of thanks the Primus Pilus folded up on to it, saying to
those of the band who, mindful of old discipline, had risen
or showed signs of doing so, 'Nay, go on as you were before. I come only as a self-invited guest, not in any official
capacity.'

Justin said after a few minutes, 'Everything seems so
quiet. And by this hour tomorrow it will be as quiet
again.'

'Aye, and in all likelihood with the fate of the province
settled in the time between.'

Justin nodded. 'I am glad the Parthica and the Ulpia
Victrix are here.'

'Why so?'

'Because they served under C-Carausius once. It seems
right that his own Legions should avenge him.'

Licinius glanced at him sideways under his helmet rim.
'When you go into battle tomorrow, will it be for Rome,
or for Carausius?'

'I – don't know,' Justin said painstakingly. 'I suppose for
the province of Britain. And yet – it is in my mind there'll
be a good few remembering the little Emperor, among the
men who served under him.'

'So, for Britain, and for one little half-pirate Emperor, and not for Rome at all,' Licinius said, '*Sa, sa*, the greatness of Rome falls into yesterday.'

Justin pulled a bracken frond beside him, and began carefully to strip the tiny lobes from the stalk. 'Carausius said something like that to Flavius and me once. He said that if Britain could be made strong enough to stand alone when Rome fell, something m-might be saved from the dark, but if not – the lights would go out everywhere. He said that if he could avoid a knife in his back before the work was done, he would make Britain as strong as that. But in the end he d-didn't avoid it; and so now we fight in the ranks of Rome again.'

They were silent a while, then Licinius drew his legs under him. 'Ah well. I think that we have been talking treason, you and I. And now I must be on my way.'

When he was gone, Justin sat for a while staring into the fire. His few words with his old Commander had brought Carausius very vividly before him; the terrible little Emperor who had yet thought to write the letter that Flavius carried in the breast of his ragged tunic.

When he looked up again, Flavius was coming towards him through the bracken. 'Have you the watchword?'

'Watchword and battle-cry, they're both the same,' Flavius said. He looked round at the throng in the fire-light, his eyes at their most blazing bright under the wild shock of flaming hair. 'Brothers, the watchword for to-night and the battle-shout for tomorrow are "*Carausius!*"'

The first light of next morning was shining water pale above the woods, as Justin headed down with Flavius and the rest, through the fern and the young foxgloves that swayed belly-high about their horses' legs, to their appointed place among the Auxiliary cavalry of the right wing. The heavy dew of the summer morning was grey on the bracken fronds, and flew in shining spray as they brushed by, and suddenly, though there was no sun as yet, all the air was shining and a lark leapt into the morning, dropping its rippling thread of song above the massing Legions, as the disreputable band sidled their horses into position behind a squadron of Gaulish Cavalry.

After that there was waiting again – waiting.

And then Flavius's head went up suddenly. 'Listen! Did you hear anything?'

Justin listened, his heart racing. There was only the jink of a bridle-bit as one of the ponies moved, the distant bark of an order from the battle-line, and then stillness again. And then, somewhere away below them in the mist that still hung about the lower ground, a faint, low-pitched murmur of sound, like the distant thunder that one feels while it is still too far off to hear. Only a moment, before it was lost in some fold of the land; then, even as they strained after it, the tension running through the massed Cohorts like a wind-ripple through standing corn, here it came again, clearer, nearer: the sound of an advancing host with many horses.

'Not long now,' Flavius said.

Justin nodded, running the tip of his tongue over a dry lip.

Nearer and nearer rolled the blurred thunder of hooves and marching feet; and then, far ahead where the Auxiliary skirmishers held the first line of defence, a trumpet sang, and from farther off another answered it, as cock crows defiance to cock in the dawn.

The opening phases of that battle seemed to Justin, looking down on it from above and apart, as Jove might do, to be quite unreal; a thing of the ordered movements of great blocks of men, more like some vast and deadly game of chess than the struggle for a province. A game controlled by the tiny child's-toy figure on the opposite hillside that he knew was the Prefect Asklepiodotus with

his staff about him. He saw far away the wavering and
billowing line where the light skirmishing troops of both
armies came together; he saw, closer in, the solid, grey-
mailed blocks of the Cohorts, each under its own standard, with the Eagle of the Ulpia Victrix in the van. He
saw the Auxiliaries, their part played, falling back, slowly,
steadily, passing cleanly through the gaps left for them
between Cohort and Cohort; saw the gaps closing like a
door. And now the trumpets were sounding the Advance,
and with a slow and measured certainty that was somehow more terrible than any wild rush, the whole battle-
front was rolling forward to meet that other host rolling
darkly towards them up the line of the ancient track and
far across the ferny hillside on either hand.

Again the trumpets were singing, ringing to the morning sky, Cavalry trumpets now, and the long waiting was
over. 'Come on, my heroes; it's our turn now!' Flavius
cried; and with the fiery notes of the trumpets still ringing
in their ears, the horses broke from a stand into a canter,
and they were sweeping forward to guard the flanks of the
Cohorts as the valley broadened and the shielding thorn-
scrub fell away on either hand. The sun was well up now;
far ahead of them it glinted on spearhead and shield-rim,
axe-blade and helmet of grey iron, striking sparks of light
from the polished bronze of horse ornaments. Justin saw
the black boar banners of the Saxons, the swarming
squadrons of Cavalry. He could make out the denser massing of standards in the midst of the enemy host, the stiffer
lines of marines and legionaries and the gleam of gold and
Imperial Purple where Allectus himself rode among his
wild barbarian horde. Vaguely in the engulfing turmoil,
he was aware of the two battle-lines rolling in towards
each other; and his ears were full of a sound that he had
never heard before: the clashing, grinding furnace-roar
of full battle.

And now, for Justin, the battle whose opening moves had seemed like a game of chess, became a bright and terrible confusion, narrowing down to his own part in it, while all else ceased to have any meaning. For him, the great battle for the province of Britain fought out that fine summer's day, was a snarling, blue-eyed face and streaming yellow hair; it was a coral-studded shield-boss and a darting spear-blade and the up-tossed rolling mane of a horse. It was a thunder of hooves and the wheeling and swerving of wild cavalry through the bracken, and the red stain growing on his own sword. It was Flavius, always the length of his horse's head in front of him, and the wingless Eagle in the thick of the press, and the little Emperor's name yelled above the tumult for a battle-cry, 'Carausius! Carausius!'

And then somehow the battle was growing ragged, scattering and spreading out over the countryside, becoming no longer one battle, but a score. And suddenly, as though a bright and raging fever had lifted from his brain, Justin was aware of breathing-space, and the sun away over towards evening in a sky puffed with white summer cloud. And they were far to the North, on the tattered fringe of things; and southward the legionaries were rounding up the beaten enemy as sheep-dogs driving sheep.

He shook his head like a swimmer breaking surface, and looked about him at the Lost Legion. It was smaller than it had been this morning, and several of those who still rode with them had some hurt. Little Cullen, still carrying the Eagle proudly erect, its crown of yellow broom long since torn away, had a gash over one eye; and Kyndylan was managing his horse one-handed, with a useless arm hanging at his side.

Turning back towards what remained of the battle, they came straggling up a long wooded ridge; and from the crest of it found themselves looking down on the Londinium road.

And along the Londinium road and all across the country below them, like a river in storm spate, was pouring a wild flood of fugitives, reserves and horse-holders probably, for the most part; mercenaries breaking back and streaming away from the battle; a broken rabble of barbarians on foot and on horse-back, flying for their lives.

Justin felt suddenly sick. Few things in the world could be more pitiless than a beaten and demoralized army; and only a few miles away the Londinium road ran through Calleva!

Flavius broke the silence that had gripped them all with something like a groan. 'Calleva! It will be fire and sword for the whole city if that rabble get in!' He wheeled about on the men with him. 'We must save Calleva! We must ride with them and hope for our chance at the gates. There's no time to wait for orders. Anthonius, get back to Asklepiodotus and tell him what goes forward, and bid him, in the names of all the gods there be, to send up a few squadrons of Cavalry!'

Anthonius flung up his hand, and wheeling his horse was away almost before the words were spoken.

'Cullen, cover up the Eagle. Now, come on, and remember we are fugitives like the rest until we are within the gates,' Flavius cried. 'Follow me – and *keep together*!'

Justin was at his side as usual; Cullen with the Eagle under his ragged cloak and the spear-shaft sticking out behind him, Evicatos and the old gladiator, and the rest hard behind, a wild-geese skein of flying horsemen, as they broke from cover of the woods and sent their horses downhill, crashing through the fern and foxgloves as though in desperate flight, swinging wide into the midst of the fleeing barbarians.

17

Eagle in the Flames

THE flood of fugitives caught them up and swept them on and away. A flood that was desperate — and wicked. Justin could feel the desperation and the wickedness flowing all about him, as he dug his heel again and again into his mare's flank, leaning forward to ease her, in a desperate attempt to force a way ahead, to out-ride the stream of sudden death pouring toward Calleva, and reach the gates ahead of it.

The gates — if only the gates were shut in time, it might be that the little city would yet be safe, for this wolfish rabble would scarcely spare the time to break them down, with Asklepiodotus and his Legions the gods knew how close on its heels. If *only* they had got the gates closed in time!

But when the road lifted over the last ridge, and Calleva lay before them on its gentle hill, Justin saw, with a sickening lurch of the heart, that the gates were open, and the barbarians pouring through. The whole countryside was alive with fugitives by now; with desperate shadows among the trees, fleeing onward and away; and, ever more thickly, that dark stream of men, turning aside from the main flood of their fellows, to the open gate of Calleva and the prospect of loot that was more to them than escape.

Riding neck and neck, with the Lost Legion close behind them, yelling with the rest, Justin and Flavius swept

through between the gate towers. The bodies of half a
dozen legionaries and townsmen lay within the gates,
which they must have sought to close too late. Allectus
had withdrawn the rest of the guard.

The wide main street running north from the gate was
already jammed with the marauders; some of the houses
were on fire, and abandoned horses, terrified by the
tumult and the smell of burning, were running loose
among the howling mob. But a large part of the rabble
had halted to sack the big posting inn just within the gates,
which, from its size and air of importance, seemed to
promise treasure for the taking.

'Down here!' Flavius shouted. 'Get ahead of them –'
and swung his horse right-handed into a narrow alleyway
beside the inn. Justin and the rest swung after him; a
small knot of Saxons also, but they were dealt with
shortly and sharply, and the band pressed on. The narrow
ways were deserted; it seemed that most of the people
must have fled to the shelter of the basilica. In the gardens
of the temple of Sul Minerva, Flavius reined up in full
career, and dropped to the ground, followed by the rest.
'Leave the horses here. If the fire spreads they'll have a
chance to keep clear,' he panted. 'Kyndylan, come you
with me – and you – and you.' Quickly he singled out
about a dozen of the band, all men who knew Calleva
well. 'Justin, you take the rest, and hold those devils back
as long as may be. It looks as though most of the town
has made for the Forum already – but we must be sure.
Give us all the time you can . . .'

They were heading back for the heart of the town,
from which came ever more strongly the reek of burning
and the shouts and cries of the Saxons. Justin remembered
after, though he scarcely noticed at the time, how Pandarus broke a crimson rose in passing from a bush beside
the temple steps, and thrust it into the shoulder-pin of

his cloak as he ran. Pandarus and his rose for the Arena!

The lane they were following brought them into a
wider one, and they swung left, then left again, the ugly
tumult swelling every moment on their ears; and then
they were back in the main street. Justin caught one
glimpse of the gleaming white colonnades of the Forum
at the top of the street, then it was behind him as he
headed his little company towards the fight which was
now raging lower down.

'Friend! friend! friend!' Justin shouted as they flung
themselves into the thin ranks of the defenders. 'Carausius! Carausius!'

There were a few among the citizens who had swords;
but for the most part they were armed only with such
weapons as they had been able to catch up: daggers and
knives and the heavy tools of their trade. Justin glimpsed
the purple tunic-stripe of a magistrate, the saffron kilt of
a countryman, and in their midst one russet-haired giant
swinging a butcher's axe. It was a most valiant defence,
but it could not last. Already they had been driven back
half the length of the street. The sudden swelling of their
ranks by Justin and his fellows with their long cavalry
swords checked the fall back for a moment, but it would
have taken a couple of Cohorts to hold that mob, mad-
dened now by the wine of the Silver Garland's cellars, so
that they forgot the danger hard behind them, forgot all
else in the wild joy of destruction. The street was full of
the smoke of burning houses, and out of it yelling Saxons
loomed to fling themselves like wild beasts on the defenders; while at any moment more of them might find
their way round by the side streets – there was nothing to
prevent them – and be between the defenders and the
Forum.

How long they held up the barbarian flood, slowly giving ground despite all their desperate resistance, fighting

back from house to house, from street corner to street
corner, Justin had not the least idea. Suddenly they were
right back into the open space that surrounded the Forum,
and there was no longer any question of holding the barbarians in check, no question of anything but somehow
gaining the Forum entrance themselves before they were
completely cut off.

And then Flavius was there, and others with him;
Flavius yelling in his ear, 'The main entrance – barricade
the rest.'

The arch of the main entrance was overhead, proud
and pompous with its marble sheathing and bronze
statues, and Flavius was shouting to the townsmen with
them, 'Back! Get back to the basilica. We'll hold the gate
for you – do you hold the door for us when we come!'

And in the mouth of the deep gate arch, the Lost
Legion turned shoulder to shoulder to hold back the yelling horde of barbarians while the townsmen gained the
basilica.

Behind him, Justin heard the retreating rush of feet
growing smaller across the sun-warmed emptiness of the
Forum. Little Cullen was beside him, the battered Eagle
raised high amid the reeling press; Pandarus with the
crimson rose in his shoulder-pin; Flavius with his buckler
long since gone, and his blade biting deep; a rock-steady
band of champions to hold back the tide of raging, fair-
haired devils that crashed and hurled against them.

It was a short struggle, but a desperate one, and several
of the band were down, their places instantly filled by the
next man behind them, before the cry went up, 'All clear
behind!'

And Flavius yelled, 'Break off! Back to the basilica –
now!' and they sprang back and turned to run for their
lives.

Justin was running with the rest; running and stumbling with a bursting heart across a seemingly endless expanse of sunlit cobbles, towards the refuge of the great East door that seemed to draw no nearer. They had a few moments' start, for in the very wildness of their rush, undisciplined as they were, the Saxons had jammed themselves together in the gate arch, yelling, struggling, trampling over each other in wild confusion, and the band of desperate men were half across the Forum before Allectus's wolves burst through like a flood released behind them. They were into the shadow of the basilica now, but the barbarians were hard on their heels. The great door was gaping before them, men massed at either side to shield their flanks and draw them in; and on the portico steps the hindmost of the Lost Legion whirled about, buckler to buckler, to do rearguard for the rest.

Justin, his shoulder against Flavius's shoulder, had a confused vision of a wave of barbarians sweeping towards them, winged and snarling heads and the evening light on spear and saex-blade and upswung axe. The forerunners of the wave were upon them, and he struck home over the rim of his buckler, and saw a man crumple down the portico steps, even as he felt the top step against his heel, and moved backward and up.

'Sa, sa! We'll just do it!' Flavius shouted.

The doors were three parts closed, leaving only room for their passage, as the two of them dropped their points and sprang back. And next instant, with the power of a score of shoulders behind them, the great carved timber leaves crashed shut, and the heavy bars were thrust into place.

Outside in the Forum rose a yell of baffled fury, and a crashing of blows against the doors that echoed in the high, empty places of the vast building above the heads of the multitude huddled there. A tall man with an old uniform sword in his hand, who had been with them through the street-fighting, turned a haggard face to Flavius as he leaned a moment panting against the door. 'In the name of all the gods, who are you?' And then, 'Roma Dea! It is young Aquila!'

Flavius pushed off from the door. 'Yes, sir. We'll give you an account of ourselves later. Just now there's not much time to spare. Help will be here soon, but we've got to hold the basilica till it comes.'

He had stepped, naturally and inevitably, into the Command; and even in that moment of stress, it flashed into Justin's mind with a glimmer of laughter that if they were not all killed in the next hour or so, Flavius would undoubtedly get his Legion one day.

Flavius, knowing the basilica and its weak places as well as anyone there, was posting men to hold the main entrance and the small side doors, and in the Municipal offices and treasure-chambers that opened all down the long side of the hall opposite to the entrance; getting the women and children cleared away from the danger points. 'Back, farther back here. We must have more fighting space.' Posting guards in the galleries above the aisle of the great hall, to watch the high windows, in case the Saxons should seek to reach them by way of the colonnade roof.

Justin never forgot that scene. There must have been eighteen hundred souls or more, slave and free, crowded into the basilica. The women and children, the old and the sick, huddled together around the feet of the columns, on the raised floor of the Tribunals at either end where in time of peace the Magistrates sat to deal justice, on the steps of the Council Chamber itself; while the men with their hastily snatched up weapons stood to the barred doors beyond which rose the wolf-pack yelling of the Saxon mercenaries. He saw huddled forms and strained white faces in the shadows; here a mother trying to com-

fort a frightened child, there an old merchant clutching
the bag of jewels he had caught up in flight. There were
family pets, too, and small pathetic family treasures. A
little dark-eyed girl had a singing-bird in a cage, to which
she talked softly all the while, and which hopped uncon-
cernedly about, fluting a few notes from time to time
above the yelling and the random thunder of blows
against the carved timbers of the entrance.

But Justin had little leisure to look about him. He was
Flavius's Second-in-Command, but also he was a surgeon;
and just now the wounded – there were many wounded –
needed him more than Flavius did; and he laid aside sword
and buckler to do what he could for them. It was not
much; there was no water, no bandage linen, and he must
have help. Looking hurriedly round the great hall, his eye
picked out a figure huddled in the shadows that he knew
for the chief physician of the place. He called to him,
'Balbus, come and help me, man.' Then, as the huddled
figure paid no heed, thinking that perhaps the man was
deaf, he rose from his knee beside one of the wounded,
and went quickly across to him. But when he stooped
and set a hand on his shoulder, the other shied away
from him and looked up with a face shining with sweat
and the colour of lard, and began to rock himself to and
fro. Justin dropped his hand and turned away with a
feeling of mingled disgust and pity. No help to be found
there.

But in the same instant two women rose in his path, and
he saw that the foremost was Aunt Honoria and the one
just behind her was the enormous Volumnia.

'Tell us what to do and we will do it,' said Aunt Honoria, and it seemed to him that she was very beautiful.

'Tear up your tunics,' he said. 'I want bandage linen;
there are men here who will live if the bleeding is stopped
and d-die if it isn't. We must get the wounded together,

too. Can't see what there is to do, with them scattered all up and down the hall.'

Other helpers were gathering to him before the words were well out; a stout wine-shop woman; a slave from the dyeworks with splashes of old dyes ingrained in skin and garments; a girl like a white flower, who looked as though she had never seen blood before, and many others.

They got the wounded together before the North Tribunal, and at least there was no lack of stuff for bandages now; bandages of the coarsest homespun and the finest flower-coloured summer linen, as the women stripped off their outer tunics and tore them up to serve the need, and set to work with him in their shifts. Most of them knew how to deal with a sword-cut or a broken head, he found, and that left him free to attend to the more sorely hurt. Thank the gods he had his instrument-case!

With the fair girl to help him, he had just finished getting a javelin-head out of the shoulder of one of the Otter's Ford brothers, when the pounding against the main door, which had slackened a little as the barbarians found the money-changers and the wine-shops in the Forum, suddenly returned tenfold. A new yelling arose outside, unearthly in its savagery and insane triumph, and suddenly the smoke-dimmed sky beyond the clerestory windows was shot with fire. The great door shook and shuddered under the new onslaught – not now the mere random thunder of war-axes and light beams torn from the nearby shops, but something infinitely more deadly. The Saxon devils must have got into the timber yard nearby, and found there something to use as a ram.

There was nothing more at the moment to be done for the wounded that could not be done as well by Aunt Honoria and the other women. Justin said to the pale girl, 'Stay here with him whatever happens, and if the bleed-

ing starts again, press where I showed you,' and snatching up sword and buckler, ran for his place among the
men at the main entrance. Flavius yelled to him above
the rending thunder of the ram, to get up to the gallery
and see what was happening. And a few moments later,
scarcely aware of the steep stairs behind the Tribunal that
he had taken two at a time, he emerged high above the
nave of the basilica. The light was beginning to fade, sul-
phurous behind the rolling smoke; and when he peered
out through the beautiful unglazed lattice-work of the
nearest window, the whole Forum seemed a pit of fire.
The Saxons, mad drunk on the contents of every wine-
shop in Calleva, and raging not only for plunder, but for
blood, with the savage, wild-beast frenzy of their kind, had
dragged bits of timber from the burning buildings to
spread the blaze, and were rushing to and fro, their makeshift torches streaming in mares' tails of smoky flame behind them. They were flinging burning stuff against the
basilica, heedless of who among their own kind it
scorched. The Forum was full of looted gear, running with
wine from broken jars and burst skins, the shops falling
into red ruin. And below, part hidden by the roof of the
portico, part plain to see, a score of men were charging
again and again at the main doors, swinging between them
the great balk of timber – almost a whole tree-trunk –
that they had found to serve as a ram.

Again the knot of barbarians charged forward, again
came the crash of the tree-trunk against the door. The
timbers could not stand long against such punishment;
but surely any moment now help would come – help
drumming up the road towards them, maybe already at
the gates ...

'It can't be long now,' he said to himself as much as to
Pandarus who was on guard at that end of the gallery.

'*Na*, either way, it can't be long now,' said Pandarus;

and looking quickly round at him, Justin saw that the old gladiator was happy – happy as he had not been since he won his wooden foil.

For himself, Justin was not at all happy. The fighting over the open downs had been one thing, this was quite another. Somehow the surroundings of polished marble and finely wrought bronze, the whole atmosphere of a place meant for dignity and order and good manners, made what was happening horrible and grotesque, and his old horror of being in any place from which he could not get out at will was jibbering most unpleasantly at his elbow. He made some sort of hurried jest to Pandarus – he was never sure what it was – and turned and plunged down the stairs again.

There was no need, no opportunity either, to tell Flavius what he had seen. The main door was going as he regained the hall; and above the splintering crash of the timbers and the sudden clash of blade on blade and the savage burst of shouting as attack and defence came together in the jagged and smoking breach, he heard the cry go up that the Saxons were breaking in from the rear into the main Court room.

And without any clear idea in his head save that Flavius was in command at one danger point, and therefore his place was at the other, he found himself heading at the run for the new menace, with a handful of the Lost Legion at his heels.

The outer door of the Court room had gone up in flames, and fiery smoke hung in a drifting haze above the heads of the fighters. And it came to his mind, even as he charged to the aid of the townsmen, that the basilica was now well on fire. Then a giant with bright hair streaming like the flames of the torches made for him, long-handled axe upswung for a mighty stroke; somehow he swerved from the path of the blow, and dived on, young Myron

behind him and Evicatos at his shoulder with his great
spear drinking deep.

It was a desperate and a bloody business, fought out
among the splintered wreckage of the solid Court-room
furniture, while ever the smoke thickened overhead and
the red glare strengthened on winged helmet and upswung
blade. Many of the defenders were down with the first onslaught, while for every Saxon who fell it seemed that
two more sprang in through the gaping doorway or down
from the torn-out window-holes. And to Justin, struggling desperately for every inch of ground that he was
forced to yield, it had begun to seem that they could not
hold the barbarians back much longer from the main hall,
from the women and the children and the wounded, when
above the tumult his ear caught the thin sweet mockery
of bells; and Cullen the Fool dived almost under his elbow
into the trampling press. And suddenly above them in the
rolling murk, blazing red-gold in the light of Calleva burning, was the wingless Eagle.

The gods alone knew what had prompted little Cullen
to bring them the Eagle, but the sense of increase was like
wine, like fire, running not only through the band but
through the townsmen who had not followed that battered standard before; and they steadied as though they
had been reinforced by a Cohort of the Legions.

But the next thing Justin saw was Cullen struggling
breast to breast with a yellow-haired barbarian for possession of the Eagle! And even as he sprang sideways to the
little man's aid, he disappeared completely in the press;
and a howl of rage burst from the Saxon, and the white-
ash spear-shaft swung aloft, with the cross-piece still in-
tact, but of the Eagle – never a sign.

Something in Justin's mind understood quite coolly that
the age-corroded talons must have snapped under the
strain upon them. And then, even as a roar of fury burst
from his own men, there came a jingle of bells above the

uproar, and a little figure sprang clear of the press, leaping for an overturned table, then up again – and Cullen was on the main house-beam above them, and in his hands the Eagle! He scrambled out along the beam on his knees, and crouched there, holding it high, the red light of the flames all about him, the Eagle burning in his hands like a bird of fire. And the cry of fury changed to shout on shout of fierce triumph, as the defenders once more closed their thinning ranks and drove forward.

Next instant a flung spear caught the little Fool in the shoulder. He swayed and seemed to crumple up, like some small gaudy bird hit by a stone, becoming a mere bundle of bright feathers; but by a miracle he clung to his vantage point just long enough to set the Eagle firmly on the flat top of the beam. Then he toppled down into the very midst of the fight.

Justin, with a fighting power he had not known he possessed until that moment, was crashing forward in one more desperate charge, sweeping the rest with him. 'Cullen! Save Cullen!' But it was Evicatos, the swan's feathers of his great spear crimson now, who reached the spot first, ploughing forward into the very midst of the enemy to bestride the little crumpled body while the rest came battling on in his wake.

And in that instant, above the tumult of the conflict, far off and infinitely clear and sweet, they caught the sound of Roman trumpets!

The barbarians heard it too, and swayed back; and with a sound that was almost a sob, Justin drove in his charge; past Evicatos and on.

When all was over, Evicatos still stood astride the body of the little Fool, beneath the Eagle on the house-beam; a great and terrible figure, red with his wounds from head to heel, like some hero out of one of the wild legends of his own people, like a Conal of the Victories.

He steadied himself upright, and with one last superb

effort, sent his beloved spear hurtling after the flying foe. But already the sure aim was gone from him, and the great spear missed its mark, and crashing into the stone column beyond the reeking doorway, shivered into fragments of iron and wood and blood-stained feathers on the pavement.

'*Sa*. It is well,' Evicatos said. He flung up his head, and there was a pealing triumph in his voice. 'We go together, back to our own people, she and I.'

And so crashed down headlong among the slain.

Little Cullen had not a mark on him but the spear-gash in his shoulder and a cut over one eye, and was already whimpering back to life as they drew him out from under Evicatos's body.

Justin lifted him – he was so small that he could handle him quite easily – and turned to the inner doorway. Vaguely he heard someone ask about the Eagle, and shook his head. 'Leave it. It has served its hour and must go back to the dark.' And he carried Cullen out into the hall.

The Nave of the basilica was full of smoke, and the rafters at the far end were well alight. Here also the fighting was over, and Flavius, with blood trickling from a gashed cheek, was struggling to call off his fighting men like a hunter calling off his hounds. 'Leave them to the Cavalry! *Leave them*, lads; we've our work cut out here!'

Justin carried the little Fool across to the North Tribunal, and laid him down among the rest. Aunt Honoria was beside him as he did so; and just behind her the girl like a white flower still knelt beside the farmer from the Otter's Ford, with his head in her lap.

The basilica was emptying swiftly, as the women and children were passed out into the wrecked Forum, but the roar of the fire was increasing every moment, and the tall man who had recognized Flavius was improvising a bucket chain from the well outside to keep the flames back from

the Records Office and Treasury while the City's gods
were got out; it was hopeless to think of doing more – the
fire had too big a hold. Justin, knotting off the bandage
about Cullen's shoulder, said to the physician, who, now
that the fighting was over, had pulled himself together and
come to his aid, 'It is growing a bit warm. Time, I think,
that we got this lot outside.'

There were many willing hands, and the task was soon
accomplished, and Justin, who had remained inside himself until the last man was out, was about to follow,
when something fell from the gallery above, from which
the guards had by now been withdrawn, and landed with
a plop beside him, and, glancing down, he saw that it was
the crimson rose which Pandarus had picked in the temple
garden only an hour or so ago. Instinctively he stooped
to pick it up – and the crimson came off on his fingers.

Next instant he was pounding up the gallery stairs, calling the gladiator by name.

He thought he heard a groan, and then he burst out
upon the narrow gallery. The western windows across
the Nave were filled with a mingled glare of fire and sunset that streamed across, turning the smoke to a billowing,
tawny fog. The nearest lattice on this side was broken in,
and beneath it lay a dead Saxon, his short sword still in his
hand, his hair outflung across the stained floor; and beside
him Pandarus, who must have lingered behind the rest,
leaned on one arm, while his life drained away from a
red hole under his ribs.

He raised his head with a twisted smile as Justin reached
him, and gasped, 'Habet! It is thumbs down for me at last.'

One glance told Justin that the wound was mortal and
the old gladiator could not last many moments. There
was nothing he could do for Pandarus, nothing but stay
with him through those few moments, and he crouched
down and laid the other back against his knee. 'Not

thumbs down! That is for a beaten fighter,' he said vehemently; then, as his gaze fell on the dead Saxon, 'Euge! that was a fine stroke.'

The rush of the flames was very near, the heat growing every moment more intense. Smoke billowed across Justin's face, choking, suffocating him; and as he glanced over his shoulder, he saw that the floor of the gallery itself had caught, and the fire was writhing towards him. Below the windows, the roof of the Colonnade was crackling into flame; no going that way if the stairs caught ... his heart was racing, and he was sweating with more than the heat. Here with a vengeance was the place from which he could not get out. Not while Pandarus lived.

He bent low over the dying gladiator, trying to shield him with his own body from the heat and the fiery cinders that were falling around them now from the burning roof, striving to fan back the smoke with a fold of his cloak. Above the furnace-roar of the flames he thought he heard something else. The beat of horses' hooves.

Pandarus turned his head a little. 'It grows dark. What is this great noise?'

'It is the people shouting for you!' Justin said. 'All the people who have c-come to watch you win your greatest fight of all!'

There was a ghost of laughter in Pandarus's face, a ghost of an old pride. He put up his hand in the gesture of a victorious gladiator acknowledging the cheers of the crowd; and with the gesture half made, fell back against Justin's knee, with his greatest and his last fight fought indeed.

Justin laid him down, and finding that he was still holding the crimson rose, laid it in the hollow of the dead gladiator's shoulder, with a confused feeling that it was fitting Pandarus should carry with him his rose for the Arena.

As he got to his feet, the first ranks of Asklepiodotus's cavalry were swinging into the ruined Forum.

He thought he heard someone calling him. He called back, lurching towards the stair, his head beginning to swim. The narrow stairs were already alight as he plunged down them, one arm upflung to shield his face. The smoke was shot with little torn-off tongues of flame, sucked upward by the draught; the heat poured up the stair-shaft, lapping him round, searing his lungs as he stumbled downward, and near the foot blundered into Flavius with a wet rag over his mouth crashing up to find him.

He heard a gasp of relief, and was not sure whether it was Flavius's or his own. 'Who else is up there?' Flavius croaked.

'No one save Pandarus, and he's dead.' Justin caught a crowing, shuddering breath, and somehow they were at the stair foot, crouching to catch the current of clearer air along the floor. 'Eagle's in – the Court-room roof – all right?'

'All right,' Flavius choked.

The whole basilica was blotted out in rolling smoke, its far end veiled in a roaring curtain of flame; and a blazing beam came down with a crash not a spear's length from them, scattering red-hot fragments in all directions. 'Got to get out! Nothing more we can do,' Flavius was croaking in his ear.

The side door close to the stair-foot was blocked by the blazing ruins of the garland-maker's shop, and they headed at a stumbling run for the main entrance. It seemed a long way off, such a long way, at the end of a fiery tunnel . . .

And then suddenly Anthonius was there, and Kyndylan and others – and they were outside, and there was air to breathe; real air, not black smoke and red flame. Justin dragged it into his tortured lungs, stumbling forward, and finding a burst bale of some kind in his path, sat down on it. He was dimly aware of men and horses, of a great throng of people, of the Forum a blackened shambles, and the sounds of strife in the burning town, and the drum of horses' hooves dying away into the distance as the Cavalry swept on after the Saxon wolves. He heard someone shouting that the traitor Allectus had been captured, but he didn't care. He was aware with surprise that it was still sunset – and that somewhere the little bird in its cage was singing, most sweetly and shiningly, like a star singing. But the whole scene was dipping and swimming round him like a great wheel.

Myron't rat-pointed, anxious face swam into his sight hovering over him, and Flavius had an arm round his shoulders and was holding a broken bowl to his mouth. There was water in the bowl, and he sucked it down to the last drop. A few moments later he was sick with all that he had in his stomach to be sick with, which was not much beside the water, because he had not eaten since before dawn; and the world began to steady.

He pulled himself together, and got up. 'My wounded – must g-go and see to my wounded,' he mumbled.

18

Triumphal Garlands

JUST over a month later, on a sweltering July day, all Londinium was waiting for the coming of the Caesar Constantius. Londinium decked as for an Imperial Triumph, her crowds in their best and gayest clothes. And all up the broad paved street from the river to the Forum, and from the Forum right across the City, men of the Legions were on street-lining duty; men of the Second Augustan and the other British Legions who had all come in to make their submission again to Rome. A thin line of bronze and russet-red up each side of the street to hold back the holiday crowds, unbroken save in one place – a place of honour – about half way up from the River Gate to the Forum, where Flavius and Justin and Anthonius stood with the valiant, tattered handful that were left of the Lost Legion.

The three of them still wore the rough barbarian garments that they had worn so long. Flavius's eyebrows, which had been singed off, were only just beginning to grow again; and Justin had lost most of his front hair and still showed on his right forearm the sore-looking shiny pink of new skin. And the little reckless band on either side of them, bearing also the marks of burning Calleva, were as tattered and disreputable as themselves. But in their odd way they were the proudest unit in the streets of Londinium that day.

Justin, leaning on his spear, could glimpse beyond the

River Gate, the long timber bridge that carried in the road from Rutupiae and the Saxon coast, the flash and shimmer of the river in the sunlight, and the prow of a naval galley garlanded with green. But all Londinium was garlanded today. Strange to think how very easily Londinium might have been like Calleva – Calleva as he had seen it last, blackened and desolate under the summer rain.

Asklepiodotus had left a company of pioneers to help clear the town, and swept the rest of his force on at full pace towards Londinium. But Saxon fugitives from the battle were well ahead of them, and bands of Mercenaries were swarming in from the forest and the coast-wise fortresses; and the Legions, despite all their forced marching, would have been too late to save the richest and greatest city of the province from fire and the sword. But Constantius's missing transports, storm-swept clear round Tanatis into the Thamesis estuary, had forced a way up-river to reach Londinium just as the first wave of Barbarians swept to its walls. And that had been the end of Allectus's wolves.

Yes, Rome had avenged Carausius most fully. Justin remembered the executions that there had been in the ruined Forum at Calleva. Allectus's as it were leading the rest, Serapion's amongst them. He was not of a vengeful disposition, but he was glad about Serapion. – But somehow, looking back on them, they did not seem real; not as the things that went before had been real. He remembered looking up from his work and feeling the heat like the blast from an open oven on his face, and seeing the roof of the basilica sinking inward like blazing canvas; the sudden hush, all the world seeming to wait, holding its breath, and then the rending, shuddering roar of the falling roof, and the basilica a black shell full of fire as a cup is full of wine; and Flavius suddenly beside him, scorched and blackened from head to foot, crying to him above the

tumult, 'See there! A fine pyre for a lost eagle!' That had
been real. He remembered the big house close by that had
escaped the worst of the fire, where they had carried the
wounded. He remembered Aunt Honoria with the paint
patchy on her grey face, saying in that jewel-cut voice of
hers, when they told her that her house had gone, 'Ah
well, I have always had a fancy to live at Aqua Sulis, and
now I shall gratify it.' He remembered men who had died
that night under his hands, and men who had lived. He
remembered them bringing Allectus through the City to
the transit camp for safe keeping; and the way the sinking fires of Calleva had seemed to flare up again at his passing, as though they knew the man who had kindled them,
and greeted him in mockery; and the glimpse of Imperial
Purple rags, and a white, staring face in which the old
charming smile had become a set and rigid snarl of rage
and torn pride and despair.

He remembered the overset and broken rose-jars in the
colonnade of the big house, and a crimson rose-spray outflung on the pavement, caught for an instant in the swinging light of a lantern, that had torn at him with the sudden understanding he had not had time for before, that
Pandarus was dead. Pandarus and Evicatos, and little
plump Paulinus a year ago, and so many others; but it was
for those three that suddenly he had been blind with
tears.

A striped wasp whining past his ear made him jerk his
head, and brought him back to the present. To the garlanded street that waited for the Caesar Constantius, who,
forced to put back into Gesoriacum by the failure of his
transports to make contact with him, was now coming
in person to take possession of the lost province that was
once again part of Rome.

Justin shifted his weight from one foot to the other,
and shifting, felt again the thin papyrus roll that he had

slipped inside the breast of his tattered tunic. His first letter from home in almost two years. The very first letter he had ever had from his father that had not made him feel a disappointment. 'It is with relief that I receive word of you,' his father had written. 'On the occasion of your last letter, you assured me that you had done nothing of which to be ashamed, and I am rejoiced to find that most fully borne out by a certain report I have had of you from my old friend and your one-time commanding officer, Fulvius Licinius. Believe me, however, that I was never in the least danger of being ashamed of you. There was a time when I was disappointed at your failure to carry on the family tradition, but I have always been perfectly assured that you would not under any circumstances give me cause for shame ...' And then further on, 'I trust that when we next meet we may learn to know each other rather better than we have done in the past.'

And Justin, turning the stiff and formal phrases over in his mind, knew that he had quite ceased to be a disappointment to his father; and was glad with a warmth that laughed a little at both of them, but principally at himself, as he could not have done two years ago.

And now there was a stirring, far away across the river; a sound rhythmic as a pulse, that grew and strengthened moment by moment into the ringing tramp of legions on the march. Excitement was running through the crowded streets, where tribesmen in plaid breeks and townsmen in Roman tunics jostled cheerfully for a better view. Now there was a flicker of movement on the bridge – white and bright and many-coloured movement – and the street-lining legionaries linked their arms into a stronger barrier. The head of the advancing column was past the gigantic statue of Hadrian at the near end of the bridge; now it was coming beneath the arch of the garlanded River Gate, and a roar of acclamation burst up

from the crowd, as the leading ranks, headed by the chief
Magistrates who had met the advancing army a mile outside the City, swung into the broad, paved street.

On they came, the Magistrates in the dignity of their
purple-bordered togas, the tramp-tramp-tramp of the
Legions' feet swelling into a pulsing crash of sound that
could not be drowned even by the roaring of the crowd.
The people were throwing green branches in the roadway,
surging forward. Justin, leaning back against the thrust
that threatened to jerk him into the middle of the road,
his arms linked with Flavius on one side and Anthonius
on the other, was thumped violently between the
shoulders by one excited citizen, while another bellowed
blessings upon the Saviour of Britain into his left ear. The
Magistrates were past now, and behind them marched
the trumpeters, four abreast, the sun glinting on the enormous ram's-horn coils of the Roman trumpets. And then,
mounted on a tall black stallion, with his staff and senior
officers about him, the Caesar Constantius himself.

Looking up past the black, arched mane, Justin caught a
rather startling glimpse of a face under the Eagle-crested
Imperial helmet, that was almost as pale as Allectus's had
been, and remembered that the troops had bestowed on
this man the surname of Chlorus, Green, because of his
pallor. Then the Caesar Constantius also was past, and
they heard the wave of cheering run before him on towards the Forum. Justin caught sight of Asklepiodotus
looking half asleep as usual; and lean, brown Licinius.
And then behind them the great silver-winged Eagle of
the Seventh Claudian Legion went by, steady as a rock
with all its weight of gilded battle honours, upborne with
rigid pride by its lion-skinned Eagle-bearer pacing between
his escort. And the spread wings bright against the
summer sky sent Justin's mind back in a moment of vivid
memory to the mutilated stump of a once-proud ensign,

beneath which Evicatos had died, the battered Eagle that lay lost for ever under the blackened ruins of Calleva's basilica. And then the memory was swallowed up in the thunderous tramp of the Legions swinging by.

The summer day passed with its drawn-out celebrations. Londinium had been eager to show her gratitude and joy in a great banquet, but the Caesar Constantius had let it be known in advance that he had no mind for a banquet at this time. 'There is over-much work waiting for us in the North, and we march not our fastest on full stomachs,' ran his message. 'Feast us when we return.' And so, when the Magistrates had made their speeches in the basilica and the sacrificial bull had died before Jove's altar, he retired at the day's end to the fort at the north-west angle of the City walls, with his staff and Senior Officers.

Below the fort a vast marching camp had been made ready for the Legions outside the City walls; and in the still summer twilight, by and by, the camp-fires sprang up, and the soldiers made merry on the extra wine that had been issued to them for the occasion. Round one such fire, down towards the horse-lines, the handful that were left of the Lost Legion were taking their ease; all save Justin and Flavius. And those two, summoned from their comrades, were standing in the lamplit Praetorium of the Fort, before a very weary man wearing the Imperial Purple.

The Caesar Constantius had laid aside his gilded breast-plate and the great Eagle-crested helmet that had left a crimson weal across his forehead. He was sitting half turned on the cushioned bench, to speak to Licinius almost behind him, but he looked round as they snapped to attention in front of him, showing a face that, for all its whiteness, had none of that look of a thing bred in the dark that had marred Allectus's features, and acknowledged their salute with a swift gesture of the hand. 'These are the two, Centurion Licinius?'

'These are the two sir,' said Licinius by the window.

'I greet you. Which of you is Centurion Aquila?'

Flavius advanced the regulation pace. 'Hail Caesar.'

Constantius turned his gaze to Justin. 'And you are Tiberius Justinianus of the Army Medical Corps?'

'As Caesar says.'

'I sent for you because I have been hearing things concerning a certain band of irregular troops, and wished to meet its Captains, and to thank them for the intelligence and – reinforcements that have reached me from time to time over the past year and a half from this province.'

'Thank you, sir,' said Flavius and Justin in one breath. And Flavius added quickly, 'But it was a one-time secretary of Carausius's who began the work, and – died for it. We took over from him, no more.'

Constantius bent his head gravely, but Justin had a feeling that there was a flicker of amusement behind the gravity. 'Have no fear that I shall give you the credit that belongs to another man ... Nevertheless, you took over, and to good purpose, and for that the thanks of the Empire are due to you. At a later date I shall demand of you a full account of these past years; it should make a tale worth the hearing. But that can wait.' He leaned forward on his crossed arms, and studied them, first one, and then the other, with a long, quiet scrutiny that made Justin at least feel uncomfortably as though the outer layers of himself were being peeled off like the skins of an onion, that this man with the white, fine-drawn face might see exactly what lay at his core and judge of its worth.

'Yes,' said the Caesar Constantius at last as having seen what he wanted, and made his judgement, and rose, with a hand on the table beside him. 'You have earned a long spell of leave, and I make no doubt that you need it. But

the North is bursting into flames again; the very Wall itself
is in danger. Doubtless you know all that. It was inevit-
able, with half the troops withdrawn to fight Allectus's
battles. In two days we march North to put out the fires,
and – we need men.'

He stood looking quietly from one to the other as
though waiting for the answer to a question. And Justin
saw suddenly that on the writing-table by his hand lay
two sealed tablets on which were written their own
names.

It was very quiet in the lamplit room, high above the
fort. They heard the challenge of a sentry on the ramparts,
and the soft rise and fall of sound that was the voice of
the City, like a sea below them, far, far below. Then
Flavius, glancing also at those tablets and up again, said,
'Our marching orders, Caesar?'

'Not necessarily. I do not order in this case; I leave the
choice to you. You have earned the right to refuse.'

'What happens if we do refuse?' Flavius asked after a
moment. 'If we say that we served the Emperor Carausius
with our whole hearts, and have not the same service to
give again?'

The Caesar Constantius took up one of the tablets. 'Then
I open this and soften the wax at the lamp here, and
smooth out what is written within. That is all. And you
shall be free to retire from the Eagles with all honour. But
I hope that you will not say that. I hope it for the sake of
this province of Britain, and a little, I find, for my own.'

There was the faintest shadow of a smile in his eyes as
he spoke; and looking at him, Justin knew that here was
a man worth following.

Flavius took another pace forward, and picked up the
tablet with his name on it. 'For myself, I am ready to
march North in two days' time,' he said.

But Justin was still silent. It often took him longer to be

sure about things than it did Flavius; and he had to be sure, quite sure, about this. And then he was sure. 'For m-myself also,' he said, and took the pace forward, and picked up the little tablet that had his fate on it.

'So. It is good,' Constantius said. He looked from one to the other. 'I am told that you two are kinsmen; but I think you are also friends, which is a greater thing. Indeed, that was told me by the Primus Pilus here. Therefore I hope you may not be ill satisfied to find yourselves once again posted together.'

Justin turned his head quickly to look at Flavius, and found that Flavius had done the same. He realized suddenly how far Flavius had grown – himself too, he supposed – from the boys that they had been when first they found each other before the great pharos at Rutupiae. All that way they had come shoulder to shoulder, and the old bond between them was strengthened accordingly.

'Caesar is very good,' Flavius said.

'It is in my mind that Rome owes you that, at all events,' Constantius said, with that shadow of a smile again in his eyes. He took up some papers from the table. 'I think that there is nothing more that we need to speak of tonight?'

'One thing more, Caesar,' Flavius said urgently.

Constantius lowered the papers again. 'Well, Centurion?'

'Caesar, we have four legionaries and another Cohort Centurion yet with us. They are as much Caesar's men as those that escaped to Gaul.'

'Send them to my Staff Centurion in the morning.' The smile that had been hovering flashed up in Caesar's face, lighting the thin whiteness of it so that he seemed suddenly much younger and less tired. 'And meanwhile, you can bid them – unofficially – also to be ready to march North in two days' time ... So! It is settled. Go now and draw your equipment and set about disbanding these cut-throats of yours. We shall both be busy in the next hours. I salute you and bid you goodnight.'

Outside, by common consent Justin and Flavius turned aside from the head of the open stairway on to the high rampart walk, the tablets containing their postings still unopened in their hands, and lingered there a few moments, needing as it were a breathing-space between one world and another. Justin thought, 'We ought to be going back to the band. Only it isn't a band any more, or it won't be after tonight. Just men – free to go their own way.'

Save for the sentry pacing his beat, they were alone on the rampart walk. Below them the darkening City was strung with lights – dim amber window squares, and the golden drops of light that were lamps and lanterns in the garlanded streets. Lights and lights and lights away to the misty river. 'Londinium rejoices,' Flavius said. 'Surely there's not a dark house within the City walls tonight.'

Justin nodded, not wanting to talk, his mind turning back to the start of it all : to that interview with Licinius, more than three years ago; the sand-wreaths in the corners of the mud-walled office, and the jackals crying. That had been the night that it began. Tonight was the night that it was over.

Over, like Carausius's brief Empire in the North that had been brought to nothing by the murdering hand of Allectus. Britain was once again part of Rome, safe so long as Rome was strong to hold her safe – and no longer ... Well, better for Britain to take her chance with Rome than fall to ruin under Allectus and his kind. And tonight, with the lights of rejoicing Londinium spread below them, and the Legions encamped beyond the walls, and the man with the thin white conqueror's face seated at his writing-table in the lamp-lit Praetorium, the idea of a time coming when Rome would not be strong seemed, after all, thin and remote.

And for themselves – they had kept faith with the little Emperor; and the world of familiar things that they had laid down, walking South from the Wall into that autumn mist of almost two years ago, was waiting for them to take it up again; and life was good.

He was just about to push off from the wall on which he leaned, when something that had been squatting unseen in the shadows uncurled and stood up with a faint chime of bells into the light of a gate tower doorway.

'Cullen!' Flavius said. 'What do you here?'

'I followed my Lords in case, as a good hound should,' Cullen said.

'In case of what?'

'Just in case,' said Cullen, and touched the little dagger beside the Silver Branch in his belt. 'What do we do now?'

'Those of us who are of the Legions march North in the morn's morning,' Flavius said. 'For the rest – the Lost Legion is finished – broke up – free to go its own way.'

'So. I go my Lords' way; I am my Lords' hound,' Cullen said contentedly.

'But you are free now,' Flavius said.

Cullen shook his head vehemently. 'Curoi said that if he died, I was my Lords' hound.'

There was a small silence, and then Flavius said helplessly, 'Cullen, we are not Emperors, nor High Kings of Erin, that we should need a Household Fool.'

'I can be much, besides a Fool; I can keep your armour bright; I can serve you at table, and carry messages, and keep secrets.'

'Would it not be better to be free?'

'Free? I was born a slave, the son of a slave. What is "Free" to me, but being masterless – and maybe hungry?'

They could not see his strange narrow face save as a pale blur in the reflected light of the doorway; but there was something in his voice that could not be denied.

Justin spoke for the first time, across the little man's

head to Flavius. 'We have never been masterless and hungry, you and I.'

'Never masterless, at all events,' Flavius said, and Justin knew that the thoughts of both of them had gone for an instant to the man they had left in the Praetorium. There was no disloyalty to Carausius in that, for they knew, both of them, that a man may give his service more than once without breaking faith, but only once for the first time.

Suddenly Flavius flung up his head and laughed. 'Well, it's a good thing we are posted together, or we should have to slice our hound in half!'

'I come with my Lords?' Cullen said. '*Sa*, it is good!'

'It is good,' Justin said.

Flavius laid a heavy arm across his cousin's shoulders. 'Come on, old lad. We must tell Anthonius and the rest how the wind blows, and get some sleep while we can. We shall have our work cut out in the time before we march North.'

They turned back to the rampart stair, and clattering down it, headed for the gate which stood open tonight between the fort and the great marching camp; little Cullen strutting behind them with his hound's tail a-swing at every step, sounding the apples of his Silver Branch triumphantly as he went.

Roman Place Names

MANOPEA – An Island in Mouth of Scheldt
GESORIACUM – Boulogne
SCALDIS – Scheldt
RUTUPIAE – Richborough
TANTUS – Thanet
AQUASULIS – Bath
VENTA – Winchester
LIMANIS – Lymne
LAIGHIN – Leinster
DUBRIS – Dover
MAGNIS – Station on the Wall
EBURACUM – York
CALLEVA – Silchester
PORTUS ADURNI – Portchester
RHENUS – Rhine
REGNUM – Chichester
CLAUSENTIUM – Bitterne
VECTIS – Isle of Wight
SEQUANA – Seine
LONDINIUM – London
THAMESIS – Thames
ANDERIDA – Pevensey
DUROVERNUM – Canterbury

Other Puffins by Rosemary Sutcliff

DRAGON SLAYER: THE STORY OF BEOWULF

THE HIGH DEEDS OF FINN MAC COOL

TRISTAN AND ISEULT

THE EAGLE OF THE NINTH

WARRIOR SCARLET

BLOOD FEUD

Heard about the Puffin Club?

... it's a way of finding out more about Puffin books and authors, of winning prizes (in competitions), sharing jokes, a secret code, and perhaps seeing your name in print! When you join you get a copy of our magazine, *Puffin Post*, sent to you four times a year, a badge and a membership book.

For details of subscription and an application form, send a stamped addressed envelope to:

The Puffin Club Dept A
Penguin Books Limited
Bath Road
Harmondsworth
Middlesex UB7 0DA

and if you live in Australia, please write to:

The Australian Puffin Club
Penguin Books Australia Limited
P.O. Box 257
Ringwood
Victoria 3134